Built on the bones of an ancient city, modern-day Everstrand is where master mage, Rowan, has set up his enchantment shop. When not hanging out with his werewolf best friend, Caleb, or studying, he dabbles in herbology and the controversial practice of blood magic. A prodigy who has already earned two masters, Rowan's bound and determined to reach the distinction of grandmaster, a mage who obtains a masters in all five Schools of Magic.

Shaw works for the Inquisition, the organization charged with policing the magical races collectively known as magicae. Recently, it has come under scrutiny as magicae begin to disappear and reports of violence increase. With secrets of his own on the line, Shaw is willing to risk everything to find out just what is going on behind all the locked doors.

When Rowan and Shaw are entangled in each other's worlds, it becomes evident that their hearts are as much at risk as their lives. They must find the truth and stop a conspiracy before it's too late.

A MAGE'S POWER

The Inquisition Trilogy, Book One

Casey Wolfe

A NineStar Press Publication

Published by NineStar Press
P.O. Box 91792,
Albuquerque, New Mexico, 87199 USA.
www.ninestarpress.com

A Mage's Power

Printed in the USA
First Edition
July, 2018

Print ISBN: 978-1-949340-20-4

Also available in eBook, ISBN: 978-1-949340-18-1

Warning: This book contains sexual content, which may only be suitable for mature readers, and scenes of graphic violence.

For Ruger B. Riddick

I will always love you, my boy.

See you at the Rainbow Bridge.

Chapter One

THE CITY OF Everstrand came into view when Rowan's dirt bike broke through the last of the forest. The engine *whirred* as he caught a little air over a bump, wind whipping at his blond hair. He laughed, leaving dust in his wake. Spring was fast approaching and Rowan was enjoying the sunshine and warming temperatures perhaps a bit too much.

The dirt roads leading from the Sacred Timber, where he lived, gave way to the paved roadways of civilization. Rowan much preferred the solitude of nature to the bustle of Osterian's capital city, so it was just as well he tended to keep his trips there to a minimum.

Not that the city was completely horrible. It was ancient, and a lot of the original structures had been well-preserved as the city expanded over the centuries. The Everstrand Mages Guild was part of the oldest section. It sat on a broken piece of land that was enchanted to float in the air above the Grey Tides—visible even now. Chains kept it bound to the cliffside so that it didn't drift away.

Rowan needed to stop by the Guild at some point, but he wanted to go to his shop first. One wouldn't think he'd be able to make a living by being open a few days out of the week; however, an enchanter's services were always a valuable commodity. Considering Rowan was the sole master enchanter in the entire city offering his services to the public, he wasn't worried about losing business.

Having timed his arrival after the morning rush, Rowan had no problems getting to the shop. He cut through a few narrow side alleys to the Orchard Street Mall. He loved that it was all outdoors, restricted to foot traffic only, instead of a typical mall complex. It gave the area a certain charm, with the unique facades and plentiful landscaping.

Rowan parked his bike in the section reserved for vendors, permit tag sealed in place with magic to prevent theft. Satchel strap over his shoulder, he made his way down the cobblestone paths, past shops of every size and type.

Nestled between a bookstore and a pastry shop—that he frequented probably more than he should have—was Charmed to Meet You. Even now, the name made him cringe a little. It had been his late grandmother's suggestion, and with no counter-name in hand, Rowan had relented. It seemed he was stuck with it too—at least his customers thought it was cute.

Once inside, he flipped on the lights and tossed his satchel onto the counter. He shrugged out of his brown leather jacket, hanging it on the rack. The weather may have been breaking, but riding his bike still required protection from the chill. It was nice enough to open the windows, which he did with a flick of his hand. A breeze swept inside, the fresh air swapping out the stale from over the weekend.

It was a small shop, designed more as a work space than a storefront, with all the shelving behind the counter holding his supplies. There were no displays or little charm trinkets lying around. Everything he did was custom. Let them go to a kitschy tourist trap if they wanted some run-of-the-mill good luck charm. He had better things to do.

Already finished with current orders, Rowan decided today was a good day to work on his own projects. He sat on his stool and pulled a thick book from his satchel before stowing the bag under the counter by his parchment, ink, and quills. It might have been old-fashioned of him, but he enjoyed the feel of a quill in his hand and handmade paper under his fingers—his grandmother's influence, no doubt, as she had been the one to give him his first grimoire filled with parchment. After that, a notebook and pen simply wouldn't do for anything involving his magical studies.

"Now, where was I?"

One of the few things he'd taken from his grandmother's cottage was her magic books, but he hadn't been able to read them until recently. Even looking at them had invoked powerful memories of her, and it was far too heartbreaking to consider. They had sat around, gathering dust, for the last half-dozen years, and Rowan thought it was about time to get over it. Thus, he'd begun pouring over her old grimoires and spell theory books in earnest.

Naturally, no sooner had he gotten settled, his cell phone chimed. It turned out to be his best friend, Caleb, and Rowan wasn't surprised at the inquiry: *"Lunch today?"*

Rowan smiled while typing out a reply text: *"Of course."* As though Caleb didn't come out to Rowan's cottage enough, the werewolf was always on him to hang out when he was in town. *"Now hush. I'm studying."*

The returned zipped-lip emoji made Rowan laugh. "Damn wolf," he said affectionately, shaking his head as he set the phone aside.

Not that the silence lasted long. From the back of the shop, Rowan heard a soft *meow*. He turned to find the brown tabby cat that roamed the neighborhood, slipping through the window and landing gracefully on a stack of books. "Hey, Badger."

The cat *meowed* again, making his way along the shelves before jumping onto the front counter. Badger purred, rubbing his head against Rowan's arm, demanding attention. Rowan scratched behind the cat's ears. He certainly was an animal magnet.

Badger had shown up in the shop one day when Rowan had opened one of the back windows to vent the smoke from a failed experiment—not one of his prouder moments. Rowan had no desire for a cat, but he couldn't just throw the guy back out into the wet snow either. Thankfully for Rowan, the cat didn't exactly want to be kept.

Badger came and went on his own whims, although it seemed he'd picked up Rowan's schedule and was sure to drop by to see him. Rowan figured part of it had to do with the fact he was keeping meat treats around. Not that he minded. Badger was a quiet, comforting presence who mostly took advantage of the warm, dry place by curling up on the counter and napping.

Caleb had saddled the cat with his name. Rowan wasn't planning to name him—after all, he had proven to be his own animal—but Caleb had pointed out they couldn't keep calling him "the cat." Badger should have been thankful Rowan vetoed Whiskers.

The bell above the door announced the arrival of a customer, one of Rowan's regulars. Most of Marian's requests were idiotic, but he wasn't about to turn down her money. If she wanted to keep wasting it at his shop, that was fine by him.

"Rowan, hon, there you are," the older woman gushed, coming up to the counter. "Did you get my message?"

"I actually just got in." Rowan may have sounded apologetic, but he wasn't in the least. Marian had the habit of freaking out over nothing and believing she needed magical interference to deal with every little challenge. *Think of the money*, he reminded himself.

"Oh, I am in desperate need of your help. It's my neighbor. The old fool has been trying to curse me."

Rowan had to hold back an exasperated sigh. This was going to take a while. He closed his book regretfully.

"Curses are serious business," Rowan said. "Are you sure?" Despite his words, he was already moving toward the shelves. They were set perpendicular to the counter, so he was still able to see Marian as he searched for various things he would require.

"I'm certain," Marian insisted, as Rowan knew she would. "It's my garden! Everything is just...*dying.* It was fine one day, and the next..." She threw her hands in the air, which was apparently supposed to mean something.

Rowan hummed in false agreement. "Yes, that does sound serious. Have you thought of reporting it?" Humoring her didn't mean he couldn't take a few jabs at her expense.

"Heavens, no. Those fools don't do a thing. You should know that, dear."

Rowan rolled his eyes. *This is what I got a masters for?*

It wasn't the first time he'd thought it, and not even with Marian's ridiculous requests. There he was, the youngest mage ever with a masters degree—now *two*—and he was humoring people who needed to keep plants alive despite their lack of green thumb, prevent a neighbor's dog from shitting in their yard, or protect from griffin attack—because somebody told them they were rampant in the south of Osterian where they planned to vacation. Money was money, though, so Rowan stomached the inane requests and prayed for those that were a good use of his time.

"Do you think you can help me?" Marian asked, before cooing at Badger. He was thoroughly unamused, relocating himself to one of the shelves near Rowan. "He is such a beautiful cat. It's so precious how he follows you."

"Yes, he is," Rowan agreed, Badger rubbing his head against his shoulder. "And, yes, I can most certainly help you out. If you have more shopping to get done, I can have it ready in about an hour."

Marian clapped her hands together. "Oh, that's wonderful. I do appreciate it."

"No trouble at all." He kept the fake smile in place until the door shut behind her. "One charm to stop you from murdering your own plants, coming up," he griped. Looking at Badger, he raised a brow. "Why is everything a curse or whatever with her? I swear I don't understand mundanes." He spoke of those without magic.

Badger *meowed* as if he understood. Rowan smiled at him, gathering up the supplies he needed to make the charm in question.

He turned to another shelf, pausing when he saw the potion sitting there. "I forgot about this." Rowan had been dabbling with potion-making lately. Despite not being an actual School of Magic, herbology—like divination and runes—was an offered course at many guilds. While anyone could learn such skills, magic could often enhance the effects.

"This...wasn't exactly the color I hoped for," Rowan admitted, turning the small glass bottle over in his hand. The sickly green liquid sloshed around, unchanged. "So much for that."

He may have been something of a prodigy—passing his apprenticeship at eighteen, and earning his first masters at twenty-one—but he was far from great at all areas of magic. Likely, his grandmother would have kept him on track, except she'd died shortly after he opened Charmed to Meet You. She missed his second masters at twenty-four, and without her around to scold him, he'd spent the last four years messing around here and there with all sorts of other magic—including intensive study in blood magic—without truly settling on a new course of study.

Perhaps two masters would have been more than enough for any mage to have, but not him. He was bound and determined to reach the distinction of grandmaster, a mage who had obtained a masters in all five Schools of Magic. First, he needed to get through his next exam.

THE CAFE ROWAN frequented with Caleb wasn't far, merely a couple of blocks away in a small square. There was no point in taking his bike, especially when it was such a nice day.

He regretted that decision the moment he spotted an Inquisition knight. "What the hell are they doing around here?" he grumbled. In the next breath, he scolded himself. "I've been listening to Caleb's stories too much."

For the last fifty years or so, most countries had an Inquisition presence. The organization was not technically a part of their governments, rather, an entity *authorized* by their respective countries. Their purpose was to deal with crimes involving magicae—those races with magic—or to help those in need of rehabilitation.

As of late, various Inquisition temples—as they called their headquarters buildings—were coming under fire. Accusations of cruelty toward magicae were followed by whispers of kidnappings. The way people told it these days, if the Inquisition took someone, they were never heard from again.

Rowan dismissed most of the rumors as folly. If they were really holding so many magicae without cause, the governments surely would have stepped in. The claims of abuse of power, beating suspects, and the like, well, Rowan had no way to explain those away quite so easily. Whatever the case, he would rather avoid the members of the Inquisition.

Apparently, that would be impossible, as Rowan watched the knight's attention zero in on him when he crossed the street. It wasn't as if he were an elf or vampire, but his unusual violet eyes still had the habit of giving him away. Any hopes that he would be able to move on without a confrontation were dashed when the knight decided to step in his path.

"Excuse me," Rowan said, attempting to sidestep him.

"No, you can stay right there," the knight replied. As the name suggested, the official dress the knights wore resembled the heavy cloth armor of their medieval counterparts. Rowan found it anything but dashing, rather a testament to how backward the organization was. They admired men who used to kill dragons for the hell of it; how was that good for magicae? "Give me your ID."

Rowan's brows lowered. "I don't have to do that."

"Sure you do. I asked for it, didn't I?"

Rowan scoffed. Clearly this *boy* assumed no one paid attention to the law. "Do you suspect me of a crime, Knight...?"

"Dansforth." He sneered. "And I haven't decided yet."

That was it. Rowan was having none of this guy's haughty attitude. He wasn't typically a confrontational sort, but when push came to shove, Rowan wasn't afraid of holding his ground. "Then have a nice day, Knight." He forced his way past, only to have his bicep grabbed. Nostrils flaring, Rowan spun around, eyes no doubt glowing with the fire that filled his belly.

"Knight Dansforth!" an authoritative voice barked. "Release that man at once!"

"Sir!" Dansforth did as he was told, jumping away like he'd been scalded. He saluted the man who approached— this one an inquisitor. Whereas the knights were the general law enforcement of the Inquisition, inquisitors were their investigative branch. They held the power within the temples and were not to be crossed.

"There a reason you felt the need to put your hands on someone?" He may have been shorter than Rowan by a few inches, but the inquisitor had more mass on him. The cream, long-sleeved shirt underneath the fitted, leather armor of his station didn't hide his muscle. Currently, all of that coiled power was at least being directed away from Rowan.

"Sir, he refused to—"

"Give you ID," the inquisitor finished, his voice holding an accent that pegged him a foreigner. "I'm aware." He turned to Rowan, looking him over. "I apologize on behalf of this git," he said candidly. Dansforth's lips pursed, but he wasn't about to speak out of turn again. "Saying he's new isn't an excuse," the inquisitor continued. "I'll personally be filing a misconduct report when I return to the temple."

It didn't do much to smooth out Rowan's proverbial ruffled feathers. "Knights like that are what's giving you a shit reputation," he pointed out.

"Well, hopefully we can correct that misconception, yeah?"

Rowan felt a prickle against his skin that he knew to be magic. Not everyone—even magicae—could sense it, but being a mage certainly meant he could. Except, that didn't make any sense. The Inquisition had strict hiring policies. Everyone in their ranks was mundane, which of course, did nothing to dissuade the claims of bigoted behavior on their part.

A calm washed over him, like a soothing touch barely there against his consciousness. "Maybe," Rowan murmured, meeting the inquisitor's gaze for the first time.

His eyes were a sparkling blue-green, a few bits of his slicked-back, dark-brown hair falling in front of them. He had a strong, square jaw, highlighted by the scruff of a beard. Rowan was surprised the Inquisition allowed him out like that, but then, the inquisitors always had some leniency.

"As ironic as this is..." the inquisitor continued, "I'm going to need your ID. When I write my disciplinary report, I need to put your name in it. Not that anyone is bound to call you and ask you to verify anything."

Sighing, Rowan pulled his wallet from his pocket and flipped it open to show the ID in the window screen. "Figures."

The inquisitor's lips quirked into a brief smile before he schooled his features and jotted down a few things from the ID into a little notepad.

"Thank you," he said with a nod. "Again, I apologize. Hope you have a better day."

It was there again, that sense of ease. Rowan only nodded, pocketing his wallet as he hurried off to meet Caleb before he started to worry.

SHAW WATCHED AS the mage left, noting the quick glance over his shoulder at them before he disappeared around the corner. Rowan, his ID had said.

Typically, Shaw didn't step in when he caught knights pushing the boundaries of the law. As an inquisitor, he was above them in rank, yes, but they were also a separate division. He had enough to worry about without dealing with the overzealous knights in the city.

Something about Rowan had made him react. Shaw's natural protective instincts flared, and he'd found himself confronting the brash young knight. He could have written it off as saving Danforth's skin—after all, Rowan had looked about ready to flay him alive—but that wasn't it at all.

No, it was Rowan's presence. It had called to him. As cliché as it sounded, that was the truth of it. Drawn in, the feeling intensified when Shaw had looked up into those bright eyes. They'd been glowing at first, easing back into a deep violet once Shaw gained control of the situation.

Now, he had Rowan's information copied into his notepad, tucked safely away in the pocket of his short-sleeve jerkin. Shaw wasn't about to pretend it hadn't been for self-indulgent reasons. Rowan was a tall drink of water in painted-on jeans. His lavender shirt complemented his eyes and his blue-gray overshirt had been left unbuttoned to show off a trim waist. A sharp jawline and a shock of blond hair falling in layers against his cheek had added to the hard stare Rowan had landed him with. Shaw had practically melted into goo right there on the sidewalk—*damn it.*

Shaw glanced over to find Dansforth standing there, appearing none too happy with his intervention. "Is there a problem, Knight?" he asked, a bit of danger in his tone.

"I was doing my job...sir."

Shaw's lips curled into a sneer. The man was being just this side of insolent. "I'd watch your step, Knight. I'm not filing a report on this. But I can change that at any time."

Dansforth immediately relaxed his stance, leaning in toward him. "I thought you were clear on your next course of action, Inquisitor."

So, now he's showing respect. Shaw barely held back from rolling his eyes. "Well, he don't have to know that, now does he?" He brushed it off, turning to leave. "Continue your patrol, Knight."

"Yes, sir."

In truth, if Shaw were to write up the report, nothing would ever come of it. The Inquisition took care of their own, first and foremost. Something as *incidental* as this would have been thrown in the garbage. If anything, it would create a target on Rowan's back, and Shaw refused to be the one to put it there. The magicae in the city had enough issues without the constant harassment the Inquisition brought them.

He wasn't in a position to do anything about it, so instead, he did his job. As an inquisitor, Shaw was afforded more freedom than the average employee, and he wasn't about to risk that by making too many waves. If he could help magicae in the process, then it was all worth it.

Shaw returned to his issued car, having been on his way there when he'd passed by that little scene Dansforth had caused. He had been out contacting a potential witness for a case and, unfortunately, it was time to get back to the temple.

In his opinion, Everstrand's headquarters was unnecessarily opulent. It had been constructed nearly thirty years back, but in the style of the castles and cathedrals of old. Its location in the historic Southern District, however, made it blend in rather nicely, as if it had always been there.

Shaw pulled into the employees-only lot behind the building, thankful to avoid the entrance at the front of the massive structure. It was all too much for him: the grand facade, the high-vaulted ceiling, and the paintings adorning the walls. It was easily the most nauseating part of the temple.

There was even a giant tapestry, complete with dragon-slaying, that paid homage to the Inquisition's roots. From famed dragon killers to experts on all things magicae, it seemed every rising government had a consulting Inquisition presence. However, *consulting* turned into full-on law enforcement fairly quickly once they proved themselves capable of the task.

The rest of the temple, while still feeling grand and out of time, was far more subtle. Long parapets led to towers at the corners of the building. There was a final square tower in the center, which jutted out above the rest. The inquisitor offices were housed there, along with the rest of the high command.

Slipping through the back entrance, Shaw nodded politely enough to those he passed. He hadn't exactly been around long enough to make friends. Honestly, he didn't even want to. Most of the people who worked for the Inquisition were undeniably assholes with a point to prove— bigots just seemed to go hand-in-hand.

He had a job to do, so Shaw would grin and bear the rest of it. He knew he could make a difference, given time. As each day dragged into weeks, however, he wondered if it would be worth it in the end, if anything would come of it.

Vaughn emerged from his office, spotting Shaw in the hall. "Inquisitor Shaw," he greeted with a faux smile. "Anything to report?"

"When there is, you'll be the first to know."

Shaw walked right by. He refused to kiss Vaughn's ass like the other inquisitors did. Assistant High Inquisitor had gone to Vaughn's head, in Shaw's opinion. No, the sole person he would even think to watch his step around was Meredeen—head of the inquisitors, and second only to Zane.

Slowing, Shaw looked over his shoulder to see Vaughn turning the corner. He waited a moment before rerouting to Vaughn's office. Clicking the door shut behind him, Shaw gave the room a cursory glance. He would have to make this quick.

After kicking the computer chair out of the way, Shaw pulled a flash drive from a small pouch inside his boot. He slotted it into the USB port, waking the computer in the process. He needn't worry about passwords; the program in the flash drive ran encryption-cracking software automatically.

Shaw let the drive do its job, turning his attention to the rest of the room. There was paperwork everywhere, along with stacks of folders filled with potential information. There was no way Shaw had time to go through it all.

Instead, he pulled a scroll from the hidden pocket inside his jerkin. Unrolling it exposed a spell written in Runic, which translated to "reveal that which is hidden." A brief glow radiated from the scroll when he pressed it to the wall. Light washed across the floor, ceiling, and everything else within the room.

Shaw looked around, hoping to find any indication that the spell had found something. Unfortunately, he was left with nothing. He pulled the now blank scroll from the wall and shoved it back into his jerkin.

The computer chimed softly, signaling the end of the download. Shaw pulled the flash drive out, reset the chair, and returned the drive to its hidden pouch, before slipping back into the hall completely unnoticed.

Chapter Two

ROWAN SPOTTED CALEB on a bench by the square's fountain. He might have appeared relaxed, but Rowan knew better. His friend was always alert, his canine senses stretched out. Caleb's nose twitched, a slow smile spreading across his face as he no doubt picked out Rowan's scent from the other people milling around. Warm, honey eyes opened, finding Rowan almost immediately.

Sitting up from his graceful sprawl, Caleb brushed angled bangs from his eyes. His dark roots were showing again, not that his hair ever *stayed* that way. Caleb had a thing for dying it any number of crazy colors—or three. At the moment, it was royal-blue—a great improvement from bubblegum pink.

"Hey, man!" Caleb greeted brightly. Evidently, Rowan was more shaken than he realized, as Caleb's brows immediately lowered. "What's wrong?"

"I see you wore the shirt I got you, finally," Rowan said in a bid for avoidance.

Caleb was rebellious with more than his hair. Today, his clunky combat boots were paired off with black jeans that had buckled straps around the thigh and calf. Completing the look was a white long-sleeved shirt with gashes at the elbows, making it seem torn. He loved anything that made a statement, as long as it was in monochrome.

Caleb shrugged. "Not my fault it's been too cold to go without a jacket and this doesn't work with any I've got." He hip-checked Rowan as he chided, "And don't change the subject."

Grumbling, Rowan held open the door to the Brew Room, the aroma of fresh-brewed coffee greeting them. They sat at their usual table near the back, where the large windows let in an abundance of light. One wave to the pretty nymph waitress and they knew their usual order would be put into the kitchen.

"What the hell's goin' on?" Caleb demanded, leaning forward on his arms and catching Rowan's gaze.

"Had a run-in with a knight on the way over," he answered. "Just freaked me out a little is all."

Caleb's eyes narrowed, trying to figure out if Rowan was being entirely truthful. "What the hell they want?"

"No idea. Some upstart looking to make a name. Flexing his power."

Huffing, Caleb turned sideways so his back was against the wall and window, arm slung over the back of the chair. "Fucking assholes," he muttered. "Surprised no one's been buggin' me yet." To Rowan's questioning look, he asked, "Don't you ever watch the news?"

"As if."

"That bill I told you about? The one that would require all were-creatures to wear collars?"

"Don't tell me they actually passed it." Rowan felt his stomach drop at the thought.

"No, but it's up for vote in Parliament next week."

It was natural Caleb would be concerned. Plenty of were-creatures wore anti-shift collars while out in public around the time of the full moon. It was a choice, however, with few exceptions, but the law in question would make them mandatory. Extremists were even pushing them to be an everyday requirement outside the home.

Caleb was staunchly against the collars. Then again, it wasn't like he needed one. He had been controlling his shifts completely for nearly a decade—being a born werewolf sure helped in that regard.

"It'll never pass," Rowan said. The bill was being backed by the Inquisition, and with all of the heat being brought down on the organization lately, Rowan couldn't see that it would get the type of support they needed.

"I hope you're right," Caleb murmured, sinking back against the wall. "We're a minority if enough magicae races want to turn their backs on us."

Rowan couldn't say that they hadn't seen it before. Fearmongering and bigotry were perhaps to be expected between mundanes and magicae, but it still surprised Rowan to watch magicae turn on their own. "It won't pass," Rowan insisted, as though that settled the matter.

Danais, their usual waitress, came over with their coffees. Rowan was one for tea, but he couldn't argue how good the hazelnut blend was here, a little vanilla cream added to make it perfect. She also had a pair of sugary pastries. "Your sandwiches should be up shortly," Danais said with a smile, before going to attend other customers.

"Anything new?" Rowan asked, nodding toward Caleb's sketchbook on the table. He always carried one with him. At least he'd stopped bringing charcoal with him, too, as it often caused messy situations.

"If I ever meet my muse? I'm going to drop-kick her into the Grey Tides."

Rowan choked on his pastry.

"I've just been so stressed out with all this political shit going on, I can't seem to get anything to work right," Caleb continued without notice. Clearly, Rowan's attempt at a distraction had backfired. "Pollock threw his hat in the ring for Prime Minister."

"And you think a guy who campaigns openly as anti-magicae is going to win?"

Caleb sent him a look. "He got into Parliament, didn't he?"

"Well, he's going to need support from more than his district to pull it off."

Caleb's frown deepened, looking down at the table. "I'm scared, Ro," he admitted quietly. "I'm scared of what this country's becoming. And I'm terrified for what it means for all of us." He shook his head. "I mean, when did it get so bad that someone like Pollock is even in the running?"

Rowan frowned as well. "I don't know." He understood Caleb's distress. It was inconceivable that things had come to this. "We have to have faith in each other." He reached out to take Caleb's hand. "If we stand together? I think we'll be alright."

Caleb's lips twisted up into a little smile. "Yeah, I guess you're right." Caleb squeezed his hand.

After a long moment, Caleb released his hand and grabbed his sketchbook, flipping open to a fresh page. Pastry in one hand and pen in another, Caleb started to doodle.

"So, are we hanging out tonight?" Caleb asked absentmindedly.

Rowan shook his head ruefully—typical Caleb. At least he was done with all the politics talk. Rowan took a bite of his pastry and was chewing when Caleb looked up at him for an answer.

Swallowing first, Rowan replied, "I'm heading out to the Guild after this. Need to set up for my next exam."

Caleb's eyes widened a bit. "Yeah? You were serious then."

"It's time to get it done," Rowan said easily enough.

"Well, good luck."

Rowan chuckled. "Little early for that, isn't it?"

"It's also you," Caleb countered. "I'll be lucky to see you at all before it's over."

"You got me there," Rowan grumbled. He had the tendency to get obsessive, he knew, but that was just who he was.

"So is that a 'no' for tonight?" he asked, attention back on his drawing.

"I'm going to have a lot of work to do." When Caleb looked at him pointedly, Rowan grimaced. "That would be a no."

Caleb rolled his eyes. "One of these days…" He took a sip of coffee before humming as he remembered something. "Oh, I got that new painting done for the shop. I'll bring it by later."

"No rush," Rowan assured him, finishing off his sweet.

Caleb's last painting, a stunning night scene of the Sacred Timber, had caught the eye of one of Rowan's customers. They had made an offer on it, a sum too good to pass up in Rowan's opinion, so he had let it go and passed the money along to Caleb. He had been a bit put out that Rowan had sold something meant as a gift, but Caleb *did* need the money—the whole reason Rowan had done it, as trying to lend Caleb money never worked.

It was Rowan who suggested Caleb make more pieces to put up. Another avenue to show his work never hurt. Besides, anything truly meant for Rowan was at his cottage. That evening piece had mostly been there because Caleb complained the shop needed more atmosphere.

"I think you'll like it," Caleb pressed on. "Floating islands with waterfalls flowing off of them into the abyss."

"I'm sure it's amazing."

Caleb gave a noncommittal grunt.

It was always like this, from the day they had met at a street faire. Caleb hadn't been in Everstrand long, and he was there selling his art. Rowan was impressed, but Caleb never thought all that much of his own work. He was far more confident in his web design skills that he used to pay the bills. After updating the website and social media for the then-new Charmed to Meet You, they became fast friends and, soon thereafter, inseparable.

Danais returned with their sandwiches—roast beef for Caleb and tuna for Rowan—promising to check on them in a bit.

Digging in, Rowan glanced at the sketchbook. It was rough, but there was no mistaking the figure on the page as anyone other than Rowan. A spell of some sort was floating above his palm, and the shape of a wolf was forming beside him.

Rowan's lips quirked. "Y'know," he mused, "if you keep drawing us together, people are going to get the wrong idea."

Caleb barked a laugh. "What? You embarrassed that people might think we're dating?"

Rowan scoffed, which made Caleb laugh harder. "You know I love you," Rowan said, "but you are not my type."

"Well, mysterious *and* handsome is a lot to handle in one man."

It was Rowan's turn to laugh. "I can't even with you. And no, you know exactly what I mean."

"Ah, yes." Caleb feigned seriousness. "I am a slut."

Rowan threw his head back and laughed, the bright sound filling the cafe. "Oh my Goddess."

"Hey, I won't argue." Caleb smirked. "I'm not ashamed of it."

"I know you aren't."

Rowan knew that better than anyone. Caleb never led men on. They were all well aware that it was nothing more than a hookup—maybe even on multiple occasions if they clicked. Caleb claimed he was having too much fun exploring himself and the world to worry about commitment. Still, Rowan would argue having regular sex with a person was some kind of a relationship.

It was Rowan who required a commitment. If they were dating, then it was exclusive. Sex for sex's sake wasn't his thing. Not that he saw anything wrong with it. Perhaps he was too busy looking for that perfect partner instead of simply enjoying life, as Caleb put it.

It was hard keeping a boyfriend with his schedule. Maybe he really *should* have been considering something a bit more casual—if only to have companionship outside of Caleb.

"And if anyone so much as looks at you crossways for it," Rowan promised, "I'll fry them."

Caleb's grin flashed sharper-than-average canines and he flipped his bangs from his face. "See, this is why I love you. You've got a devious streak hidden under there."

Rowan smirked in reply.

HAVING PARKED HIS bike in the lot for the Mages Guild, Rowan walked to the brick and wrought-iron archway. It wasn't a physical barrier, rather one that was enchanted to grant or deny entrance as visiting hours allowed. His brows lowered when he saw the notice on the event board that said they were closed to non-guild members for the day.

"What's that about?" The air rippled around him as he passed through the archway, responding to his magic.

The floating rock the Guild sat upon was accessible by a slatted bridge, enchanted to be stable even in high winds. Regardless, it was slightly disconcerting to walk across, suspended in the air over the cliffs where the waters of the Grey Tides crashed. The heavy wooden doors of the Mages Guild hadn't been closed in nearly twenty years, since a crisis involving the accidental summoning of five honey badgers and one angry, rampaging moose—even now, they stood open and welcoming.

The Guild itself was made of stone, with warm wood features and glowing torches of magic light. There were three buildings set around a courtyard that boasted beautiful landscaping and a fountain at its center. Rowan particularly loved the night lilies and moondrop flowers that glowed after sunset, along with the fireflies that were attracted to them, creating a magical atmosphere that had nothing to do with the mages' powers.

The building on the left was quarters for those who stayed within the Guild, mostly apprentices and journeymen who would have left home to study there. The larger one on the right was used for classrooms and practical applications.

"Have you seen Masters Ieus and Frey?" Rowan asked the first apprentice he saw.

She pointed toward the Hall of Enlightenment, across from the entrance. "The Masters Board has been in session for a while now. They canceled classes for the rest of the day." If Rowan hadn't been worried before, he certainly was now.

He cut a direct path through the garden to the Hall—their indoor amphitheater—a circular arena with raised seating. Demonstrations were held there, and testing administered, but it was also a place to hold meetings or, on rare occasion, an internal tribunal.

Once inside, Rowan was stopped at the inner doors by one of the guards. There were only a few on duty at any given time as there wasn't much need for them. "Closed session, Rowan," Tate said.

"What the hell's going on?" he demanded all the same. "What's happened?"

Glancing over his shoulder at the doors, Tate sighed. "I don't know much. Just that there's something shady going on. The board is discussing what to do about it. I'm assuming they'll tell the rest of us once they've come to a decision."

"How long have they been in there?"

"Over an hour now. Ieus was worked up. Jorah looked murderous. Frey and Quail were both clearly concerned. And Sacha looked about ready to throw up."

"Well, that's disturbing," Rowan said.

Ieus was the oldest on the board, and thus often looked to by the others as a defacto leader. Jorah was a former battlemage, his experience affording the Guild a unique perspective. Frey had been Rowan's sponsor as an apprentice, a level-headed woman who didn't get rattled easily. To that end, Quail was very much the same, far more focused on mentoring than the politics. Sacha was a master from a guild to the east, a more recent transplant, who had proven to be a positive asset to them.

For something to have them all worried, it must have been big.

Rowan leaned against the wall next to Tate. There was nothing left to do but wait, so he asked, "Did you put in for your Alteration exam yet?"

Tate seemed grateful for the change in subject. He had already passed with summoning, giving him a Masters in the School of Conjuration. "Been trying to come up with an appropriate show for the board. You?"

"Leaning toward Spirit." It was probably the next strongest of his schools, yet he was having doubts. "But, same issue as you. My counter-curses and hexes need more work. My healing abilities suck. And blood magic, well..."

"Not much you can really do with that, huh?"

The inner arena doors opened. Quail walked by, pushing his glasses back up the bridge of his nose and looking pale. He barely gave Rowan more than a nod, which was quite different from his usual energetic self. Sacha followed in his wake, not looking much better, a frown marring her otherwise pretty features. The youngest of the masters, she was still Rowan's senior by two decades.

Jorah stalked past next, looking downright murderous, indeed. He spun on his heels, barking, "Tate, with me."

Tate jumped. "See ya 'round," he said in apology, before jogging to catch up with his mentor.

Ieus and Frey were, unsurprisingly, the last out. His gray hair and bushy beard gave Ieus a grandfatherly, if not slightly eccentric, look. Frey's white-blonde hair and prim appearance gave her a similarly instant credibility as someone who would look after and mother everyone in sight. In both their cases, that held true.

"Rowan!" Frey exclaimed. "What are you doing here, dear?"

"I think the better question is what's going on?"

She pursed her lips, clearly debating on what to say. Then she sighed and motioned him to follow. "We have a problem."

"There's a dark mage running around Osterian," Ieus explained, as Rowan fell into step between them on their path around the courtyard. "We've been getting reports for the past couple months. Scattered, and few at first, so we didn't pay them much mind. Now, the mage has apparently arrived in Everstrand, and they've stepped up their game."

"What's been happening?" Rowan asked, already worried by the amount of secrecy.

"There have been questionable deaths, mostly. Afflictions with seemingly no explanation."

"But, they haven't found any evidence of magic," Rowan guessed.

Frey confirmed, "The original reports were of animals dying under similar circumstances. Mostly in outlying areas, like Appleby and Riverpost, or wild game found by hunters in the Timber."

"A lot of the game," Ieus added, "was torn to pieces, shredded, like an animal attack, but not consumed."

"Then it stepped up to domestic animals." Rowan put the pieces together. "And now it's people."

"Precisely."

"We need to handle this fast," Frey said. "We can't let the Inquisition get wind of it."

Rowan didn't need to ask why they would avoid reporting it. The Inquisition already watched them enough as it was. Plus, reports of a dark mage would incite panic and misplaced suspicion toward other mages. The Inquisition would probably like nothing more than for the people to turn against the magicae. Causing a frenzy in the city would sure help do the trick.

"How can I help?" Rowan asked instead.

"I don't think there's much for you to do at this point," Frey said. "Jorah will be heading up the investigation. We need to track down where this mage is, first of all, and we can go about taking care of the problem from there."

"All of this remains internal," Ieus stated firmly. "And no apprentices are to be alerted to the situation."

"Agreed." Rowan didn't want to imagine what would happen if this got out of hand. He merely hoped Jorah worked fast.

"But, enough about all this," Frey huffed. "It's giving me a headache. What is it that you needed, dear?" She slipped into the matronly role Rowan had come to find comforting.

"I need to set up another masters exam."

"Already?" Ieus's words were amused rather than disbelieving.

Ieus and Frey understood, more than anyone, that they needed to invest in the next generation of mages. It was what made them both such wonderful teachers. Frey had taught him a lot during his apprenticeship—however, she argued that fact—and Ieus was a patient mentor.

"What have you been working on?" Frey inquired.

"I'm going to try for Spirit."

"Incarnum has never particularly been your strong suit," Ieus replied, using the traditional name of the school.

"I've been doing a lot of work with my blood magic."

"That's near impossible to demonstrate."

"I know." Considering it was mostly used as a way to enhance other spells, it made for a tricky prospect. "But, I'm hoping all that work translates into my hexes, curses, and counters."

Frey gave him a considering look. "It won't be easy, dear. But, then, I don't have to tell you that."

"Jorah won't pull any punches," Ieus agreed. As a Spirit master himself, it would be Jorah who would test anyone who wanted to add that particular masters onto their mantel. "At least you won't have to beat him."

"Comforting," Rowan muttered.

Frey put a hand on Rowan's shoulder, stopping them in their walk around the garden, shaded from the late afternoon sun by the overhangs from the buildings. "Perhaps ask Tate to study with you? He's been working closely with Jorah for his own studies. You might be able to help each other."

Rowan hesitated. It wasn't that he didn't like Tate—he was talented and pleasant to be around, perhaps even a friend—but Rowan was rather finicky when it came to his studying. Deviating from his usual methods could potentially backfire.

"Or you could hold off," Ieus suggested. "You could put your focus into Alteration like you've been talking about ever since Sacha joined us. I'm sure she would make time to help you."

"I want to make high master," Rowan balked. That required him to receive a third masters, and it would get him that much closer to grandmaster. "Sooner rather than later. So that makes Spirit my best bet. Alteration and Conjuration I'd spend too much time on."

"What's the rush? You have plenty of time, Rowan."

"You're already the youngest mage recorded in any of the guilds to hold two masters," Frey pointed out. "You'll get there."

"I can do this," Rowan replied stubbornly. "You know I promised Gram."

Frey let out a little sigh, nodding. "Alright, dear." She rubbed Rowan's arm briefly.

"There's no harm in trying," Ieus relented. "I just don't want you to set yourself up for failure."

Rowan nodded. He took a deep breath, looking at the garden as he tried to keep focus. "I planned to ask Jorah for study suggestions, but..." Jorah was going to have his hands full with the dark mage problem for the foreseeable future. Rowan wished it would leave Jorah distracted for the test, but the man hadn't gotten a masters for nothing.

"I can email you a few study guides," Frey assured him, ever the support system, despite how long it had been since Rowan was her apprentice.

"Quail would likely be willing to go over things with you," Ieus suggested. "It might benefit him as well to have a distraction."

"Thank you," Rowan told them both, feeling relieved.

His request for an exam before the Masters Board had been granted. Now the real work began.

A FEW DAYS passed before Shaw finally got around to doing a database search on Rowan. His record came back clean. At twenty-eight, he was five years younger than Shaw. It appeared he was a business owner as well, the address on file coming back to a shop in town—Charmed to Meet You. That was a rather cute name, actually.

Shaw was fairly certain no one had living quarters above the stores at Orchard Street Mall. Given that Rowan owned a dirt bike, Shaw assumed he lived outside the city. It would explain everything being registered to the shop, at least, since most places out in the Sacred Timber weren't serviced by Everstrand in any way.

Looking at the ID photo on the computer screen, it didn't do Rowan justice. The guy was attractive, no doubt. It had been a spur of the moment decision to grab his name. Now that Shaw had information on him though, he wasn't particularly sure what to do with it.

Maybe he could visit this shop of Rowan's? While browsing the website, Shaw realized he didn't have much need for a charm. Apparently, Rowan had a masters in enchantment, so there was likely very little he couldn't do. Perhaps Shaw could ask for something simple, to see if Rowan would take the bait.

Shaw scoffed, clicking out of the windows he had open. This was all so stupid. First, this wasn't the way to go about trying to get a date. Second, and more importantly, he couldn't afford the distraction right now.

"Speaking of..." Shaw looked at the time. Meredeen should have left for her appointment with the district attorney. That meant her office would be unoccupied.

Shaw double-checked his pockets before leaving his office. As head of the inquisitors, Meredeen would be privy to even more information than Vaughn. No one else ranked higher, save for Zane, the head of the entire temple.

As if appearing by mere thought, Zane turned the corner in front of him. With him was a man Shaw didn't know. Hoping to pass by, Shaw nodded to them. "Knight Commander."

"Ah, Inquisitor. I would like you to meet someone. Pollock, this is our newest inquisitor, Shaw." Pollock offered his hand and Shaw shook it—although he didn't want to, considering the vibes he was getting from the man. "Senator Pollock is one of our most valued supporters."

Oh, joy, Shaw thought sarcastically.

"We were just discussing his campaign for Prime Minister."

Double joy. Aloud, Shaw said, "Well, more supporters of the Inquisition in power can only be a benefit."

Pollock grinned, a look even more animal than Shaw had seen on were-creatures. He was a portly man, wearing a fine suit that was likely above his means, with the bearing of someone who thought much too highly of himself. "I'm glad you agree. Where is it you hail from, might I ask, Inquisitor?"

Shaw's accent had the habit of making him stand out. "Rouvalon, originally, but I was just transferred from Shadewind."

"Commander Larus seemed very unwilling to let him go," Zane supplied. "Best case man they had."

"Excellent." Pollock beamed. "We could use fresh blood in these halls."

Shaw nodded. "I was actually on my way to look into a new lead..."

Zane waved a dismissive hand. "Carry on."

He went around the corner, waiting until the pair had gotten out of sight before resuming his original mission.

Meredeen's office was at the end of the hall, conveniently placed where the inquisitors would have to pass by going in or out of the building, allowing her to pull them into her office if the need arose. Knowing there were no cameras in this area of the temple, Shaw took a quick look around as he rubbed at his left forearm. Picking the lock was an easy feat to deft hands such as Shaw's—the skills of another lifetime.

The blinds on the windows were already closed, and the glass on the door fogged over upon closing for privacy. The desk was hardwood, the chair large and plush, and there was even nice carpeting instead of the cheap stuff the rest of them were stuck with. Arrogance.

Unlike Vaughn's office, Meredeen's was spotless and organized to a fault. Everything would have to go *exactly* back into place.

He slapped a reveal spell scroll on the wall. "There we are." The brief light that ran across the room bounced back, showing a small glowing outline of something behind a filing cabinet.

Working fast, Shaw put a flash drive into the computer tower, allowing it to automatically hack and download the contents. While that did its job, Shaw pulled the cabinet out. There was a section of the wall that housed a secret compartment—hard to see if you weren't looking for it.

Opening it revealed a bundle of documents, along with a flash drive that was likely encrypted. He didn't have the skill to hack it himself. It was just as well he knew someone perfect for the job. The computer beeped, signaling the end of the data transfer, so he plugged in the mystery flash drive and a fresh one of his own for the information to copy onto. Shaw had to know what was on it.

While that was working, he snapped photos of the documents using his phone. He wouldn't worry about looking at what was on them until later; he was already pushing his luck doing two data transfers. Everything of potential use would get sent in a data package tonight, and afterward he would scrub the evidence.

Once everything was back in place, with no trace he'd ever been there, Shaw checked that the way was clear. He slipped back into the hall, the door clicking shut behind him. Breaking into Zane's office would have been pushing his luck, but Shaw was willing to risk it if nothing better turned up. Hopefully it wouldn't come to that.

Chapter Three

"STOP BEING AN ass," Shaw heard Rowan's friend telling him. "You know, you'll actually enjoy yourself if you stop worrying about your damn studying for two seconds."

"I have less than four weeks before I'm called before the Masters Board." Rowan sounded as if he were reminding the other man for the nth time.

"And you'll do *fine*. Now lighten the fuck up." He held a glass up to Rowan—some blue concoction the same color and vibrancy as his hair. Resigned, Rowan accepted the drink, clinking their glasses together before taking a sip.

When the line of Rowan's shoulders relaxed and the pair appeared ready to settle in, Shaw moved to the bar. "Dhangan Ale," he requested.

"Good choice," the bartender complimented. Not that Shaw needed to be told. No one made ale quite like the dwarves.

He smirked when he noticed Rowan glance his way and perform a double-take.

"Oh, what the—? Seriously?"

Shaw raised a brow.

Rowan scoffed, "Out of all the pubs in this town you just happen to pick the one I frequent?"

"Hello to you too" was Shaw's reply, complete with easy smile. "Name's Shaw, by the way."

"Why, hel-lo," the lithe stranger at Rowan's side replied, leaning on the bar to look around him.

"Down, Caleb," Rowan said dryly. "This one's an inquisitor." Caleb *growled* at that. "If it's any consolation, he was the one who got that other asshole off my back the other day."

Caleb's nostrils flared and he begrudgingly said, "Well, thanks for that." He took a gulp of his drink before adding as a warning, "Ro's pack. So, if anything happened to him..."

"Pack, huh?" Shaw took a drink of the ale set in front of him while he studied the pair. It appeared Caleb was a werewolf—certainly not someone he wanted to be on the wrong side of, especially if he claimed a mage as pack, of all things. "I'll keep that in mind."

"Smart."

Rowan rolled his eyes, having already downed half his drink and looking about ready to chug the rest. "What in the hell are those?" Shaw asked, nodding toward the drinks. He was attempting to make conversation, but he was also genuinely curious.

"River Hound," Rowan answered. "Don't ask what's in it. Where Caleb's concerned, I've found it's best not to."

"You're a riot," Caleb said. He looked over as a few people got out of a nearby booth, smacking Rowan's shoulder. "Our table's open."

"Grab it before I shoot lightning at somebody." As Caleb went to do just that, Rowan downed the rest of his drink.

Shaw raised a brow. "That kinda night, huh?"

"What?" Rowan looked at him, apparently catching his meaning as he shook his head. "Oh, no, I'm not really big on drinking. Caleb always insists I have at least one whenever we come out. So, I amuse him, but I'd rather just get it out of the way."

The bartender gave Rowan a sympathetic smile as he passed over a large mug that smelled of coffee with a whipped foam on top. "Elven coffee?" Shaw guessed. It was a style rather than anything grown or brewed by the elves. The coffee didn't matter so much as the fact it had starleaf steeped in it, a plant common in regions the elves favored. It added a magical spark to the beverage, which those sensitive to such things would draw on.

"Natural energy boost." Rowan smiled over his mug as he took a drink. Shaw would take that as a positive.

"Mind if I join you?" he asked, tilting his head toward where Caleb sat waiting.

"I guess since you went to so much trouble to stalk me..." Rowan teased.

"Stalking is completely the wrong way to put it." When Rowan raised a brow in challenge, Shaw explained, "I did a standard check after our encounter. For the report, you know?"

"Nice try. But, curious all the same."

"What's to be curious about? You're attractive. I was intrigued."

"I'm also a mage."

"So?"

Rowan gave him a skeptical look and walked away.

Shaw followed. "Look, just because I'm an inquisitor doesn't mean I have some...*hatred* for magicae. I've nothing against any of you. I'm just doing a job."

Rowan turned to him, those violet eyes glinting when the low bar lighting hit them exactly right. They were just as enchanting as that first time they met. And like then, Shaw silently willed the man into seeing that what he said was true. After what seemed like an eternity, Rowan consented. "Have a seat."

Shaw grinned as he slid into the booth across from Rowan and Caleb.

"You're not from around here," Rowan noted.

"Did the accent give me away?" Shaw joked, watching Rowan smirk a little in amusement. "My family's from Rouvalon. Moved to Calagon as a teenager." He spoke of the countries across the ocean from Osterian. "And here I am now."

"Always wanted to go to Rouvalon," Caleb mentioned, taking a sip of his drink.

"Beautiful country," Shaw said. "I miss it sometimes. The wilds here seem very similar from what I've seen."

"The Sacred Timber is lovely this time of year," Rowan said fondly. "But, I have to say, autumn's the best. The colors are gorgeous."

"You grew up here?" Shaw asked, more than curious about Rowan. He was intriguing in a way that Shaw couldn't explain.

"I did. Raised in the Timber." Rowan's fingers played with his mug, shadows crossing his face. "My parents died when I was ten—car accident—so, my grandmother raised me."

"I'm sorry."

Shaw couldn't imagine being a young boy losing a parent, let alone both at once. It wasn't like he had a stellar relationship with his folks these days. Once they'd decided to return to Rouvalon and he'd chosen to stay behind in Calagon, it had caused a rift. But, growing up the way he had—poor, and barely scraping by—would have been miles harder without them there, that was for certain.

Rowan raised a shoulder. "I had a good life out there. Gram taught me everything she knew about magic. By the time I went to apply for apprenticeship with the Everstrand Guild, I was able to test out of a lot of the basic courses." The corner of Rowan's mouth ticked up. "Guess that's how I pissed a lot of people off, passing my apprentice tests and becoming a journeyman by eighteen."

"Seriously?" Shaw's brows rose. "Isn't that supposed to take until you're like twenty, twenty-one?"

"Yup," Caleb answered for him, clapping Rowan on the shoulder. "Became the youngest mage with a masters, and then he decided that wasn't good enough, so he had to go and get a second."

"Two masters?"

Rowan smirked at him. "I thought you did your homework, Inquisitor," he teased.

Shaw chuckled, pleased that he had made Rowan relax enough to joke around. "A standard check wouldn't come back with something like that. Though your website mentioned the masters in enchantment. I actually swung by the shop earlier, but you were already closed." He shrugged. "Asked around and somebody told me you usually come here after you close."

"Well, it's not really a big secret where we hang out," Caleb admitted. He readjusted himself in the corner as he subtly pressed his scent into the cushions, essentially claiming the booth.

Rowan nodded in agreement before answering Shaw's original question. "Two masters for now. Hoping for the third here shortly."

"Was Enchantment your first?" It was the School of Magic that covered everything from charms and wards to imbuing various magics into weapons.

"Yup," Rowan confirmed. "I fixed the levitation charms under the Guild."

Shaw's eyes widened. "You...? The floating rock out there is floating because of you?"

Rowan attempted to shrug it off, but there was no missing the slight curl to his lips. "I can't take all the credit. The Guild has been floating for almost a hundred and fifty years. I just shored up all the enchantments that were losing power, fixed the wards, that sort of thing."

"He's being modest," Caleb said. "If he hadn't done it, that thing would probably be in the Grey Tides by now."

"I may have found a fault or two," Rowan conceded. He took another sip of coffee. "Mastered in Primal Magic after that." Journeymen could show proficiency with a few of the elements, but a mage had to show mastery of *all* to get a distinction for it.

"How'd you do that?" Shaw snarked. "Find a new element?"

Rowan barked out a laugh. "I set up a battlemage test. Except it was scaled down to focus solely on Primal magic."

"That's still impressive. Those tests are no joke."

He lifted a shoulder. "It was a civilian version. No one was shooting at me or flinging curses. It was me against dummies and stuff like that."

"Doesn't make it any less impressive," Shaw insisted, toasting him with his glass, before taking a swig.

"Not as much as anyone who passes the real thing. And to think they don't even get the masters out of it." Because of their military status, battlemages weren't allowed to hold membership in a guild. That meant that they couldn't hold any titles—be it apprentice to master, or beyond.

"So, you're basically a badass," Shaw mused.

Caleb laughed, choking on his drink.

Rowan made a face at him and groused, "Thanks."

"I mean, you've got amazing skills," Caleb said. "But I'd never use that word to describe you."

"Why not?" Shaw was curious. Friends usually gave the best insight into people.

"Badass has the implication of being a fighter. Ro's a lover." Caleb threw Shaw a wink.

Rowan huffed.

"Come on, now," Caleb insisted. "Nerd is a better word for you."

Rowan muttered under his breath, "Not arguing there."

Shaw was grinning, and it caught Rowan's eye because he asked, "What about you? What's your story?"

Shaw raised a shoulder. "Nothing quite so interesting, I'm afraid. Brand new to Everstrand. And, well, utterly bored out of my mind, to tell the truth. I don't know anyone here. Don't really know the city yet. Just...lonely, honestly."

"So, you pick a couple magicae to hang out with?" Caleb baited at the same time Rowan inquired, "Why come here if you don't know anyone?"

Shaw's fingers drummed on the table. "Suppose it was time for a change. Shadewind was boring." He spoke of Calagon's capital. "My friends were going their own way; my only family moved back to Rouvalon. It seemed like...an adventure."

That made Rowan smile a bit. "Just like that?"

"Just like that."

Rowan took a drink, seeming to mull everything over. "Why the Inquisition?"

"Easy enough job to get being law enforcement. I kind of did this all on a whim and they were hiring." It was more complicated than that, but this was neither the time nor place to get into it—if ever.

"We need to find you a better job," Caleb concluded.

Shaw laughed. "I'll take it," he replied honestly. "You think I like being around those bigots all day? It's enough to drive a man to drink." He toasted them with his glass pointedly, finishing it off.

"Here, here." Caleb returned the gesture, throwing his own drink back.

The tone of the place had changed, slipping into a more lively late night atmosphere. Even the music had moved from mellow tunes to something with more kick. "Is that...?" Shaw's brows scrunched together, head tilting. "Armored Night?"

"Hell yeah, it is." Caleb was enthusiastic about it, while Rowan rolled his eyes.

"Not a fan?" Shaw asked.

"They're a bit much for me." Rowan's reply was mild; the side-eye he gave Caleb—who was bobbing his head—was anything but.

"I can go put something better on," Shaw offered. "What do you like?"

"Anything that takes it down a decibel?"

"So, trollhop's out then."

Rowan threw him a look like he was contemplating setting Shaw on fire with his mind. Shaw threw his hands up, though the fact he was laughing was likely not convincing.

"Try the local section," Caleb suggested. "Lots of good stuff to choose from."

Shaw discovered that Caleb wasn't kidding. The song selector had a whole section devoted to Osterian-based bands of all types. Staying away from shrieker and trollhop, Shaw instead found the rock, figuring folk wasn't something this crowd was going to stand for.

"I hope you like Hex," Shaw said when he returned.

"Perfect!" Caleb beamed, and Shaw was happy to see Rowan approved as well. "We're gonna be seeing them at the Equinox Festival. Bunch of the local bands play here, too. You should check them out sometime."

At least they didn't have to wait long for his selections to start playing. Caleb literally howled. "Shaw, this is the best!"

"So, let's dance."

Caleb practically shoved Rowan out of the booth. Rowan stumbled and Shaw caught his arm. He grinned up at Rowan, watching those vibrant eyes of his.

"After you," Shaw mused.

Rowan licked his lips and nodded, trailing behind Caleb, who was already swaying to the pounding beat.

Once they were out on the floor proper, Rowan offered him a little smile, body starting to move. Shaw had never truly been good at dancing, but he liked to do it anyway. He was blocky in his movements, while his two dancing partners moved like sinew. They were liquid grace, and rather enchanting. Still, his focus was drawn to Rowan.

The song was about magic—apropos, given current company—and made mention about casting spells on the listener.

Shaw reached out, placing a hand on Rowan's waist, making him freeze a moment, eyes flashing as he looked at Shaw. Then Rowan smiled, dancing closer to him. Shaw breathed out in relief, allowing himself to become lost in the music. Rowan was absolutely hypnotizing. Shaw pressed closer, his hands flaring possessively over Rowan's hips.

He felt a back against his—Caleb swaying to the music behind him—but Shaw only had eyes for Rowan. It was bewitching—as cliché as it sounded. Their gazes locked and Shaw didn't release him, emotion bubbling to the surface and threatening to burst from his chest.

Both of Shaw's selections passed before he realized it— *when had the song changed*? At least Rowan appeared just as dazed, both of them shaken out of it by Caleb. He was grinning from ear to ear. Shaw figured had his tail been out, Caleb would have been wagging it furiously.

"Good choices, Shaw. Let's get some more drinks!"

Shaw smiled momentarily, eyes cutting over to Rowan, who was flushed as he pulled away. "Yeah," Shaw answered, "sounds great."

Shaw got another ale, and Rowan another elven coffee. Caleb's new drink was even more colorful than the last. It was bright purple, but as Shaw looked closer, he saw blue swirling inside. Caleb smirked knowingly. With the tap of his finger to the glass, it came alive with pinpricks of shimmering light, the entire drink appearing to be a rotating galaxy.

"Wow!"

"Nice, huh? One of the mages at the Guild invented it. Called a galaxy shot."

"Appropriate name. What's it taste like?"

Caleb wiggled his brows, smiling over the glass. "Magic."

Rowan shook his head, amused. "Acai berry and blueberry with vodka," he supplied, "and a pinch of magic. It's in a dissolving capsule they add in."

"Thought you didn't like to drink," Shaw said.

"Don't. But, kind of had to try it when they created it. Horus, the bartender, makes it with half the liquor for me, and it tastes pretty great."

Caleb was licking his lips. "So awesome. Oh, watch this." He blew out a breath, little sparkles coming from his mouth to float in the air. They twinkled a moment before dying out. "An unintended side effect, but really freakin' cool."

"Agreed." Shaw was impressed. "Might have to try one of those later. I'm more an ale man than cocktails, but..."

"Worth it at least once."

Shaw was used to being able to talk with practically anyone. At the same time, it was far more rare to find people he truly connected with. He could fake it—or coerce it—but the real thing was a different story. Whatever it was about these two, he was feeling it.

Granted, Rowan had his attention for entirely different reasons, but Caleb was an interesting character in his own right.

It was getting late, and Shaw could tell the pair were winding down. Figuring it was now or never, Shaw leaned forward across the table. When Rowan met his gaze, Shaw said, "Come back to my place."

Rowan froze. "I don't kn—"

Caleb shoved him roughly. "Go," he encouraged with a goofy grin.

Rowan huffed at his friend before looking unsurely back at Shaw. "I'm not... I don't just..."

Deciding to save him, Shaw assured Rowan, "No expectations." Taking a chance, he reached out and laid his hand over Rowan's. "Coffee and more talking."

Rowan licked his lip, biting it a moment. The way his head was angled, his violet eyes gazed back at Shaw from under his lashes. Shaw inhaled sharply, knowing he wasn't imagining the heat there. "And if I want more than that?"

Shaw swallowed. "Whatever you want."

That made Rowan grin slyly. "Let's get going."

"Call me in the morning." Caleb leered, not even complaining when Rowan punched him in the shoulder.

Shaw was already standing, offering a hand. Rowan's expression softened and he accepted, lacing their fingers together. Caleb's laughter followed them out.

BECAUSE SHAW DIDN'T have his own transportation, he had to flag a cab, and Rowan followed on his dirt bike since he didn't want to leave it at the bar overnight. "Would have been nice if you had room on the back of that thing," Shaw mentioned, nodding at the bike that Rowan sat straddling at the curb.

He smiled up at Shaw. "If you weren't so built, we might have been able to squeeze on." He looked Shaw over from head to toe, pointedly.

"I don't hear any complaints."

Rowan laughed, shaking his head. He gestured for Shaw to lead the way. "Shall we?"

The apartment building was in the Southern District, overlooking the bay where the ships came in. It was unsurprising that an inquisitor would pick a home so close to the temple. It had been tactically placed, the Order wanting to keep a watchful eye over the comings and goings of the city. Rowan chose to ignore the temple he could see in the distance, instead focusing on the man he'd decided to follow home.

In the elevator, Rowan looked over at Shaw leaning against the side. "I don't just go home with people like this, you know."

"You don't really seem the type," he agreed. Shaw tilted his head. "So why'd you come?"

Rowan lifted a shoulder, looking away. He followed Shaw off the elevator when they arrived at the fifth floor. "Guess I'm curious."

"Well, I did say no expectations," Shaw reminded him, slotting the key in the lock.

"I know." When the door opened, Rowan pushed Shaw through it, kicking the door closed behind them. He captured Shaw's lips with his own, intent clear as he pressed against him. Shaw's arm wrapped around his waist, hand coming up to tangle in his hair, kissing back just as fiercely. "I might have a few, though," Rowan gasped as he dragged his lips away.

"You won't hear any objections from me." Shaw's eyes were slightly glazed over as he looked up at Rowan.

Decided, Rowan walked Shaw backward. It was a studio apartment, so there was no hunt for the bed that was tucked behind a slatted room divider. With a little shove, he sent Shaw back onto it, both of them grinning like complete fools.

Shaw was infinitely more attractive out of that inquisitor uniform. He was all muscle underneath a tight gray long-sleeve shirt. His jeans were loose-fitting and hung low on lean hips, and his hiking boots, Rowan had noticed, were covered in dry mud.

Rowan helped Shaw remove his shirt, tossing it aside. It revealed an array of tattoos previously hidden from view. Getting on the bed, Rowan threw his leg over Shaw to straddle his hips. "You have a lot of these," he mused, tracing the tattoo over Shaw's heart. It was a dragon skull with a dagger through it.

"I've been collecting them awhile." Shaw took hold of Rowan's shirt, so he bent forward to allow Shaw to remove it.

The tattoos on Shaw's forearms caught his eye next. On the underside of each, there was a word printed in Runic: *shadow* and *shield*. Rowan's fingers ran over the first one, feeling the tingle of magic in response.

"Mana-infused," Shaw explained. Rowan nodded, knowing it was the sole way for non-mages to use spells. Typically, that meant magic scrolls, but in this case, it was placed directly into skin to use over and over again.

Shaw took Rowan's necklace in hand, the blue crystal standing out against stark skin. "What's this?"

Rowan closed his hand around the aqua aura crystal, its rough-cut state rubbing against callouses. "It's a power charm," he answered with a tilt of his head. "It was one of the first things I made on my own when I was younger." He opened his hand, allowing Shaw to run his finger over the pendant and the silver wire that wrapped around it to hold it in place on its leather lanyard. "Never go anywhere without it."

"It's beautiful," Shaw spoke softly. His gaze traveled from the necklace up to Rowan's eyes. "Kind of like you." Rowan felt his face heat up and Shaw chuckled in response. "What? No one ever tell you that before?"

"Been awhile," Rowan admitted. "For a lot of things, in fact." He was always so busy with his studies and the store that any boyfriend got put to the back burner. Not many seemed to appreciate that.

Smiling up at him, Shaw ran his fingers through Rowan's hair. "I think we can fix that." He tugged lightly, bringing Rowan down so their lips met again. Unlike their first kiss, rushed and heated, this was exploratory. An ember of desire traveled straight up Rowan's spine, making him melt against Shaw.

Rowan felt tingling against his fingertips as they traveled over Shaw's bare skin. Teeth tugged at his lower lip, drawing his attention. Rowan smiled against Shaw's mouth, pressing against his touch. The hand running down Rowan's spine caused a full body shiver. Everything seemed to light up along his nerve endings, pleasure seeping into every pore. Rowan sank into the sensation, allowing it to pull him under.

ROLLING OVER IN the morning, Shaw expected to find Rowan still in bed with him. Instead, he found Rowan sitting at the end of the mattress, studying something in his hand. Sitting up, Shaw stretched and grinned lazily. "Morning," he said. When Rowan gave him a piercing look, Shaw's face fell. "What's wrong?"

"I knew you were too good to be true." Rowan tossed what he was holding onto the bed. It was Shaw's ID. "Human," Rowan said flatly. "That's what it says, but I don't buy it. I know magic when I feel it."

Shaw felt his mouth go dry. "What are you—?"

"I don't know how you did it, or why, but I'm not about to stick around to find out."

Shaw snagged Rowan's hand when he stood. "Wait, wait! I can explain, okay?" Rowan gave him a long hard look, but when he didn't try to escape, Shaw took it as a sign to continue, carefully releasing him. "The *how* is complicated. It involves bribery, a lot of groundwork, and plenty of practice concealing myself. Though, apparently not well enough to fool you."

"What are you?" Rowan was guarded, and Shaw couldn't exactly blame him.

"A witch," Shaw admitted. Unlike mages, witches were born with one particular magical ability. They were also of the mental variety—clairvoyance, telepathy, and the like. "I'm an empath."

Rowan actually growled—a thing he most likely picked up from Caleb—and backed away. "So, you manipulated me," he accused. "You tricked me into coming here. Into..."

"No, not at all," Shaw quickly reassured him, getting out of bed. "I can only *influence*. I can't force someone to do anything against their free will." Shaw tried to move closer, but with every step he took, Rowan retreated. Holding his palms up, Shaw pointed out, "Like the day we met. I compelled you to calm down so that bullshit with Dansforth didn't get worse."

Rowan's nostrils flared as Shaw tried to do the same thing again. "Don't even!"

"Rowa—"

"No!"

Magic crackled in the air, a witch like Shaw able to pick up on it. Even if he was a mundane, Rowan's glowing eyes would have given it away. Shaw held up his hands again in a show of peace.

"Why?" Rowan demanded. "Why hide? Why work for the Inquisition?"

Shaw worked his jaw back and forth, knowing Rowan wouldn't like his answer. It was the one he had to give. "That's my business."

"Bullshit!" Rowan spat. "That's not the way this works."

Shaw knew that it was likely impossible to have a relationship going forward like that. Still, all he could offer was "I can't tell you."

As expected, Rowan looked anything but pleased. "Forget it," he snarled, shaking his head. Rowan headed for the door.

When Shaw went to follow, Rowan whirled on him. A force field of energy hit Shaw, slamming him back into the wall. Its spell didn't release until the front door shut behind Rowan. Shaw crumpled to the ground as the pressure lifted, his lungs fully inflating once again.

"Damn it," he hissed. He didn't know why Rowan's rejection stung so much, but he couldn't let it lay like this.

Shaw was completely unaware of his actions until his phone was already ringing in his ear. When Thalanil's voice came over the line, he couldn't say he was surprised. "Hey," Shaw greeted softly. "How're things?"

"You okay?" Thalanil deflected, concern lacing his voice.

"Yeah, Mum. I'm fine."

Thalanil snorted.

"I, uh, I might be compromised. Not entirely sure."

"Then get your ass back here," Thalanil ordered. "We can't take that chance."

"Not with the targets," Shaw explained. "It's... There's this guy I met. A mage."

"Oh, hell." Thalanil sighed. "What have you done, Shaw?"

"Oi! It's not my fault!" Shaw ignored the scoff. "And I believe I asked how you guys were."

"Last mission went fine. Rhys is gonna send us out again in a couple weeks. I'll send you the encrypted data." Shaw wouldn't argue as they were far from being on a secure channel.

"But how are you?" Shaw pressed. "How're they holding up?"

"About as well as you'd expect."

Shaw didn't have anything to say to that.

"Hold on." There was noise on the other end Shaw couldn't make out. "Alright, alright," Thalanil laughed. Back on the phone, he said, "Orion says 'Hi' and 'We miss you.'" Thalanil laughed even more. "Oh, and 'Hurry back already.'"

There was no helping the smile that came to Shaw's face, momentarily forgetting his growing array of problems. "I miss you guys too."

Chapter Four

ROWAN WAS SITTING on the stool behind the shop's counter, leg bouncing a little. An elbow rested on the counter, his other hand turning the pages of the book he was perusing. The bell above the door chimed, grabbing Rowan's attention. He froze when he saw who it was.

Shaw's eyes locked onto his, hesitating before coming inside all the way. "Hey," Shaw greeted, walking up to the counter.

Rowan wasn't exactly thrilled to see him. After what happened two days ago, he didn't figure he could be blamed either. "Can I help you with something?" he managed to ask with forced politeness, gaze shifting away from Shaw.

"I, uh, I wanted to apologize for what happened."

"I don't want your—"

"I also wanted to see if you could make a few charms for me."

Rowan's teeth *clicked* together audibly. A customer was a customer, and he couldn't exactly turn one away. Still, he was a little suspicious on the timing. "Really?"

"Yeah." Shaw rubbed at the back of his neck awkwardly. "I need four. They're for my old squad."

That piqued Rowan's interest and he sat up a little straighter. "Your squad? You were military?"

There was no hiding the pride that filled Shaw at that. "Spec ops for Calagon, stationed out of Tolhallow."

"Spec ops?" Rowan was impressed. He recalled the conversation they had at the bar, though, and lowered his brows. "Didn't you say you were law enforcement?"

"Was," Shaw replied. "After I left them. Don't really like to talk about it." He shifted uncomfortably, rolling his shoulder.

The motion drew attention to Shaw's chest, and Rowan tapped his own as he said, "Your tattoo."

"The division emblem."

Rowan had wondered about the tattoo's origin. Granted, he was too focused on other things at the time to get further into it. The man had been quite distracting, in fact. The thought twisted Rowan's lips upward for a moment before he caught himself. Clearing his throat, Rowan inquired, "So, what is it you were looking for?"

"They're gonna be deployed again soon," Shaw replied, brows drawing together. "Don't like not being there, but my miss— My reason for leaving... They understand." Shaw looked at him, tongue swiping nervously over chapped lips.

Rowan watched him carefully. There was something else Shaw was hiding, but Rowan couldn't begin to guess what. Shaw was worried about his friends, that much was clear. Perhaps he knew the details and was simply trying to respect the secrecy their job entailed—or maybe he knew nothing at all, and that made him all the more concerned.

Picking his battles, Rowan prompted, "You want them to have extra protection."

Shaw nodded, taking a deep breath and allowing the tension to bleed out.

"I assume you don't want a run-of-the-mill charm." Rowan pulled some parchment from under the counter. "Otherwise, you could pick those up almost anywhere."

"I want protection on them, yeah, but I figured to make it more personal than that."

"Enchantments related to their jobs specifically, their skill sets." Rowan pulled his quill and inkpot over.

"Exactly."

Rowan glanced up to find Shaw smiling, that same bright and open one he remembered from the bar. He cleared his throat and reminded himself to focus. "Well, I can certainly do that." He rubbed the phoenix feather quill between his fingers, little sparks coming off as it spun back and forth. Shaw eyed it carefully but didn't comment. "The more I know about them, the more effective I can make the charms. Pictures and personal items help too."

"You meditate on the person the charm's meant for?" Shaw rested his hand on the counter, close to where Rowan's sat holding the quill. There was almost a tangible spark in the air at the proximity, Rowan concentrating on not giving into the temptation to reach out for the source.

"I do," he finally replied, hoping Shaw missed his hesitation. Rowan licked his lips before focusing on the task at hand. "Who do you want to start with?"

"How about Thalanil? He's team lead now. An elf from the Redwood. He's also the best sniper in the entire division."

Rowan chuckled. "Bold words, I'm sure."

Shaw smirked. "Oh, he can back it up. Might barely be past his first century, but I'd put money on 'im. Also has a thing with throwing daggers."

Rowan nodded, marking it all down. "Next?"

"Well, that would have to be Orion. He and Thal are mates. He's a Redwood Pack werewolf."

Rowan stopped writing midsentence. "You just said a lot of things that I'm not sure go together."

Shaw laughed. "Right?"

"Correct me if I'm wrong, but isn't the Redwood Pack—?"

"Feral? Ruthless? Devoid of pretty much any interaction with anyone else? Yup."

Well, chalk one up for Caleb's were-creature intel, Rowan thought sarcastically. "There's also the fact I don't think I've ever heard of an elf getting mated to a wolf before."

"Believe it. It's something to see. They're full-on mated the elven way, too—soul bonded and all." Shaw frowned, fingers drumming on the counter. "Their anniversary is coming up soon, actually. Doesn't look like I'm gonna be there." Softer, to himself, Shaw added, "Five years already? Has it already been that long?"

Rowan didn't reply, instead, he dipped his quill to continue his notes.

Shaw leaned over and furrowed his brows at the runes he saw instead of script. "Do you always write in Runic?" he inquired.

"A habit I picked up during my apprenticeship. At first it was to protect my grimoire from prying eyes, but I find it nice to use to protect client information as well." He was perhaps a little paranoid of somebody stealing his notes. Wards only did so much and those at the shop were basic ones that wouldn't do anything against a physical break-in.

"But, anyone who studied Runic could translate it," Shaw reasoned. "Even a mundane."

Rowan's smirk was borderline cocky. "Who said it was translated from Standard?"

Shaw's eyes widened a little. "So, you're translating into another language before putting it into Runic? How many languages do you know?"

"Including Standard and Runic? Four."

"Well, at least I don't have many to sift through if I want to learn all your hidden secrets," he teased in turn, pulling a smile from Rowan's lips. Leaning forward onto his forearms, Shaw said, "There's that smile I like so much." Rowan felt the blush color his cheeks. Not commenting, he shifted the topic back on course. "I believe you were about to tell me about the third team member."

Shaw allowed the deflection. "That would be Keenan. He's the resident battlemage. Primal and summoning magic are his specialty. He has a thing for glamours too."

With little effort, Shaw braced his hands on the counter and popped up, twisting around to land his butt right on the surface. He smiled down at Rowan who rolled his eyes in turn. "That leaves us with Haxos," Shaw continued. He paused for dramatic effect, Rowan raising a meaningful brow. "Centaur."

That certainly surprised Rowan. "You got a centaur to leave his herd?"

"Not sure on the details of *how*, just that he's one of three the herd gave up to be soldiers. He's the demolitions expert. And, as you can imagine, he's pretty handy in a brawl." Shaw thought a moment. "Think you can add something so he isn't such a pain in the ass?"

Rowan snorted, shaking his head. "I'm afraid there isn't much to do about that." Before he could filter the comment, he added, "I can only influence. Not make someone into what they're not."

"Pfft, thanks," Shaw grumbled.

When Rowan peeked up at him, he found Shaw appeared amused at having his own line turned against him. A self-satisfied smile crossed Rowan's face while jotting down the last bit of information he needed. *Focus, you idiot.* Shaw's proximity was enough to be distracting, and it was making Rowan forget about the fact he was meant to be angry with him.

Getting back on track, Rowan inquired, "Do you have any pictures of them?"

Shaw brought up a group photo on his phone and passed it over to Rowan. They were dressed in black combat gear, covered in mud. Shaw pointed out each member in turn, all of them rather attractive in their own right. Orion was glued to Thalanil's side, grinning from ear to ear while Thalanil looked tired but pleased. Keenan's arm was slung around Haxo's shoulder as he flashed the camera a peace sign, Haxos's face set in stone. Last was Shaw, his arm thrown across the shoulders of a sixth member, the man laughing with his arm around him as well.

"Who's that?" Rowan asked when Shaw didn't introduce him.

"Marcus. Vampire."

"Doesn't believe in charms?" Rowan guessed. It was an honest question, as vampires were typically a superstitious bunch—an ingrained fear from long ago when their race was still hunted.

"He's gone" was all Shaw said, taking his phone back and looking away.

Rowan sensed the heaviness in the air, deciding it best to leave alone. Instead, he looked down at the list. "Do you need one too?"

Shaw shook his head. "I'm fine. It's them I'm worried about." After a moment he hopped off the counter, shaking off his earlier funk at the mention of Marcus. "So, how long do you think it will be?"

"I can do them now." Rowan stretched as he stood. "As long as I have everything I need, that is."

Shaw's head snapped around to look at him. "Shouldn't you be busy? I expected to wait a couple weeks, at least."

Rowan brushed it off, turning to look at the rows of shelves behind him. "I have a few orders at the moment, but those are all on hold until I get additional ingredients." He glanced over his shoulder. "You can hang out if you want. If you're busy, leave your number and I'll let you know when they're ready."

"I can stay."

Rowan slipped down the first aisle between the shelves, feeling Shaw's gaze trailing him. There were crow feathers down there somewhere. *There you are*, Rowan thought, spying one sticking out from a drawer higher up. Rather than using a ladder, he simply blew out of his lips, watching as the feather wafted upward like it was caught by a breeze before drifting down into his hand. It was followed by a second.

When Rowan placed them on the counter, he noted Shaw's expression. "What?" Rowan asked, barely managing to keep it innocent. He turned around before his face broke into a grin. He would show Shaw just what he was made of.

Rolls of fabric ribbon filled a drawer and he grabbed the royal blue immediately. He hemmed and hawed over the others, trying to think of the proper corresponding color meanings that he wanted to use. He pulled out a roll of gray and a shade of dark purple, levitating all of them over to the counter. He grabbed a spool of leather cord from a cubby and snagged the bucket that held his paints on the way by.

"What in the world are you even doing?" Shaw inquired, pulling a bottle of paint out of the bucket.

"I thought I was making charms." Rowan hadn't meant to sound coy, but it was worth it to see Shaw's expression. With a chuckle, Rowan went back to gathering things.

He started to idly hum a tune, sifting through a drawer full of crystals and stones. Meanwhile, the parchment he'd written on earlier hovered over to him, allowing him to reference it.

Satisfied, he snapped his fingers, a Bunsen burner coming to life. Various roots and flowers came out of their tins and floated into the beaker of water already set on it. "Tea?" he asked Shaw, finding the man positively speechless as he watched the goings-on.

Admittedly, Rowan hadn't been able to help himself. He had been pissed at Shaw, no doubt about it, but after talking with him again, Rowan realized Shaw's deception hadn't been out of malice. Whatever it was Shaw was hiding, Rowan could understand his hesitance. It wasn't like they'd known each other long enough for Shaw to trust him with obviously sensitive information.

Rowan was willing to give him another chance. To say he had a great time with Shaw was an understatement. And, if he were being honest with himself, Rowan sensed *something* about him. He wanted to keep Shaw close, if only to figure out what this was between them.

The beaker chimed, letting him know the tea was ready. It wasn't the most traditional system to make tea, but Rowan had never seen the point in trying to install any type of stove in order to put a kettle on. The beaker and burner did its job, and it doubled as a way to brew his experimental potions.

"Tea?" he asked again, gesturing to where the liquid was straining into a mug on its own. "It's herbal."

"Sure?"

Rowan passed the first cup over to him, placing another down for the enchanted objects to strain a second.

"That's a neat trick," Shaw mentioned, blowing on his mug.

Rowan shrugged. "Honestly, I get myself so engrossed in work that it's just easier to get my things to whip up tea mostly on their own so I don't have to break my concentration." Rowan's lips twisted into an amused grin. "Basically, I'm lazy."

Shaw chuckled. "Dunno 'bout that one. But can ya enchant my vacuum into running itself?"

"Child's play."

"For you, maybe." Shaw took a sip of tea, humming his approval. "So, what exactly are you planning here?" He nodded his head toward the growing number of supplies.

"Well," Rowan said, setting his own mug down on the counter, "Orion and Thalanil are bonded, so a lot of theirs will be the same. Would they prefer to wear them? Carry them in their gear?"

"They have mating cuffs already." Shaw tapped his own wrist. "And Thal likes necklaces. Keenan wears these enchanted gloves"—he wiggled his fingers—"so, maybe a charm that would work with those?"

Rowan nodded.

"And Haxos... I honestly have no idea."

"Does he wear tail adornments?" It was supposedly a common thing among the centaur herds to braid things into their tails or wear bands at the base like a hair tie.

"Nope, and he doesn't wear any other jewelry. That's the problem."

Rowan chewed on his lip a moment before concluding, "Well, I'll go with the tail then. It'll be out of the way, and since he's not used to wearing anything..." Rowan shrugged. "Worst case scenario: he can send it back and have it changed up the way he wants it, since I'm sure you didn't tell *them* you were doing this."

Shaw looked innocently over his mug. "No idea what you're talking about."

"Mm-hmm." Rowan didn't believe it for a second, but it was neither here nor there. It was the thought that counted, and Rowan could understand wanting to keep the ones you loved protected.

Getting started, Rowan took the two crow feathers and laid them in a clear space. "Do you know the Elvish word for 'mate'?" he inquired casually, digging through his paint bottles until he found the gold.

"*Sœurâme*," Shaw answered. "Thal calls Orion that all the time."

"That's cute," Rowan said, dabbing a thin paintbrush into the paint. "Well, mate bonds are one of the strongest natural magics there is. Tapping into that increases the power of any spell, and it replenishes itself simply by them being together." He smiled softly, painting the Elvish symbol for *mate* across each feather. "I could only imagine a bond like that."

"Me too," Shaw answered, just as softly. Rowan glanced up, Shaw licking his lips as he looked away. Rowan felt his stomach do a strange little flip.

Going back to the task at hand, Rowan grabbed the royal-blue ribbon. He cut two lengths, nimble fingers securing them to the base of the feather shafts before weaving them around what remained. "Necklaces, huh?"

Nodding to himself, Rowan reached for one of the stones he had collected. It was a shining fire opal. It was the perfect choice to help channel the magic to the wearer, the added bonus of protection properties already woven into the stone. Rowan marked the circumference with a Sharpie, before concentrating on the stone. The opal split straight down the center, falling away in two halves.

"You do that like it's nothing," Shaw said in disbelief.

Rowan shrugged. "For me, it really isn't. It's all part of Primal magic." He took the first opal half and smothered the back in glue. He placed it on the ribbon-covered feather shaft. "Being the same stone," he explained to Shaw as he applied pressure so it bonded properly, "will allow a natural transfer of energy."

"Feeding on the bond," Shaw gathered.

"Exactly." Rowan applied the second opal, as well. "While those set..."

He summoned the gray and dark-purple ribbons, deciding to start on Keenan's charm next. The first color was especially useful with glamours, a skill Shaw had specifically made mention of, while purple was perfect for mages. It was associated with channeling magic and building power, which would help aid the spell Rowan planned to put into the bracelet to help fortify Keenan's mana.

Rowan thought it over a moment before going down one of the rows, opening a drawer where he kept the sheets of leather. "You wouldn't happen to know how big Keenan's wrist is, would you?" He returned with black leather and a knife.

"Umm, 'bout the same as mine I s'ppose?"

Rowan motioned for him to hold out his arm, wrapping the leather and marking the length and width he wanted. He purposefully left it a little long, figuring on putting two different sets of snaps so that Keenan could adjust it to fit properly. Next, he sliced small slits down the length, making sure there was enough edge that the leather wouldn't break.

"So, was this always what you figured on doing?" Shaw asked. He was leaning with his elbows on the counter, watching Rowan intently. Shaw seemed especially absorbed with his fingers.

"Not really. There was never truly a *plan*. Gram was the one who encouraged me to do enchantment work. Said I had a natural ability and an eye for detail."

Rowan's fingers worked deftly to weave the gray and purple ribbons through the slots, braiding them together with the leather itself. Occasionally he still surprised himself at what he came up with. He cut another leather piece to size, adding the snaps and gluing the two pieces together. When it dried, he would finish the edges.

"Why don't you just enchant premade items?"

"A journeyman can do that," Rowan scoffed. "I'm a master. I hold myself to a higher standard. As should others." He met Shaw's blue-green eyes. "Besides, when you make something yourself, you put more of your imprint on it. And it allows you to customize to whatever you need, to whoever it's for." He gestured to what he had done pointedly.

"Fair enough," Shaw conceded. "I can certainly see the advantages." He smiled. "And I happen to like homemade things. It was more of a conversation starter."

Rowan bowed his head to hide his amusement. "If it's conversation you're after, why not tell me more about your squad. What is it they do?"

"Special Operations Division? It kinda runs the gambit."

"Like what?" Rowan fished, going to look through another box filled with ribbon.

"Gather intelligence, perform recon, stage rescues, capture high-value assets, even assassination."

Rowan paused, looking over at him.

"Some things are called 'black ops' for a reason."

Plausible deniability. He hated politics.

"Deploy at a moment's notice wherever needed... We get trained to do just about anything. Most of the time that involves working completely on your own, with your squad alone to rely on."

"That's..." Rowan couldn't find the words, instead settling on "That sounds like a rough life."

Shaw raised a shoulder. "Nothing I'm not used to. My folks, well, we were pretty poor in Rouvalon. We moved to Calagon when I was twelve? Thirteen? They had a dream of restarting and finally making it."

"Did they?" Rowan worked to wrap an elastic band in green and black ribbon, yet his attention was most certainly stuck on Shaw.

"We weren't starving anymore." Noticing that Rowan was waiting for more of an answer than that, he added, "My dad worked for a large fabrication plant. Made good money. Mum was always a gardener. It was how we survived in Rouvalon. So, we had a huge garden and whatever we had extra, she would sell at the farmer's market."

"What did you do?" Rowan started to run braided strands of leather from the elastic band, placing glass beads periodically.

"Joined the military at sixteen."

Rowan paused again.

Shaw's lips pulled up at the corners. "I didn't want to break my back in a mill or factory all my life, and I suck at gardening. For an uneducated kid from Rouvalon who knew how to scrap? Seemed like my best bet."

"I suppose," Rowan replied softly.

After a moment, Shaw said, "They moved back to Rouvalon when Dad retired. Missed home, I guess, I dunno. I stayed behind. I was already with Special Operations and was happy with my position. Our relationship has been a bit, well, nonexistent ever since."

"Sorry." Rowan offered him a brief half smile.

Shaw waved it off. "I made peace with it a long time ago." Changing the topic, he pointed at the charm that was nearly done. "So, Hax is supposed to wear that on his tail, huh?"

"It's not too flashy is it?" Rowan was concerned the glass beads were a bit much.

"Nah, I think he'll like it."

"But it's not...I don't know, *untactical* or whatever?"

Shaw chuckled, an easy smile back on his face. "It'll be fine."

"Sure you don't want one?" Rowan asked as he set it aside.

"I appreciate the thought, but..."

"Well, maybe another time." Rowan gave him a little smile.

There was noise at the back window and Rowan turned to find Badger dropping down onto the stack of books there. "Hey, Badger," he greeted casually, starting to clean up his workspace before he got to the actual enchanting itself.

The brown tabby *meowed*, looking over at Shaw in what amounted to curiosity. Apparently deciding the newcomer wasn't all that interesting, Badger sat down and began licking at his paw.

"Pretty cat," Shaw complimented.

"Something of a neighborhood feline it seems. Comes and goes as he pleases." Rowan pulled the small bag of beef jerky from the drawer, giving it a shake. When Badger *meowed* and hopped up onto the counter, Rowan chuckled. "I'm pretty sure he just likes the food." Badger purred and rubbed against his arm, demanding treats. "Yeah, yeah... Pushy thing."

Shaw chuckled, reaching out and giving Badger's head a scratch as he chomped on the offered jerky strip. "So, no pets at home?"

"Nope. Not that I'm against the idea," Rowan was quick to add. "I do practically have a live-in dog."

That startled a laugh out of Shaw. "I wouldn't let Caleb hear you say that."

Rowan's lips quirked in turn. "Oh, it's all in good fun."

Rowan had finished cleaning up, confident that everything he'd glued was set enough to continue. He pulled his cushion out from under the counter, pointing toward the door as he asked, "Flip that sign and lock the door, would you?" Rowan walked around the counter to the uncluttered customers' side. "I don't want to be interrupted while I'm enchanting."

"Makes sense," Shaw said, doing as asked. "Do you want me to go?"

"You're fine," Rowan assured him. He settled onto the cushion cross-legged. It was best to be comfortable for what came next. Rowan laid the charms out in front of him one by one. "I'll cast a general protection spell on all of them," he explained. "First, each will get their own personal touch. Could I see that photo again?"

Shaw passed over his phone after bringing the group shot up. Rowan studied them in order to keep their images in the back of his mind while he worked.

Giving the phone back, Rowan took a deep breath and shut his eyes. He took a moment to center himself, opening his eyes when he felt the magic inside him unlock easily at his behest. There was a soft inhale from Shaw, no doubt in reaction to his eyes glowing with magic.

Rowan started with the mated pair, deciding to enchant the charms at the same time so they would be tied as closely as possible. It would be a challenge to imbue them with two different sets of spells simultaneously, but he was confident he could handle it. While Orion's would call for strength and agility, Thalanil's would require dexterity and speed, being the squad's werewolf and sniper respectively. Once the fire opals on both charms glowed a brilliant orange in response to being filled, Rowan sealed them in protection magic before setting them aside.

Next, he picked up the leather cuff meant for Keenan. As a mage, no one knew better than Rowan the things they required. He beefed up the charm with a mixture of spells. They would allow Keenan to better channel his magic and replenish his mana stores quicker and easier. Rowan layered them with a spell to aid in concentration and the same protection one that he had placed on the others.

The charm for Haxos was the most curious one. Rowan knew next to nothing about centaurs, but he figured a little help with moving silently couldn't hurt. He added on a powerful stamina spell, and sealed it with protection, hoping it would be enough.

With the last charm laid aside, Rowan closed his eyes. He took a deep breath, centering. He gave himself a minute to relax and come down from his power output. Once he felt stable, Rowan opened his eyes, finding Shaw was watching him closely.

"You good?" Shaw asked, reaching his hand out.

Rowan took it, allowing Shaw to help him up. "Perfectly fine," he assured him.

Shaw grinned brightly. "That was... That was pretty damn incredible."

Rowan covered up his blush by bending down to gather the charms. He retreated behind the counter, setting them aside to find a box and packing material.

"So, hey"—Shaw began, leaning across the counter—"wanna go with me for an early supper?"

Rowan hesitated, looking over at him. After a long moment, he went back to work. "I'm not sure if—"

"Only food. I promise." When Rowan bit his lip, Shaw reached over and covered Rowan's hand with his. "Please? I know I fucked up, but I'd like the chance to make it up to you."

Rowan met his gaze. Shaw was being sincere.

"At the least, I'd like to be friends."

Rowan could admit that he was still interested in pursuing a relationship with Shaw, even after the misunderstanding they had the other day. Clearly *something* was going on that Shaw couldn't talk about. It was perhaps a little reckless to get himself involved, but after so many years of being buried in his studies, he supposed he owed himself a little risk or two.

"Yeah, okay," Rowan agreed, turning his hand so their palms touched. "I'm not opposed to seeing where this goes."

Shaw smiled, opening his mouth to reply, when he yelped in pain, jerking his hand away. Badger had swatted at him, leaving behind nasty looking claw marks.

"Badger!" Rowan admonished. "What's wrong with you?"

The cat hissed, raising his hackles, before bolting out the back window.

Rowan's brows furrowed, looking from the window back to Shaw, who was holding his hand. "Are you alright?"

"It stings, but yeah, I'll live."

Not accepting that answer, Rowan took Shaw's hand gingerly to look it over. "Yikes, he got you good... I'm sorry. I dunno what got into him. He's never acted like that before."

"Maybe your magic got him spooked."

"Maybe."

Rowan wasn't so sure about that. Badger had been around before when he enchanted things or casually used his magic like he did. To be fair, Rowan hadn't enchanted so many things at one time while the cat was there. Perhaps all that energy *did* make him nervous.

"Here," Rowan offered, his fingertips warming. "I suck at healing magic, to be honest. But little things..."

Unlike his enchanting work or playing around with Primal magic, Rowan had to concentrate on closing the small cuts on Shaw's hand. The skin managed to stitch together, leaving behind light-red lines that would fade over the next couple of hours. "It might itch a bit," Rowan apologized, pulling away.

Shaw snatched Rowan's hand. "Thanks." He smiled warmly at Rowan, the pair staring at each other for a long while. "So," Shaw ventured, "about that food?"

Rowan caved. It might have been crazy, but he couldn't resist. "Let me finish this," was all he said, ignoring Shaw's ridiculous fist pump. After a minute, he was handing Shaw the box of freshly made charms, all packaged and ready to ship. "Hope they help."

Shaw was gazing at it with mixed emotions, but it was clear that he was grateful when he looked back at Rowan. "How much do I owe you?"

He shrugged. "I should have really done a quote with you beforehand, but you were distracting."

"Just bill me the damages, Ro. I was aware it wasn't gonna come cheap."

"I'll remember you said that," he teased, chuckling when Shaw rolled his eyes.

Rowan grabbed a few things he wanted to take home, shut all the windows with a wave of his hand, and ushered Shaw out the door. "Hold these," he said, shoving some books at Shaw.

While Rowan was locking up, Shaw grunted, "No enchantment to make these bloody things *lighter*?"

Rowan chuckled. His grimoire was indeed on the bulky side, and two of his grandmother's books on top of it didn't help. "A bit of studying for the weekend."

Shaw raised a brow, not complaining when Rowan took them back.

"I believe you mentioned food," Rowan prompted with a little smirk.

"There's a nice dwarven place a few blocks up," Shaw said. "If you're into that kinda food."

"Meat, meat, and more meat." Charred over open flame, that was the way to go with dwarves, be it meats of all kinds, or vegetables that grew in the darkness of caves. "If you're talking about the Mountain Gem, then I'm in."

"Great. I kinda stole the car from work so I can drive us."

"Stole?" Rowan teased. "Why, Inquisitor..."

Shaw laughed. "Since it looks like I'll be sticking around, I've been talking to people about finding a used vehicle for cheap."

"Well, you might want to consider a truck. Outside the city, there's still a lot of country roads." It was a bit of a hint, one Shaw seemed to understand, although he didn't say directly.

"A good idea."

As they walked, Rowan figured it was best to get it off his chest now, rather than embarrass himself later, or become even further attached. "If we're going to be friends, we're going to need some rules."

"Rules?"

"About using your empathy. I don't appreciate being manipulated."

He looked over to find Shaw frowning. "I wasn't trying to— Look, I know it's no excuse to say 'I'm used to it,' but it's the truth. It's just natural to use it to help de-escalate a situation."

"I get it. And I imagine it's very useful for that." Rowan pressed a hand to Shaw's forearm, stopping him so he could meet his gaze. "It's one thing to use it on the job, it's another to use on someone you know. Or, want to know." Rowan felt heat on his cheeks and looked away—that hadn't come out the way he wanted it to.

"I know. At the risk of sounding like a broken record, I'm sorry. I got so used to using it casually, and it was alright to use with my squad, so... I guess I have to get used to refraining until told otherwise."

Rowan's lips quirked briefly. "Well, I don't mind if it's trying to get me to focus. But outside that..."

"I promise not to do anything on purpose," Shaw assured him immediately. "Unless it's an emergency."

"Good. That's settled." Rowan was satisfied, but as he started to walk off, Shaw snagged his hand. Rowan looked from their hands, up to Shaw's face.

"Thank you." When Rowan merely stared at him, he added, "For giving me another chance."

Rowan gave him a gentle smile, squeezing his hand. "Everyone deserves a second chance."

Shaw chuckled, dropping Rowan's hand as they started to walk. "I dunno 'bout everyone, but I'm glad you consider me worthy of another shot, at least."

Chapter Five

QUANTUM HALL WAS where classes were held. Apprentices were filing in and out, and Rowan caught sight of a few journeymen as well. Likely, they were there to take an advanced course with Ieus, who handled a good number of them.

"Rowan." He jumped, whirling to find Jorah had snuck up on him. "Here for my lecture on transmutation?"

"Um, no." Why did Jorah always make him feel like a child who got caught sneaking out after curfew?

Jorah raised a brow, his face otherwise a stony mask. "I don't have a class on hexes today."

Oh, that was a low blow. Rowan thought he managed not to flinch. "I actually came to speak with Quail."

"He has a theory class right now. Room three."

"Thanks." Rowan hesitated before slowly turning away.

"Rowan."

He turned back.

"You should stick around. I have a journeyman Primal practical after lunch. I could use another demonstrator."

Rowan could tell from the way Jorah phrased it that it wasn't exactly up for debate. "Yeah, sounds good." It was just as well he'd made the trip to the city on one of his days off.

"See you then," Jorah replied, not even the hint of emotion on his face or gratitude in his voice.

Rowan huffed air through his nose, shaking his head at Jorah's retreating form. "Great."

Getting back to the reason he had come to the Guild in the first place, Rowan made his way through Quantum Hall to one of the small classrooms designed for bookwork. The upstairs rooms were open, meant for practical application, unless it was particularly dangerous or in need of a larger space—in those cases, they used the Hall of Enlightenment.

The class was already in session, Quail holding up his hand in greeting when he walked in. Rowan smiled, leaning against the side wall. A few of the apprentices glanced his way, but Quail commanded attention through charisma alone. There was a reason he often taught magic theory courses—as boring a subject as it could be—Quail made everything fun.

They were on mana studies apparently, Quail continuing on his point about training. "It's like any other skill. If you jog every day, you'll get better stamina. If you go and lift weights, you'll be able to lift more over time. Learning to paint or play an instrument gets easier with practice, and you can move onto more complicated techniques." All of this was said with broad, sweeping gestures, filled with enthusiasm.

There was no helping the smile on Rowan's face.

"Hence the need to master the basics of any school before trying to move on. Besides that, a good foundation is what success in magic is based upon. Take Rowan, here, for example."

Naturally, all eyes turned to him and Rowan shook his head in amusement. He should have seen this one coming.

"As a master enchanter, I've watched Rowan enchant item after item without feeling any effects. Even if it is a brand new charm, or one he rarely uses, the drain to his mana is minimal. This all comes from years of study dedicated to the basics and building up a tolerance to draining."

One of the apprentices raised her hand.

"Yes, Tabitha?"

"What about mana boosters? Enchanted items, stimulants, energy drinks?"

"Certainly most of the marketed boosters or replenishers work—to varying degrees—but in the learning stage, they're nothing more than a crutch. To get better means to push past walls. Think of your manara as more than an organ; think of it as a muscle that needs exercising or else it will get out of shape."

The glandular organ that all mages had, the manara, was what produced mana, the essence that powered their magic. By working at it, a mage could use less and less mana for the same type of spells. It was all in the practice and basics, as Quail stressed.

"In the end, you're better off doing the work," Quail continued. "You'll have better results in the long run."

Another teen raised his hand. "Why can witches use magic, then, without mana?"

"Not all magic is made the same. Elves, for example, have their own form of magic, yet possess no gland or mana. Millennia ago, vampires were purveyors of blood magic. Mers have a type of water magic we have yet to understand."

"Hard to study," Rowan mused, "when they want nothing to do with being poked and prodded." He knew full well how the mers felt about their "topworlder science."

"Indeed," Quail agreed. "The point is we all have our own ways of harnessing magic. Mages are unique in that we can learn multiple forms of magic. We have a large variety in our arsenal. Other races can only perform very specific forms of magic.

"Witches, as you know, possess a single ability—usually mental in nature. And, while they do not require mana to perform these tasks, it can be just as draining on their bodies as on ours without proper training and conditioning." There was a reason witches tended to get tutoring from mages.

One of the boys in the back spoke up. "So, basically, this is your way of telling us to study."

"That is exactly my point, Iswyn. How astute." His classmates chuckled, and Iswyn shrunk back in his seat, grumbling.

"You get out what you put in," Quail reiterated. "Keep that in mind for when we start practical exercises tomorrow. Until then..." He waved his hand, the apprentices not needing to be told twice, quickly gathering their things to make their escape. It appeared at least one or two were lingering, eyeing Rowan as he joined Quail at the front of the room.

"How is my favorite student?" Quail inquired.

"How's my favorite teacher?" Rowan grinned, accepting the bear hug Quail yanked him into.

"I'm going to guess you're here about your exam."

"I appreciate the email." It had been filled with study notes. "I wanted to follow up with you in person, though."

"Never hurts to have a practical lesson," Quail agreed. "Was there any particular area you wanted to work on?"

"Really, I'm just hoping not to die."

"Don't be silly." Quail brushed him off. "Jorah will only maim you at worst."

"You always have a way of making me feel better."

"Happy to help." There was a twinkle in Quail's eyes.

"I got wrangled into helping him with class later."

The humor left Quail's face. "He would pull a stunt like that." Quail huffed, scrunching his nose. The pair never had seen eye to eye on teaching styles. Frankly, Rowan wasn't entirely sure they could even stand each other most days. He was of the opinion Jorah's background as a battlemage butted up against the values of the rest of the board more often than not.

"Let's go up to a practice room," Quail offered, pushing his glasses up the bridge of his nose.

Rowan certainly appreciated Quail making the time. Granted, once they'd finished, Rowan felt completely drained—they had stopped twice for him to recoup.

Rowan crunched into a Replenish Bar as they walked outside, trading an amused look with Quail. "Didn't we just yell at the apprentices about this?"

"You're done with training. Giving yourself a boost won't hurt you. Besides"—Quail grinned—"you'll need it if you're going to be working with Jorah. He won't go easy on you, not even for practicals."

"Why do you gotta be right?" Rowan complained, sighing as he took another bite of his mana-infused granola bar.

"Well, somebody in this place has to be." Quail chuckled while Rowan shook his head. "If you want to have more sessions, let me know." He patted Rowan's back, heading off to Temperance Hall, the living quarters.

Rowan took a deep breath, letting it out in a drawn-out sigh. The Hall of Enlightenment awaited, as did Jorah and his class.

It turned out that Tate was among them, and he asked, "What are you doing here?"

"Jorah *invited me* to help out."

Tate burst out laughing.

"Laugh it up," Rowan gruffed.

"Sorry." Tate bit his lip. Despite the laughter, he was at least looking sympathetic.

"Just remember that when I accidentally put you on your ass." If there was one thing Rowan had complete confidence in, it was his Primal magic. Mana drain be damned; it wouldn't matter here. "Try to keep up."

WHEN A NAME he'd seen before came across the screen for the new intakes, Shaw knew he had a way in. It wasn't often he had a reason to be next door at the jail—he rarely booked anyone or needed a follow-up interview. This was a chance he couldn't pass up, and it had the bonus of earning him more clout with the other inquisitors.

He called over to the jail, alerting them about who he would be coming to see, before gathering his things and heading to Meredeen's office. He rapped his knuckles on the doorframe.

She gave him a kind, half smile. "What can I do for you, Inquisitor Shaw?" He had to give her credit, Meredeen was professional and good at her job. If the circumstances were different, she might have been a person Shaw would like to know.

"Wanted to let you know I was heading next door for an interview."

"Oh?"

"Werecat came up in the system this morning. Baza? I recognized the name. She's a known associate of that other cat you've been looking for—Langa."

Meredeen's smile grew. "Excellent catch."

Shaw nodded, starting to step out when she stopped him.

"Inquisitor? I'm not sure how Commander Larus runs that outfit in Shadewind, but here? You do whatever you have to, understand?"

"Yes, High Inquisitor."

Shaw let his hackles rise after getting outside. Why he was even surprised by a statement like that, after seeing what he had already, was beyond him.

The jail was across the parking lot, and he was led to a private room reserved for interrogations or, supposedly, prisoners meeting with family or a lawyer. Shaw doubted they were allowed to see either. Baza was already there waiting for him, hands cuffed to a chain in the middle of the table. The anti-shift collar around her neck looked painfully tight and her dark eyes bore into him.

"Baza, I'm Inquisitor Shaw. I understand you were booked last night for disturbing the peace."

She scoffed. "That's what they call it when you're the victim of a hate crime, now?"

Shaw's brows lowered. He would get to that. For now, he said, "I need to ask you some questions about Langa."

Baza rolled her eyes. "I don't know anything."

"Sure you don't." Shaw sneered. He made a show of walking over to the corner where the camera was set up while continuing to talk. "Long way from home for a cheetah. What are you even doing here anyway?"

She snarled at him, showing off impressive canines. "Fuck you, asshole. You and all your bigoted friends."

"Have it your way." Shaw pulled the cord out, the light on the camera dying as it stopped recording. "There." He relaxed, dropping the act. "Now we can talk."

Baza's brows drew together. "I don't understand."

"Look, I don't give a shite where that friend of yours is. I was using your arrival as an excuse." She started to speak, but Shaw barreled ahead. "Now, what's this about being victimized?" He set his hands beside her on the table as he leaned forward to listen.

Baza considered him a long moment, probably trying to judge if it was a trap or not. Finally, she replied, "My friends and I were out for a night on the town. Some anti-magicae prick comes up and starts harassing us. Even smacked me"—she pointed to the puffy area under her eye, the bruising hard to see on her dark skin—"and when the law shows, a group of knights follow and decide to haul *us* in instead."

Shaw frowned, straightening. "Sorry." He walked behind her, careful in his movements. "Hold on. Lemme loosen this stupid thing." He undid the buckle of the collar, not worried about her shifting and trying to maul him. He knew full well those cuffs would be silver, or at least magically enhanced. "Can't take it off," he added apologetically as he refastened it, "but at least I can do this."

Baza looked at him like a puzzle piece she couldn't place as he sat down across from her.

"I'll see what I can do about the charges," Shaw promised. "In the meantime, I need your help. I know it hasn't even been a full day, but have you heard anything since they brought you in?"

"Like what?" she asked carefully.

"Anything. About the guards, about what they might be doing with prisoners..."

"Whadda you care?" she challenged. He could practically taste the skepticism pouring off her. "What the hell do you want?"

"I want the wankers who are abusing their power." It was a half-truth, but it was all he was willing to say.

Baza laughed. "Try all of them, Inquisitor. What makes you so different?" She showed a fang as she growled. "You think by loosening this collar and saying you'll try to fix my charges that I'll—what?—spy for you?"

"As a matter of fact, yes. I need people feeding me information. I need evidence I can use."

Once again, Baza seemed to be measuring him. He carefully added calming energy into the room, trying to bring her down a notch. "Only thing I know?" she finally offered. "The ones that get dragged to the back cells? They don't get seen again."

Shaw would take it. "Where?"

"Main level of A Wing."

"Alright." He reached out, setting his hand on top of hers. That time, Shaw didn't skimp on the energy transfer. The calmer he could make Baza, the less likely she was to find herself in further trouble before he could get her released. "Thank you," he said sincerely. "I'll see about getting you out of here."

Baza actually curled her lips into something like a smile. "I don't know what it is, but I believe you."

Shaw flashed her a grin and stood to go to the camera. "Just, act all resigned and whatnot," he mentioned before plugging it back in. "Remember what I said, Baza," he dropped his tone into calculated cold. "Watch yourself."

Stepping outside, Shaw told the guard on watch, "Take her back to her cell."

"Yes, sir," he replied. "Let me walk you out first."

"I can find my way."

"Yes, Inquisitor."

When the guard went into the room, Shaw took the opportunity to go in the opposite direction he was meant to. Instead of going back through the processing area, he ducked around the corner toward the housing wings. Cameras were everywhere, as were guards on rounds, but no one would question an inquisitor being there.

Besides, Shaw had another trick up his sleeve—literally. His fingers ran along the Runic tattoo on his left arm: *shadow*. The mana infused into the ink activated, magic prickling across his skin. It wasn't as powerful as a mage's spell—he wouldn't be able to become completely invisible—but it was the next best thing.

People simply didn't notice him. Their eyes could pass right over him, but they wouldn't care to pay attention. He wasn't important.

As such, he walked straight down the row of cells to the double doors that sat at the end. Not a soul paid him any mind. Shaw pushed the doors open, finding a small room beyond. There were a half dozen holding cells, cramped, with nothing to sit on but the concrete floor. There was a loading bay door at the other side, and given the layout of the building, Shaw was willing to bet it led to the outside.

This had to be it. It was a step toward what he was looking for.

A scan of the area showed no cameras—the Inquisition wouldn't want anyone to see what they were up to. Shaw remedied that with a tiny hidden camera, tacking it up on the wall. He was going to find out exactly what these bastards were up to.

Like the word on his arm, Shaw slipped out the way he had come, no one the wiser.

Chapter Six

"I'M GOING TO die." Rowan's head fell to the open book in front of him, and he let out a frustrated groan. He rolled his head to the side, looking at Badger, who was laying on the counter. The cat gave him an unimpressed look, flicking his tail.

Even though Badger couldn't reply, Rowan often found himself talking aloud to his frequent visitor. Rowan worked problems out better when he talked them through. With stacks of books on one side and a sheet of parchment and his quill for notes on the other, he was feeling himself slipping into a study fog.

"I know I need a break," he admitted, "but I feel like I'm nowhere near ready for this."

He had been going over old textbooks, refreshing his memory on various hexes and curses taught at the Guild, along with their counters. Then, he started to browse through other books he had, marking the spells he didn't know. It wasn't a surprise there were quite a few, given Spirit wasn't anything he'd ever had a passion for.

"I think these outdated spells are promising at least." Rowan tapped the page of one such hex he came across. "It's likely that Jorah doesn't even *know* some of these. If I can brush up my counters to protect myself, maybe I can use these to catch him off guard."

His only chance at passing his exam, as far as Rowan could tell, was to either put Jorah down quick or survive long enough to impress the board. It was just as well that Rowan's main strength was his knowledge of magical theory. He knew that, more than anything, had a lot to do with why he was so good at learning new spellwork.

With a heavy sigh, Rowan got up from the stool, pacing back and forth behind the counter. He ran his fingers through his hair. Perhaps he was going about this all the wrong way.

"I know Jorah's gonna use mana-draining." It wasn't traditionally considered a hex, but it was still in the School of Spirit, so it was fair game to use. "If I miss the counter for it, I'll be screwed. I need too much mana to use any of these new spells. Not that I won't be using more than usual with even the basic ones."

He paused, looking at Badger who was watching him blankly.

"That's it! I need a way to keep my mana levels up." Blood magic. It would have to be blood magic. "But, if I try to use my blood to supplement..." No, it would need to be blood magic, but using a more indirect method.

"No one said I couldn't use potions right before my exam," Rowan reasoned, dropping another of his grandmother's grimoires onto the counter. "So, if I whip up a few fortifying and resistance potions, it might give me an edge."

Badger *mewed*, tail whipping impatiently.

"I know it won't be enough," Rowan admitted with a sigh. "But, I have to try *something*, don't I?"

Badger still looked unimpressed. Rowan huffed, flipping the grimoire open.

"Now, I know Gram had good recipes for that kind of stuff. Just to find them."

She had been a talented mage, specializing in what his generation termed "green witchcraft." They were ancient ways of magic, nature-based. It was her love of plants that had influenced Rowan's own curiosity on the subject of herbology. If it were an actual School of Magic, his grandmother would have been a master.

"Here we are," he said. "This is supposed to fortify mana, so it should help against mana-drains." Looking at the ingredient list, he groused, "I don't have any of this." Well, he had luna moth wings, but they were currently setting up with resin to make a charm for a client.

Badger stood and stretched, before yawning.

"I guess I could substitute some of this." Rowan knew he should probably forget all about it—or actually order the proper ingredients—and get back to his studying, but he was determined now. "Let's see what I've got…"

He tried his best to find ingredients with similar properties. He had very little on hand at the shop because most of his herbology experiments were at his cottage. "Moon sugar! That should work well." He was assuming it was the lunar energies he was supposed to be harnessing. "Maybe some thistle? Wintersbreath flowers?" What was he going to substitute for lotus blossom?

He turned to check Gram's notes, finding Badger sitting on the book. Rowan smiled, shaking his head. "You're in the way, you know. Come on." He tried shooing Badger off, but it wasn't working. "Badger." He got the cat to move, only to have Badger bat at the page as he turned it. "Feeling playful today?"

Badger *meowed*.

"Let me finish this and we'll take a break, okay?"

Sure enough, as soon as Rowan was finished looking at the book, Badger moved right back in, laying on it.

Rowan gathered up the substitute ingredients, mashing the dry with his mortar and pestle. He threw those into a glass bottle, adding in the liquid ingredients. It fizzed a little but otherwise didn't react. "Now, for my own twist," Rowan announced.

He took the silver knife from behind the counter, murmuring a spell under his breath that heated the blade to sterilize it. "Here we go." He pricked his finger on the tip, wincing.

Holding his finger over the bottle, Rowan used his other hand to squeeze a few drops of blood out. From his mouth fell words long since memorized, a blood magic spell to transfer power. If he could add his own magic to the mix, hopefully it would enhance the potion.

He watched the swirl of color, the potion turning from blue to purple. Rowan started to repeat the incantation for the third time. A couple more drops should have been enough.

The bell above the door *tinked*, causing Rowan to jump and curse. The potion reacted in kind, exploding and shattering the glass. "Fuck!"

"Bloody hell, are you alright?" It was Shaw.

"Fine," Rowan replied automatically, despite being unsure. "I'll be fine." He looked around at the mess—glass and potion thrown everywhere—and noted the cat was missing. "Badger? Badger?" He heard growling and Rowan looked up to find the brown tabby hunkered on top of one of the shelves, ears pinned back and fur standing on end.

"Forget the cat," Shaw griped, reaching across the counter and snagging his wrist. "You're bleeding." The blood on Rowan's finger was now going down his palm. "The glass musta got ya."

"No, I did that." Rowan pulled out of Shaw's grasp. Glass crunched under his feet as he grabbed a paper towel from its roll on the shelf, wiping off the blood and wrapping it around his finger. "Guess I'm lucky this is tempered glass." He and Badger would have been shredded for sure if it had shattered into sharp pieces instead of chunks.

"Here," Shaw offered, "lemme help."

Rowan flicked his hand, the broom from the corner and a few rags from a drawer levitating over to the mess. "I've got it." Despite his words, when the broom started to sweep up the glass on the other side of the counter, Shaw took hold of it to do it himself.

Leaving it be, Rowan turned his attention to Badger. "Hey, buddy," he said gently, reaching up toward Badger. "It's alright. Come on down."

Badger's growl got louder.

"I'm sorry. I know you're scared, but it's safe now. Come on. I need to make sure you didn't get hurt, little guy." Rowan wiggled his fingers enticingly.

Badger finally came close enough for Rowan to stand on his tiptoes and pick him up. "That's it. There's a good boy. I'm sorry." He held Badger to his chest, listening to the purr that started. "You okay?" He pulled Badger away to look him over, not finding any obvious injuries. When he started to squirm, Rowan held him properly again.

"What in the hell were you doing, Ro?" Shaw asked. The dustpan had floated over, holding itself in place for Shaw to sweep the glass into.

"I was trying to make a potion for my exam. I was infusing it with blood magic when you—"

"Blood magic?" Shaw froze, gaze turning slowly to Rowan.

"Yeah. You walked in and I lost the place in my incantation. Clearly, there was a bad reaction." Badger rubbed his head against Rowan's neck, prompting him to scratch behind the cat's ear.

Shaw picked up the dustpan and came around the counter to empty it in the trash before starting to clean the glass on that side. The entire time, he didn't say a word, wouldn't even look at Rowan.

"Something wrong?" Rowan prompted, ignoring Badger's paw on his face.

"Blood magic? I didn't know you practiced it."

"Does it matter?" Rowan had a feeling he knew where this was going. Despite modern thinking, it was quite common for people to still get the wrong impression of blood magic.

"It doesn't exactly have the best reputation." And there it was. "For good reason."

"So, if a dark mage uses fire spells to burn down an entire city, should we ban the use of such magic?"

"Of course not."

"Then why would it be any different to shun a perfectly benign type of magic because dark mages abuse it?"

"I dunno that I'd call it benign," Shaw ventured, from the looks of it, treading carefully.

Rowan's hackles lowered, realizing he had been gradually raising his voice, becoming defensive. Shaw wasn't slinging derogatory remarks at him or making judgments; he was repeating concerns many people voiced. Most of them were genuinely curious, ignorant of the subject, and easy enough to put at ease once it was explained to them.

"Shaw..." Rowan sat on his stool, setting Badger in his lap, and patted the counter with his hand. Getting the hint,

Shaw released the broom—which was happy enough to go about the rest of the cleaning on its own—and hopped up onto the counter, legs dangling.

"I have a feelin' I'm about to get lectured. So, fair warning, leave the technical mumbo jumbo out of it."

Rowan's lips twitched. "I'll do my best." He took a breath, as he thought of how to put it simply. Finally, what he came up with was: "It's like any other magic, you know. It can be used for good or ill. Just because I'm studying hexes"—he gestured to the stacked books—"doesn't mean I want to actually use them against someone else."

"I get that. But, having that kind of power... It can drive a mage insane."

"That's any power, Shaw." It was rarer these days, with all the guilds and the fact mages no longer had to hide what they were, but it was possible for a mage to become addicted to the power they wielded, to become unhinged.

"You have me there," Shaw murmured. He drummed his fingers on the counter a moment. "But, isn't blood magic supposed to be more addictive? Infinite power?"

"In theory, a mage could have infinite power, but, again, you're implying that the mere use of blood magic would lead somebody to abuse it. It's a magical enhancement, Shaw, nothing more."

"And a mana substitute."

Rowan sighed. "You worked with a battlemage, surely—"

"Keenan never used blood magic, and the use of it in the Calagon military is heavily regulated. He uses mana tablets to stabilize in battle."

"That still doesn't change the fact mages can use it without any ill effect." Rowan unclenched his hands, once again reining in that natural reaction to snap and snarl.

"Look," he continued, calmer, "I get that it's an easy scapegoat, but the fact is that it doesn't hurt anyone, not when you're using it ethically. We use our own blood. Or that freely given. We don't take blood."

Shaw looked at him, appearing thoughtful. After a moment, he nodded. "I get what you're saying."

Rowan let out a breath he hadn't realized he was holding. "Yeah?"

"Yeah." Shaw's nod was more confident that time. "A dark mage doesn't play by the rules. Most mages do. If you say that blood magic can be performed ethically, then I have to believe you."

"It is. Using our own blood to enhance a spell, or to keep from draining our mana, doesn't hurt anyone but ourselves." Rowan hated to admit, "Could we use someone else's for the same purpose? Of course. That's where the whole mess with blood magic being 'evil' comes from in the first place."

The fact a mage could have a constant source of power by draining another person's blood—rather than using their own mana—was a disgusting reality. It had occurred before: dark mages waging wars, using the blood of their enemies and allies alike to create chaos. That hadn't happened in the last four centuries and, frankly, Rowan felt it was time to let it go.

"But, like you said," Shaw repeated, "an ethical mage would never do that without permission."

"Exactly." Rowan gave him a little smile, feeling a weight leaving now that Shaw at least understood, even if he didn't accept it. "Shouldn't Keenan have explained all this to you?"

"He knows I suck at the technical bits, first off, so him explaining shit to me doesn't happen much. And second, like I said, he doesn't use blood magic, so no reason to ever bring it up. Only ever known one other bloke that used it—some colonel with the marines. Apparently, had to get special clearance too."

"Fair enough." Badger relocated to the counter, rubbing up against Rowan's shoulder, who reached up to scratch under his chin absentmindedly. "So, we're okay?"

Shaw's lips turned up at the corner. "Course we are."

Rowan smiled. "Good." The broom was finished cleaning, making its way back to its corner while Rowan sent the wet rags to the sink. "Well, so much for my potion, it looks like."

"What were you even trying to do?"

"I was attempting to make something to fortify my mana, to take before my exam."

"And pulling a blood magic trick during a fight might get you dead."

"I've always used it in a controlled setting. It would have to be a true emergency to make me risk doing something like that. I could bleed out easily enough, otherwise."

Shaw looked a little sheepish as he said, "Well, I'm sorry I made that one explode."

"Was my own fault for getting distracted." Rowan smirked. "Though you certainly didn't help."

"Well, how about I help you make a new one?" Shaw put one hand over his heart while holding up the other. "Promise to be a good assistant."

"I was already substituting ingredients. Honestly, I should just order the right ones. Save myself the chance of doing even more harm if it goes foul."

"What am I going to do with you?"

Shaw reached out and brushed his fingers lightly over Rowan's cheek, causing him to inhale sharply. The simple touch left Rowan's nerve endings tingling. He met Shaw's blue-green eyes and felt the air leave his lungs.

Shaw smiled, pulling his hand away, and asked, "Why don't we go to lunch? You look like you could use a break."

Rowan remembered to breathe, coming back from his zone at the loss of contact. He would have accused Shaw of using his powers, but there was no prickle of magic. Apparently, Rowan was genuinely growing attached to him.

"I'm supposed to meet Caleb." He checked the time on his phone. "Soon, in fact. I'm sure he wouldn't mind if you come along."

"Sounds good. Need help closing things up?" Shaw inquired, hopping off the counter.

"I've got it." He waved his hand to close the windows and lock them, save for one of the small back ones in case Badger wanted to get out. Rowan paused, looking at Shaw. "Is that why you came?" He had never bothered to ask why Shaw had shown up in the first place.

"Was the plan, yeah."

"And if I didn't want lunch?"

"I would have had to go out and bring food back, force you to eat, and watch you work."

Rowan chuckled, shaking his head. "Come on." At the door, he called over his shoulder, "See you later, Badger."

THE BREW ROOM was apparently a frequent lunch spot for Rowan and Caleb. Rowan needn't have told Shaw, since the nymph waitress not only waved them to their usual place but already knew what they wanted to order. "What would you like, hon?" she asked Shaw when she brought over a pair of drinks.

Shaw was a simple man. He tended to stick with traditional dark roasts. "What's your favorite?"

She lit up, eyes sparkling. "We recently got in more of this great elven blend from Thalas Naren. It's dark and rich, very earthy."

Shaw nodded. "That sounds nice. I'll give it a go."

When she left, Rowan mentioned, "Danais likes you."

"That's 'cause he's with us," Caleb said.

Shaw allowed the teasing. Sitting between them at the end of the table, he leaned over to see the open page of Caleb's sketchbook. "Didn't know you were an artist."

"Yup. Or, try to be."

Thus far, there was merely a tree on the page, but it was filled with details in the bark, grass blades between the protruding roots, and leaves halfway finished. "You got a good eye."

Danais returned with his coffee, asking about food. Once again, Shaw took a recommendation—this time from Caleb, who swore by their steak paninis.

"Mmm, this is great," Shaw commented on the coffee. He admittedly shouldn't have doubted the elves. "Thalas is the big elven city here, right?"

"It's their seat of culture," Rowan confirmed. "It's a ways from here. Past the Southern Hills."

Caleb hummed mildly, but his face was pinched with tension.

"Something wrong?" Shaw asked, feeling waves of bitterness flowing off of Caleb.

"No."

Well, that was an outright lie. He looked to Rowan.

"Caleb's from the Southern Hills Pack."

"Oh." Shaw looked back at Caleb. The set jaw and flared nostrils were enough to tell it was a sour subject, even without the negative waves flowing off him.

"Left them a long time ago," Caleb muttered. "Shouldn't be such a big deal."

"No one leaves pack easily," Shaw reasoned.

"I did." Caleb licked his lips, frustration added to the mix of emotion in the air. "Or I thought I did. Cut ties with everyone, except my little brother, Kyle."

Shaw knew it wasn't his place to pry, but he wanted to know Caleb better. He was such a big piece of Rowan's life, and if Shaw wanted to be a part of that, well, he was bound to find out at some point or other. "What happened?"

Caleb's honey eyes flicked to Rowan for a moment, then met Shaw's. "I ran away. I was nineteen."

"That's rough."

"Not as rough as living there." Caleb paused. "I'm an Alpha."

Shaw blinked. He hadn't expected anything like that. Caleb wasn't like any alphas he'd ever met, whether status-earned or bred—after all, there was a difference. While any werewolf could rise to lead a pack as an alpha, a born Alpha was a step above. Centuries of special breeding had created a type of werewolf that was naturally faster and stronger, who possessed powers unique from other wolves.

"Given your lack of pack," Shaw ventured, "I'm guessing you mean the born kind."

"Unfortunately." Caleb scoffed and took a sip of his drink before continuing. "My dad's an Alpha too. Tried breeding his own little empire of Alphas, but I'm it."

"I can guess the pressure," Shaw sympathized.

"Yeah, times it by ten. I had zero interest in leading the pack, but I was being groomed for it. There was an expectation for me to take a mate—a female, of course. Try to make more Alphas to 'strengthen the pack.'" A growl played on Caleb's lips, but he reined it in when Danais returned with their food.

Alone again, Shaw said, "So, you decided to leave."

"It was the only choice I had. I wasn't going to be his puppet. I wasn't going to deny who I was. All my preparation meant I wasn't leaving much behind anyway. I was never allowed to be close to anyone. All I had was my brother."

"Do you see him?"

"Occasionally. My parents know we're in contact. As of yet, they haven't done anything to stop us or to try and find out where I am. Not that Kyle knows. We meet in neutral locations, away from the city. Otherwise, our sole communication is by phone or email."

"I can't imagine..." Shaw shook his head. "I don't have any siblings. My folks— It's not that we're on bad terms, but we don't really talk much. My friends have always been my family."

Caleb's shoulders drooped, strands of his royal-blue hair falling in his face. "And now you've moved away from them."

"Yeah." Shaw looked down at his untouched food. He was surprised when Caleb laid a hand on his. Looking back up at him, Caleb appeared to be forcing a half smile on his face.

"Well, you've got us."

Shaw managed a brief upturn of his lips.

Caleb nodded to Rowan. "This one found me shortly after I got to town. Been mine ever since."

Rowan smirked. "Not like I could leave you looking all sad." To Shaw, he said, "He's got some mean puppy eyes."

Shaw laughed along with Caleb. Feeling a bit more at ease—and sensing the same echoing from Caleb—Shaw started to eat. "Damn, this is great."

"Right?" Caleb's mouth was stuffed with his own sandwich.

"Swallow first," Rowan chastised.

Caleb's grin was lewd. "Usually do."

"Goddess, how do I put up with you?"

"We're still trying to figure that out."

Shaw laughed again, asking Caleb, "Aren't you too old to be making such horrible puns?"

"Twenty-six."

"Ouch. You make me feel old." At Caleb's raised brow, Shaw confessed, "Thirty-three."

"Yup, old as dirt."

Shaw laughed even louder that time. Caleb's blunt delivery was simply too much. "I think we'll get along just fine."

There was no missing the way Rowan was grinning as he looked between them, despite how he attempted to hide it.

"Y'know," Caleb mentioned, "full moon's in a couple nights. You should come out to Ro's."

"Oh?" Shaw raised a brow. "Am I to be the official sacrifice?"

"You got it." Caleb winked.

"In all seriousness, though," Shaw checked, "will you be fine with me being there? With me not being pack and all?"

Over time, were-creatures could learn to control a full moon shift to varying degrees. Until then, they were wild and unpredictable. It was why many were-creatures in urban settings wore anti-shift collars or spent time in special full moon facilities. Not all of them lived in the wilds, in packs or clowders or other types of clan groups.

"You're safe," Caleb assured. "My mind's my own."

"That's debatable." Shaw smirked.

Rowan wasn't even trying to hide his smile now. Caleb muttered for him to "shut up," despite Rowan not saying a word.

"Yeah, stop being so chatty." Shaw nudged Rowan's arm.

"Need I remind you both," Rowan mentioned, "I'm currently practicing curses?"

"Not *it*," Shaw replied at the same time Caleb said, "Kill him first."

The conversation devolved quickly after that into mindless banter. Overall, Shaw considered it a successful day.

Chapter Seven

THE GROUND BENEATH Shaw's back was slightly damp. Above him, late morning sunlight cut through the leaves of the trees. Birds were chirping, and a sparrow was hopping from one branch to the next within his view.

Shaw took a deep breath, letting it out slowly. Smiling, he commented, "This is really nice."

"Can't beat it," Rowan agreed. He was lying on the ground beside Shaw, while Caleb lay at Shaw's other side.

It had been a long night of literally running around in the forest. Rowan and Shaw had no hope of keeping up with Caleb's leggy wolf form, but it had been fun, nonetheless. They had stopped for food and naps—twice—a large gray wolf making quite a comfortable pillow. Despite knowing he was going to be feeling it for the next few days, Shaw was grateful to have been invited along for the full moon.

They were behind the cottage, the scent of baking bread drifting from the open windows. "That smells so good, Ro," Caleb whined, wiggling a little.

Rowan fished his phone from his pocket and said, "Still has another ten minutes. Then it's gotta cool."

"*Gah*!" Caleb groaned, rolling over to his stomach and bumping up against Shaw. "This is torture!"

Shaw chuckled, bringing a hand up to ruffle Caleb's hair. "I think you'll survive. Didn't you have enough to eat already?"

Caleb pushed himself up onto his elbows and put on a faux glower. "Didn't anyone tell you that wolves get hungry after a full moon shift?"

"One of my good friends is a wolf. So, yeah, I've seen how you blokes can put it away."

Caleb blinked. He looked across Shaw, over to Rowan, and raised a brow.

"What?" Shaw defended. "I can't have friends that are magicae?" Clearly, Rowan hadn't mentioned the squad.

"Makes sense, I guess," Caleb said. "What with bein' how you are to us." He flipped his bangs out of his eyes.

"Just don't tell him about the elf you know," Rowan mentioned off-handedly.

"Elf?" Caleb perked up.

"Caleb has a thing for elves."

"I don't have a thing. They're pretty, okay?"

"Mm-hmm."

Shaw grinned. "Sorry, this one's taken. He's actually mated with said wolf, so..."

"Yeah?" Caleb smirked. "You just got a little more interesting, Shaw."

He gave Caleb's shoulder a shove, knocking him over onto his side. Caleb laughed in response.

Rowan teased, "I happen to think he was interesting."

Shaw grinned at him.

Caleb wasn't having it, though. He huffed, crawling over Shaw in order to get to Rowan.

"Personal space?" Shaw griped.

"Nope." To Rowan, Caleb asked, "More interesting than me?"

"Is there anyone more interesting than you?"

Shaw shook his head, watching the pair. It was no wonder people thought they were dating all the damn time. It didn't help their cause when Caleb leaned in, rubbing their faces together. "I *am* one-of-a-kind."

"I see how it is," Shaw threw out. "I get my boyfriend stolen, hm?"

Rowan ducked his head, color on his cheeks. Caleb smirked, throwing his leg over Rowan pointedly. "Sorry, he's mine," Caleb declared, sitting there on Rowan's lap. "I saw him first." Rowan's blush deepened.

Shaw laughed. "You're incorrigible."

"Part of my charm."

Shaw's fingers drummed against Caleb's thigh as he rolled onto his side. "Charm is one way to put it." It was so tempting to use his empathic gifts, to increase Caleb's pliability so that he'd continue approving of Shaw's presence—and Shaw's place in Rowan's life. But, he refrained, fingers moving away.

Rowan inquired, "Since when are we boyfriends?" The look on his face was a little playful.

Shaw leaned in, pressing a kiss to Rowan's jaw, murmuring, "Call it wishful thinking." As he pulled away, he considered Rowan's smile a success.

Caleb stuck his tongue out, making a noise. "Keep wishin', Shaw. He's mine until further notice." Caleb sent him a sultry look. "*Although*... I'm up for sharing."

"Oh, that's it," Rowan laughed. He canted his hips to the side, rolling him and Caleb. "You are horrible."

"But, you love me."

Rowan gave a long-suffering sigh. "Sadly, yes."

Caleb was scenting with Rowan again, his tongue laving at Rowan's jaw. Not only was Rowan allowing it, but he nuzzled his nose against Caleb's cheek in return. Nor did

Rowan fight it when Caleb rolled them back, pinning Rowan to the ground with his entire body. Rowan simply let Caleb snuggle, arms resting low around his waist.

Rowan's head lolled to the side, lips quirking in amusement. His expression faltered, eyes flicking to Caleb and back to Shaw. "You're not...? You're not weirded out by this, right? Not upset?"

Shaw gave him a reassuring smile, reaching out to brush hair from Rowan's face. "I think it's sweet."

Rowan smiled hesitantly. "Yeah? Lotta guys don't get it" He bit his lip.

"They get jealous," Caleb complained. "They don't get pack."

"Well, I'm not most people." Shaw's fingers threaded with Rowan's, still resting on Caleb's lower back.

"No," Caleb agreed, "you're not."

Then, Caleb surprised Shaw by leaning over and rubbing their cheeks together. Caleb was scenting him, accepting him as pack. He knew full well what a big deal this was. Shaw moved his nose to nuzzle under Caleb's jaw. "Thanks."

Caleb's laugh was a short huff. "Yeah, yeah. Just keep taking care of my Ro, and we'll be good."

Shaw chuckled. "Promise."

"Do I get a say in this?" Rowan asked, amusement written on his face.

"Not really," Shaw replied, while Caleb said, "Nope."

Rowan smiled, shaking his head. "Dunno why I put up with either of you." His phone chimed, Caleb sliding off of him—and flopping over onto Shaw in the process—so Rowan could get it. "Ah, bread should be done."

"What are we waiting for?" Caleb dragged both of them to their feet, before jogging off toward the cottage.

Shaw looked over at Rowan, finding he was already gazing back. He felt himself being lost in violet eyes. Not for the first time, Shaw had to wonder if he was the only one with the ability to charm somebody—it sure seemed like Rowan had done something to him, which was the lone explanation Shaw had for falling so deep, so fast.

Rowan offered him a little smile, along with his hand. Shaw ignored it, sliding his arm around Rowan's waist, pressing them together. Rowan hummed, ducking his head to kiss Shaw's cheek. "Come on," Rowan murmured in his ear, pulling him along.

The urge to send his emotions through their connection was almost maddening. Shaw stopped, arm falling away. Rowan turned to look back at him in question. "I need— I want to..." Shaw reached out and grabbed Rowan's hand, giving it a squeeze, and Rowan's expression shifted to understanding.

"Oh." Rowan bit his lower lip, gaze drifting down to their hands.

"I want you to feel how I'm feeling right now. And I know you're leery about influencing and—"

"It's okay." Rowan met his gaze again, lips quirking.

Shaw was momentarily shocked. When it passed, he threaded their fingers together. His eyes fell shut as he pressed his emotions out and into Rowan. All the attraction, the contentment, that sense of right, was all bared for Rowan to see.

The small gasp caused Shaw's eyes to open. Rowan's lips were slightly parted, his eyes glowing with magic. Shaw was about to apologize for overwhelming Rowan—it wasn't as though he was used to empathic exchanges—but Shaw felt a returning trickle of energy.

It was muddy, at first, just raw power. Then, they came through. Rowan was... *He was sending emotions back.* Affection was front and center, with a sprinkling of humor, excitement, and what Shaw tentatively identified as fascination. There was something fond overlaying all of it, something akin to longing.

Shaw wrapped his arms around Rowan, shutting down the link before all the emotions could start looping around on themselves. "I..." Shaw was, for once, lost for words. Instead, he allowed all those feelings to spur him forward, pressing their lips together.

It was brief, and Shaw had to clamp down on his empathy so that it wouldn't flair to life again after experiencing such an intimate connection. Rowan's breath was against his lips, eyes shimmering with an array of emotions that Shaw didn't need to be an empath to read.

"Thank you" was all Shaw could think to say. "For sharing that with me."

Rowan smiled, brushing their lips together once more. "I'm not complaining."

"Hey!" Caleb called from the window. "If you two are gonna keep making gooey eyes at each other all day, I'm eating all the bread."

Shaw chuckled. "Yeah, yeah, we're comin'."

He took Rowan's hand again, not another word said between them. But he didn't imagine the prickle of emotion against his skin while Rowan's thumb rubbed back and forth across his knuckles.

THE GREY TIDES had many small, mostly flat islands scattered about that made them hard to navigate by boat, especially when the low fog lay across them. Large ships had to travel the long way around to port in Everstrand, the entire northern side being protected by rocky outcrops.

Rowan loved coming to the shoals. He found plenty of things to use for charms and potions, as well as simply taking pleasure from the sea. With a whispered incantation, Rowan stepped out on top of the water so he wouldn't soak his shoes and pants going farther out. Trying to navigate on the slippery rocks was a plain bad idea.

A small splash caught his attention as a familiar mermaid leaped up onto a rock shelf. "Good morrow, Varina," he called the traditional mer greeting.

"Ah, my tree of the water arrives," she joked. Her smile was friendly, despite the razor sharp teeth similar to a shark's.

"I am but your humble servant, my lady," he replied, complete with a flourished bow.

"You need to stay in touch better," Varina chastised as he sat on the mostly dry stone across from her.

"Well, until the mers create an underwater telephone system, I suppose we can communicate by notes floating in bottles."

Varina huffed, flopping her ebony tail against the water to splash him, which caused him to laugh. "You're horrible, you know. Sometimes I wonder why I put up with you."

"Because I'm one of the few topworlders you find interesting?" Rowan supplied. "As well as being charming and handsome—"

"And unfortunately can't breathe water, so I would kill you if I tried to bring you home with me."

"There's that too." Rowan chuckled, Varina's lyrical laughter joining in.

"I suppose it hurts my chances further that you're gay."

"I dunno; you mers sure do have pretty tails."

"And you like Leith's better than mine," she pouted. Rowan couldn't argue that he'd loved the merman's emerald tail glinting in the moonlight the night Rowan had arranged to meet Varina for a swim. A group of her friends had joined them, and Rowan was admittedly attracted to a few of them, tails and all.

"Hey, now," he argued anyway, "I happen to love your tail." That was true. "Speaking of... I was hoping you would be willing to part with a scale for me?" Mers were always rubbing off worn scales to make way for new ones so it wouldn't hurt. Even so, he knew it wouldn't be *that* easy to obtain, despite them being friends.

"Oh?" She got a coy look about her, tail swaying back and forth in the water as fingers slid through her long black hair. It was a careful maneuver, with her sharpened nails like small spikes—mers may have been beautiful, but they were equally as deadly. "And why would you need something like that?"

Rowan knew he was walking right into a trap but answered anyway. "I want to make a charm for someone."

Varina gave him a bright, knowing grin. "This person must be pretty special."

"He might be," Rowan replied honestly, softly.

It was merely a couple days ago that they'd spent the full moon together—that Shaw had bared his soul—and Caleb had blatantly told him to "go for it." Rowan had never tasted raw emotion before—it was a heady thing—and while it had been slightly terrifying, it was also an honor.

After a moment, he looked up and said, "I did bring you a present if it's any consolation."

That piqued Varina's interest. "Well, now, I was already going to give you one, but I'm not above bribery either."

Rowan smiled, pulling the gift from his pocket and tossing it to her. It was a nautilus shell strung on a treated leather cord, smaller pieces of shells on either side. "Remember that pub song I sang that you liked? Well, I had one of the tavern girls sing it much better, and you can have it with you now." To her questioning look, he told her, "Press the center of the shell."

When Varina did, a lovely voice resonated out of the nautilus, singing the song that she had favored so much. Her eyes widened, staring at the shell. A bright smile crossed her face as she looked at Rowan, squealing with joy.

She slipped into the water, then leaped onto the rock next to him, arms flinging around him. "You are the best!"

Rowan grinned right back, although he joked, "So much for staying dry."

With a roll of her eyes, she pressed the necklace into his hand. "Put it on me." Varina rotated her body, lifting her long tresses. "It's gorgeous, Rowan. Truly." Once it was clasped in place, she pressed a kiss to his cheek. "Thank you, *amiqueri*," she said, using the mer term of endearment for "beloved friend."

She adjusted to lie on her stomach, curling her tail up before stretching out on the rocky shelf. Black scales gleamed in the light, starting at her hips and covering her tail. There were also scales covering her vertebrae, sharper and made for protection, just like the spines down the back of her forearms that could be used as a slashing weapon. The rest of her body was smooth, almost rubbery skin like a porpoise, but with a tanned skin tone—mers' skin varied in range of color as any human's did.

"I have a loose scale back there that's starting to be a pain, and I can't quite reach it." Varina twisted her torso, curling her tail again and reaching out toward the place in question. "Right in there."

Rowan trailed his fingers carefully over the scales until she indicated he was on it. Sure enough, when he gave it a test wiggle, it was already coming out.

"Just keep working it back and forth," she encouraged, and Rowan gently did so until it came free. "Ahhh, that feels so much better." Varina rolled onto her back and stretched, tail sliding back and forth against the rock.

"Glad to be of service," Rowan said, receiving a stuck-out tongue in return.

"What are you going to do with it anyway?" Varina asked, sunning herself.

"I told you: a charm." She gave him a look, causing him to chuckle. "I'm not quite sure yet. But, I wanted it to be unique."

"Well, I doubt many topworlders have jewelry made of mer scales, so you're off to a good start."

Rowan smiled a little, gazing down at the scale that glittered in the sunlight as he tilted it. He couldn't explain how Shaw had gotten under his skin. Then again, maybe he didn't have to.

Chapter Eight

AZMAR HAD BECOME quite the destination spot. Originally a dwarven settlement meant to strengthen trade routes, these days it was populated by people of every shape and size. In the summer it was hopping with tourists. Being the Spring Equinox, it was a little too early for many non-residents to be there. Nevertheless, they still attracted people from nearby Everstrand and the other small towns along the coast.

With the Equinox came celebration. There was a street faire going on, complete with games, vendors, and lots of food. A stage was set up on the beach where performers would play throughout the day. It was a time of renewal, welcoming the spring and the rebirth of life.

Shaw walked through a row of vendor stalls, barely glancing at their wares. He wasn't particularly interested in the many magical items on display or buying any trinkets. He did, however, graciously accept the strand of fresh flowers from one of the event organizers, smiling softly as she kissed his cheek and murmured a traditional blessing.

Shaw had never been very interested in the holiday on a spiritual level, but he appreciated the idea of it. Besides, he would never turn down an excuse to have good food and spend time having a bit of fun. After all the stress of his newest assignment, well, Shaw figured he could use a break.

Perhaps he had an ulterior motive for traveling down to Azmar. That was highly evident when spotting a banner with a familiar logo brought a smile to his face. He was disappointed when he got closer, noting it wasn't Rowan at the small stand for Charmed to Meet You.

"Where's Ro?" he inquired of the young woman sitting there reading a book.

She seemed annoyed at the interruption until she looked up at him. With a bit too much flirtation in her tone, she answered, "Oh, he went to the concert. But I can help you."

"I didn't know he had an assistant," he replied, mildly annoyed himself now. The woman was quite the beauty—dark skin and bright eyes—and while he had no right to feel that way, Shaw felt a twinge of jealousy sneak up on him.

"Oh, well"—she frowned, hands twisting together—"I'm not. I'm a mage apprentice at the Everstrand Guild. I volunteered to help Rowan to get my hours for class."

"So, he didn't take on an apprentice?" Shaw ignored the fact he was relieved to hear it. Without giving her a chance to reply, he said, "Well, I'll go look for him on the beach then. Thanks."

"You're welcome?"

Making his way down to the boardwalk, Shaw looked out toward the stage. It was nothing more than a mass of bodies, all dancing and singing together. As Shaw got closer and was able to make out the music clearly, he thought he recognized the song. Sure enough, when the lead singer moved aside, the band name "Hex" was visibly emblazoned across the bass drum. The easy rock sound blended seamlessly with lyrics about nature and magic, a perfect fit to an event such as this.

Shaw found himself moving a little to the beat as he looked around all the different groups dancing together. With so many people, it was a wonder he was able to find Rowan—granted, Caleb's shocking blue hair certainly helped.

"Hey!" Rowan voiced his surprise when he joined them. "I didn't expect to see you here."

"Why not?" Shaw pitched his voice to be heard above the music.

"'Cause it's mostly magicae?" Caleb said. "And yer supposed to be some kinda inquisitor?"

Shaw reached out and pinched Caleb's side. He yelped and jumped closer to Rowan. "Don't be such a smartass," Shaw scolded, albeit his smile gave him away. Rowan laughed at Caleb's expense.

It had been nearly a week since Shaw had seen them, yet now it seemed like no time at all had passed. Granted, he had been keeping in contact via the occasional text—even with Caleb, who had deemed it necessary to exchange numbers after their romp in the woods.

"Wanna go grab something to eat?" Shaw asked. "My treat."

"I'm always up for free food," Rowan said. "Caleb?"

Caleb waved him off. "Go enjoy your date. I'm gonna prowl around here more." It appeared Caleb already had his eyes on a pretty naiad that was dancing with his friends.

"Happy hunting!" Rowan called back, taking Shaw's hand boldly in his own and weaving a path through the crowd. Released from the throngs of people, Rowan laughed. "So, what are you really doing here? You didn't come out here just to see me."

"Who says I didn't?" Shaw tugged his hand, halting Rowan, who looked at him questioningly. "I like you, Ro. I've never... I've never been drawn to anyone like I've been to you. There's something about you." He puffed air through his nose in a little laugh, shaking his head. "If I didn't know any better, I'd say you must have cast a spell on me."

Rowan chuckled, grinning at him. "Nope, no spell. Guess that's just my natural charm."

"Ugh, not puns," Shaw mock complained. "Please, no puns."

Rowan's laughter grew in volume. "I couldn't help myself. Pretty sure Caleb's been a bad influence."

"You think?" Shaw reeled him in flush, suddenly serious as he gazed up at Rowan. "I felt something about you when we met, something about your magic... It drew me in. After we talked that night at the bar? I just knew I had to make you mine, that I'd do anything to keep you."

Rowan's brows rose in surprise at the confession. "I... Wow." He wet his lips. "I don't really know what to say."

"That I'm utterly ridiculous?" Shaw suggested. "Total rubbish?"

Laughing a little, Rowan shook his head. "Far from that." He touched their foreheads together, closing his eyes as he admitted, "I feel the same way. It just feels so...right when I'm with you. It's a peace I haven't felt in a long time."

Shaw swallowed, hand running along Rowan's spine. "So, whaddya say? Wanna give this a go?"

Rowan smiled, pressing a soft kiss to his lips. "Yeah, I do." Straightening, Rowan pulled something from his pocket. "I've been hanging onto this until I saw you again. Thought about calling, but..." He gave an embarrassed shrug.

Curious, Shaw accepted the item, which turned out to be a necklace. "What—?" His brows lowered. "A scale?"

Rowan chewed his lip a moment, before explaining, "It's a mer scale."

Shaw's mouth fell open, and his gaze fell back to the necklace. The black scale glittered in the sun. He wasn't sure if it was due to the natural color of the scale itself or the magic he could feel prickling on his skin. It was attached to a stainless steel chain, and there was a rune written on it in silver that Shaw knew to mean "unseen."

"I know you insisted that you didn't need one," Rowan said, "but I got the sense that you're doing something dangerous." Shaw looked up to meet his eyes again, finding concern there. "I wanted to do something to help keep you safe."

Feeling emotion bubbling up, Shaw looked back down at the necklace. "I can't believe— No one's ever done anything like this for me."

Rowan urged gently, "Put it on."

Doing as he was told, Shaw inquired, "What kind of enchantments did you put on this, anyway? Or does me knowing somehow"—he circled his hands around—"make it not work?"

Chuckling, Rowan replied, "Think of it as reinforcement to your tattoos, as well as being swift on your feet."

He nodded. "I can work with that." Shaw pulled Rowan in to press a soft kiss to his lips. "Thank you, darling." Rowan's smile was too sweet, causing Shaw to kiss him again.

Rowan nipped at his lower lip, backing away with a playful grin. "Now, I believe you mentioned food."

"Always food with you. Between you and Caleb, you'll eat me out of house and home." Shaw dodged a swat. "How soon do you have to get back to your stand?"

Rowan brushed it off. "Cora can handle it. It's just some bullshit exposure thing Caleb harps on me to do every year."

"And you skip out on it every year, don't you?" Shaw took Rowan's hand and led him toward the boardwalk in search of lunch.

"That's what the apprentices are for. Believe me, they'd rather be doing this for their credit than what other masters will give them." He raised a shoulder in a half-hearted shrug. "I've got business cards and pamphlets and other stupid shit like that. If somebody wants to place an order, she'll write down their info and I'll call 'em tomorrow."

"In that case..." Shaw stopped at a vendor selling burgers. "I'm stealing you for the rest of the day. Consider it our first official date."

Rowan grinned from ear to ear. "Get me a venison burger with the works." He slapped Shaw's shoulder. "I'll grab us drinks from Makroth."

Makroth, as it turned out, was a dwarf who sold alcoholic beverages. They walked along the faire, drinking their beers and eating their burgers, talking idly between bites.

Once the food was gone and the wrappers tossed, Rowan twined their fingers together. He sipped his beer, looking out toward the Grey Tides. "Been a long time since I've been on a date," he mused. "Almost forgot what it was like."

"The way Caleb talks it's a wonder you ever had time to date."

"I didn't. That was the problem." Rowan looked over at him in brief amusement, before saying seriously, "I'm always studying, always pushing to know more, to do more, to take my magic to that next level." He shook his head. "It's selfish, I know—"

Shaw squeezed his hand. "It's not selfish to have a dream and go after it. And if your other boyfriends couldn't accept that, it's their loss. You're an amazing guy, Ro," he said sincerely. "You'll make grandmaster. Of that, I have no doubt."

Rowan didn't reply, but his smile said enough. He nestled against Shaw's side, cheek resting on top of Shaw's head as an arm wrapped around him.

Shaw figured it was his imagination that he felt the scale necklace warm against his skin. It was enough to make him realize he had to come clean to Rowan if they were ever going to make anything between them work. "Come with me," Shaw prodded softly. "I need to talk to you."

They went off the beaten path, away from the crowds. Finding benches at a little overlook of the beach, Shaw sat. As Rowan did the same, he asked, "Can you use a silence spell?"

"Sure." Rowan simply snapped his fingers and Shaw looked around them. There was nothing different, no physical sign that there was anything amiss, yet no one would be able to overhear them. Still, it was impressive that there was no need for an incantation or even anything close to a gesture—just *snap* and done.

"I knew you were powerful," Shaw mused, Rowan smiling softly in turn. Sobering, Shaw looked away as he confessed, "I've been undercover with the Inquisition here for the past two months."

"Undercover for who? Why?"

"Marcus..." He looked back at Rowan. "He got taken by them on junked up charges. Called it a blood crime." He growled and snapped, "Marcus would *never* take blood by force. He's far more controlled than that. Hell, someone could be bleeding out in front of him and he wouldn't even drop fang."

Rowan frowned. "Wasn't there a trial? Did he—?"

"There was nothing. One day Marcus is there, the next he's taken. He wasn't ever booked into Shadewind's jail. There was no record of him being brought to Redspire or any of the other nearby posts either. He just vanished."

"And you think they brought him here?"

"Our commander—Rhys—is in the same coven. He's an intelligence officer. Hale, Marcus's sire, is a coven leader. They have a huge influence in Shadewind, so when Hale started making waves..."

"Why didn't they just give Marcus back if the coven holds that much power?" Rowan reasoned.

"Because they took him out of the country."

Rowan put two-and-two together. "And brought him here."

"But, he's not in Everstrand," Shaw said. "I've been through the prison from top to bottom. I got my hands on records. Nothing shows that Marcus has been there."

"Then, where did they take him?"

"That's what I'm trying to figure out." Shaw sighed. "In the meantime, I've found evidence of the corruption everyone has feared. The disappearances, the excuses... The Inquisition is kidnapping high-powered magicae and holding them somewhere."

Rowan dropped his brows. "Why?"

"They're experimenting on them, trying to harness their abilities and put them into regular humans."

Rowan's jaw fell. "They..." His eyes darted around, unable to find any words.

Shaw stood and went to the railing. He looked out at the Grey Tides, feeling his chest tightening in a mixture of pain and anger. "These bastards made it personal," he spat. "And now there's even more of a reason to bring them down."

"Let me help."

"No!" Shaw spun around. "No way. I cannot get you involved."

"You involved me when you decided to tell me all this."

"I told you because I didn't want to lie to you." Shaw bracketed Rowan with his arms, looking down at him. "You were right, I am in danger, and you deserved to know the truth. But this?" Shaw shook his head and backed away. "I can't let you do this."

Rowan looked down at his hands settled in his lap, not saying anything for a minute. "So that's how you got your fake ID. You never left spec ops at all."

"Rhys set up my cover. And before you ask"—Shaw was quick to clarify—"this isn't an official op. Completely off the books. If I'm found out, Calagon disavows me." Shaw paused. "I'm on my own here."

"No, you're not," Rowan insisted. He spoke over Shaw when he tried to argue. "Does the rest of the squad know what you're doing?"

Shaw huffed, looking away and shoving his hands in his jeans pockets. "Bits and pieces. Rhys is the only one with details. Well"—his lips twitched into the hint of a smile—"and Hale. But, it's not like Rhys can tell him no." It had nothing to do with Marcus being Hale's childe and everything to do with the fact Rhys had sworn an oath of service to the near millennial old vampire.

"Then, with so much at stake, I guess you can't afford to tell me no," Rowan replied smartly, standing as well.

"Rowa—"

He pressed a finger to Shaw's mouth. "No," Rowan said firmly, meeting Shaw's gaze unwaveringly. "I'm no soldier. Far from it. But I am a master with Primal and enchantment magic. I can—and I will—be helping you."

"I can't risk you," Shaw all but pleaded.

"If what you say is true, we're all in very real danger. And someone like me? How long before I'm the Inquisition's next target? How long until I'm the one to disappear?"

That did it. Shaw yanked him into a crushing embrace. "I won't let anything happen to you."

"I know you wouldn't. It's why you're the one here, isn't it?" Rowan pulled back to look at him. "You said you were their team leader. You feel responsible. You want to protect them. I get it. But, that doesn't mean you need to be bullheaded and refuse help to do it!"

Shaw couldn't argue; Rowan was right. Shaw wasn't getting anywhere on his own and he couldn't help feeling like Marcus was running out of time. If he was even alive at all.

"Well," Shaw finally answered, "technically I had to do it 'cause furry tails, elf ears, hooves, and the like would kinda give it away." Rowan shoved him, Shaw chuckling before admitting, "I could use your help. But"—he pointed his finger at Rowan—"I need you to keep your mouth shut and do *exactly* as I say."

Rowan pretended to think about it. "Have I mentioned I don't take orders very well?"

"You and my men would get along just fine." Although Rowan smiled, it quickly faded when he saw the expression on Shaw's face. "I need to find him, Rowan." Shaw could hear his own heartbreak in his words, but he didn't care. "The things they could be doing to him..."

Rowan tugged him back to sit on the bench. "We'll figure it out, alright?" He rubbed at Shaw's arm, up and down. "I'm not sure what help I'll be. Especially now."

"Whaddya mean?"

Sighing, Rowan confessed, "There's...a problem I've been trying to solve myself. Well, the Masters Board, actually." He looked a bit guilty as he said, "There's a rogue mage. We're trying to locate them and deal with it before the inquisitors find out."

Shaw wet his lips. "Well, I can't really say anything 'bout not telling me..."

"No. You. Can. Not."

They looked at each other a long time. Eventually, Shaw's lips curled upward and he let out a huffing laugh. "Looks like we've got a lot of work to do."

Rowan nodded in agreement. "Bring what you've got to my house tomorrow night and I'll make the tea."

Chapter Nine

IN THE MIDDLE of scanning one of his grandmother's books, Rowan froze. There was a presence right outside his wards.

They weren't a barrier spell, rather an alarm system. Being out in the middle of the forest, he didn't want to do anything to impede the comings and goings of the wildlife. Some woodland creature wouldn't have tripped them, however.

Whatever was out there started skirting the edge of the property. It could have been innocent enough—a person not wanting to trespass—but there was always the possibility it was something that didn't *want* to be detected. Unfortunately, because it didn't seem inclined to breach the ward perimeter, Rowan couldn't tell exactly who—or what—it was.

Already uneasy, when the wards *were* crossed about ten minutes later, Rowan was out on the porch waiting. The wards relayed back someone had turned off the dirt road into his long drive, the second set of inner wards alerting when they grew close enough to hear the crunch of the tires on the gravel. Sparks danced across Rowan's fingertips, hand tucked behind his back.

He breathed a sigh of relief when it was the faded red pickup truck Shaw leased that broke through the tree line. When Shaw got out, backpack in hand, Rowan asked, "Did you get lost?" It was a fair enough question since Shaw had only been to the cottage once. It wasn't like there were street signs out on the trail system, and at night it would have been easy to get turned around.

"No, I remembered the way." Shaw stepped up onto the porch. There must have been some concern still on Rowan's face, as he asked, "Why? What's' up?"

"Something's out there. My wards picked it up a little bit ago." Rowan shifted. "Thought it might have been you. Trying to find the turnoff or something."

Shaw followed his gaze out into the woods. "Is it still there? I'll go take a look."

Rowan shook his head. "It started to circle around, then left. Probably nothing."

Shaw gave him a considering look, stepping closer. "Who you tryin' to convince? Me or you?"

Even though Shaw made a good point, Rowan brushed it off. He gestured for Shaw to come inside, not wanting to think it was anything more than it was. He understood Shaw's paranoia—he was playing a dangerous game.

So was Rowan for that matter. All the mages were. If they didn't catch this dark magic-user soon, they were looking at an Inquisition investigation. The idea of that was even less appealing now that he knew for certain about the corruption going on behind the scenes.

"Tea?" Rowan fell back on his routine of studying, with a hot cup of tea so as not to dwell on the situation.

"You realize that avoiding shit doesn't make it go away, right?" Shaw said, following him into the cottage.

"Are you starting first, or am I?" Rowan asked instead.

Shaw set his backpack on the dining table, which took up a good portion of the kitchen. The cooking area was nothing more than an L-shaped counter with basic appliances. After setting the kettle to boil, he looked at Shaw expectantly.

Relenting, Shaw asked, "Do you have a computer?"

"Laptop's on the coffee table." Rowan pointed into the living room, which was open to the kitchen.

The centerpiece of the cottage was certainly the stone fireplace. Rowan's well-worn recliner faced it, while the loveseat near the door had been claimed by Caleb. Honestly, Rowan wasn't sure why he bothered having a couch too—he rarely had company—but it had been a memento from his grandmother's house.

Shaw returned with the laptop, setting it on the table. "I didn't have room for mine in my pack," Shaw explained, having a seat before opening the backpack to reveal the large stack of files crammed inside.

Rowan's eyes widened. "Holy shit." Rowan sat across from him and asked, "What the heck is all this?"

"You said to bring everything I had." Shaw dropped his hand onto the files. "Personnel records for everyone at the temple, all official documentation on Marcus—including the false arrest record that's since disappeared from the system—blueprints of known Inquisition facilities in Osterian, etcetera."

"Wow." Rowan didn't even know where to begin. "And you've been doing all this on your own?"

"What Rhys didn't already have, I sent to him as well. Including this." Shaw pulled a flash drive from a zipper pocket. "I've been stealing data from top Inquisition members. A lot of it is bullshit, but it was how I learned what they've been doing."

"With the kidnappings?" Rowan clarified.

"And what their plans for the victims are. I haven't found anything in the files that indicates how far they've come with their experiments or even if it's started yet."

"If they've been taking people, then I'm willing to bet it has."

Shaw nodded solemnly. "I hope you're wrong, but..."

The kettle whistled and Rowan got up to make them both tea, his mind racing. He didn't want to believe anything like this could be going on; however, the proof didn't lie.

The more Shaw showed him what he'd gathered, the more sickened Rowan became. The Inquisition was very clearly working on trying to harness the various abilities that magicae possessed. Everything from the simple—like shielding or advanced healing—to the downright absurd—like harnessing immortality—was on that list.

"Do you realize the number of people they would need to make these experiments work?" Rowan's question was rhetorical.

"Have anything stronger than this?" Shaw asked, finishing his tea.

There was a cabinet in the living room where a few bottles of liquor were kept that Rowan rarely drank. He waved his hand, calling the Rouvalon whiskey over. When Shaw saw it, he gave an amused huff. "A good choice."

"Also, perfect in the tea." Rowan ought to know. He added a splash to his and didn't say a word at Shaw drinking straight from the bottle.

"Well"—Shaw wiped his mouth with the back of his hand—"now that you get the general idea of my lovely problem, what about yours?"

"Unfortunately, there's not much more to tell." He brought Shaw up-to-date on what little he knew of the dark mage. "Now, we gotta wait for Jorah to find them."

"That's it?" Shaw asked incredulously. "You have one guy on this?"

"Well, the rest of the Masters Board is helping out, and there's Tate, but...no one else is supposed to know."

Shaw shook his head. "Maybe I can—"

"I think the bigger problem here is this," Rowan interrupted, nodding his head toward the computer. "Won't have to worry about the Inquisition finding out about this rogue mage if they're out there stealing people to experiment on."

"You've got me there." Shaw sighed. All the same, he offered, "I'll do what I can to keep things off the radar down at the temple. But, I can't guarantee anything."

"I understand." Rowan laid a hand on top of Shaw's, who turned his over, fingers curling around Rowan's. "Maybe I can help you, though," Rowan continued. "At the very least, it'll take my mind off of all this dark mage business."

Shaw seemed to force a smile. "You might be regretting that after you start digging through all this stuff."

"Shut up and pass me a file."

Shaw's grin was a lot more genuine now. "We're gonna need a lot of coffee for this one."

SHAW PADDED FROM the bathroom, scratching his stomach. He debated between returning to the bedroom, with its nice warm bed and Rowan, or going for the kitchen in search of something to make for breakfast—or brunch as it were, given the time. His stomach growling made the decision for him.

At least Rowan kept the fridge and cupboards stocked from what Shaw could tell. He supposed living all the way out in the Sacred Timber made running to the store for milk a little more difficult.

He was chopping bell peppers and mushrooms—perhaps from the garden Shaw could see out the kitchen window—when he heard activity in the bathroom on the other side of the wall. Rowan appeared shortly thereafter.

Shaw smirked at Rowan's rumpled, sleepy appearance. "Somehow, I expected you to be a morning person."

Rowan grunted in reply. He moved past Shaw to grab the kettle, filling it and putting it on one of the stovetop burners. He pulled a mug from the cupboard, glanced at Shaw, and grabbed a second one. As he was getting the tea leaves prepped, Rowan finally commented, "Usually not dragging so bad, but it was kind of a long night."

Well, Shaw wasn't about to argue that one. He figured Rowan was rather used to late nights with all his studying. Shaw certainly was capable of going days without sleep. Stress, of course, made that harder to accomplish, especially to an untrained individual as Rowan was.

"Sit," Shaw urged gently. "I'll do that."

Rowan hummed gratefully, pressing a kiss to Shaw's cheek before following instructions. Sighing, Rowan's upper body was draped onto the table, one arm pillowing his head while the other was kept straight. "Going back to bed sounds good," he mumbled.

Shaw smiled. "You'd miss out on my amazing omelets."

There was a wry twist to Rowan's lips as he opened one eye. "Can't have that."

"So, plans for today?" Shaw broke eggs into a bowl.

"Not really. I'm not opening the shop for another couple days. I've got a few orders to work on, but nothing pressing. Probably will end up studying."

"You need a break," Shaw chastised. The whisked eggs had gotten a splash of milk and fresh herbs. He dumped the mixture into a preheated pan, pushing them around a bit.

"But, I like studying. Caleb doesn't seem to get that."

"You must have some other hobbies." At least Rowan seemed to appreciate the fact he hadn't said his studies couldn't be a hobby. It was a strange one, sure, but who was Shaw to judge what somebody else liked to do?

"There's my garden. Easier to grow your own vegetables and herbs. And my gram always had flowers. I read a lot too." Shaw turned to find Rowan looking at the rather impressive bookcase on the back wall.

"Quiet, relaxing, solitary hobbies." Shaw took the kettle off the stove when it whistled, pouring them into the waiting mugs with tea leaves. "Not an adventurous bone in your body?"

Rowan laughed. "Not so much, no. It's not like I don't get out at all," he defended. "I go on walks quite often. Fish in the pond. Walk around the old neighborhoods of Everstrand."

"And get drug out for social activities by a certain werewolf."

"And that." Rowan was smiling fondly. "It's in Caleb's nature to be social. He doesn't have his pack, so that means mixing it up with other people. He drags me along because he thinks I need to get out of my head, or 'Heaven forbid you socialize,'" Rowan tried for a poor imitation of Caleb. "Then I drag him back here 'cause I know he likes to get away from the city noise and be in nature where he feels more at home."

Shaw smiled softly; Rowan couldn't see it. "You two make a good pair." After a moment, Shaw chuckled. "Honestly, you're more than opposites attract. It's almost impossible to imagine you becoming friends, but here you are." He set the mugs on the table. "You balance each other out well. Don't think Caleb could find a better friend."

There was a flush on Rowan's face when Shaw turned back to plate up the omelets.

"Besides," Shaw continued, "someone has to make sure you have a good time. Don't mind if that could be me though." When he looked, Rowan's blush had deepened. Shaw set a plate in front of him. "Eat up. And, if you don't have any particular plans, maybe I can play hooky and spend the day with you."

"I'd like that." Rowan took a bite, making an approving noise and quickly taking another. "You weren't kidding. This is great." He took a sip of his tea and hummed thoughtfully. "But your tea skills could use work."

"Well, we can't all be perfect."

Rowan shook his head, shoving another forkful in his mouth as Shaw started to dig in too. "I really enjoy spending time with you," Rowan said between bites. "Doesn't seem to matter what we're doing. I just like being with you."

Shaw smiled softly, looking down at his plate. "Same. You're... Damn, I suck with words."

Rowan stopped, food halfway to his mouth. Slowly, he set the fork down, looking over at Shaw thoughtfully.

"What's wrong?" Shaw asked when Rowan remained silent.

"We're..." Rowan licked his lips and tried again. "I know we talked about seeing how things worked out between us, after our fight. And I-I think it's been going well?" He cleared his throat, eyes darting away. "I mean, it's been going better than any of my other boyfriends have, as of late. Not that that's saying much—"

"Hey." Shaw reached over and laid his hand on Rowan's. "There's no pressure here, okay?"

The vulnerable expression on Rowan's face was almost too much. "Yeah?"

"Ro, it's not a secret I care about you." Shaw smiled gently. "I want you. If you'll have me."

Rowan grinned, turning his hand to hold Shaw's. "I will." He chuckled, shaking his head as he looked away. "Honestly, I think I'm the one who should be asking if you'll have *me*. I'm awkward and too focused and—"

Shaw leaned over the table, cutting off Rowan's rambling with a kiss. "Ro? Shut up."

Rowan shoved him, unable to hide his continued smile.

"Finish up," Shaw said. "Maybe we can watch a movie, or go out by the pond."

Rowan relaxed. "Sounds good to me. I want to check on a couple things in the other room first." He popped the last of the omelet into his mouth pointedly.

"What you got in there anyway?"

"Potions, spell supplies, my books." Rowan lifted a shoulder. "You're welcome to come check it out."

After Shaw cleared the dishes, he did just that. Rowan was already there, bent over a table with an array of potions laid out on it.

The room was a turret-style addition to the cottage. Oversized windows provided a beautiful view of the woods and pond. One wall was covered by a large bookshelf. Unlike the one in the living room, this appeared to contain magic textbooks—both new and old. Other shelves had various canisters, boxes, and the like, with unknown supplies. A decoration made of bones and feathers hung from the ceiling. If Shaw had to guess, it was likely enchanted.

"This is nice," Shaw commented. It was clearly newer than the rest of the cottage.

"Caleb talked me into expanding," Rowan said, confirming his suspicion. "I used to have everything scattered around the house."

"Doesn't exactly allow for company," Shaw reasoned.

"Wasn't used to that before Caleb."

"Not even with the other mages?" Surely Rowan had study sessions at least.

"Kept that to the city. Wasn't ever that comfortable bringing people out here." Rowan grunted. "Not that I did much with the others, anyway. I didn't care for their study habits."

"Didn't take it seriously enough?" Shaw guessed.

Rowan only smirked.

"*So*, these aren't gonna blow up too, are they?"

"I'm never living that down, am I?"

"Not likely." Shaw stood by Rowan, a hand on his lower back. "What are all these, anyway?"

"Mostly basic potions. Trying to get the hang of making them. I do have a few experiments, though."

"Is that smart? I mean, at this stage of doing things?"

"Probably not."

Shaw scoffed. He had nothing to say to that. Instead, he reached out toward a particularly interesting looking bottle which glowed a bright yellow with swirls of orange. "This one looks cool."

"I wouldn't touch that one." Rowan grabbed his wrist. "It's, um, a little unstable."

"You are so not helping your cause," Shaw deadpanned.

Rowan picked up a smaller bottle filled with a light-blue liquid. "Here, try this one."

"You completely ignored me," Shaw pointed out, at the same time Rowan was whispering a word.

Light burst from the bottle, startling Shaw and projecting all around the room. It was pretty neat, but he found himself teasing, "You may have heard of these things called flashlights."

Rowan chuckled. "Yeah, well this thing doesn't run out of batteries." He murmured a different word, and the light appeared to fold itself back into the bottle.

"Point taken."

Music started to play and Rowan reached into his jeans pocket, pulling out his cell phone. "Ieus? Wonder what he wants." After answering, Shaw watched Rowan's face change before his eyebrows shot up. "Yeah, yeah, I'll be there as soon as I can."

"What's wrong?" Shaw asked when Rowan hung up.

"The board's called an emergency meeting with all the Guild masters."

"Did he say why?"

Rowan shook his head. "I'm assuming it has to do with this dark mage business."

"I'll drive you," he offered immediately.

"Are you sure?"

"I want you to be safe." Shaw licked his lips. "I guess I'm going into work after all. See if there's any rumblings there."

"I can get Caleb, or somebody else, to bring me home," Rowan said.

"You should come back to my apartment where I can keep an eye on you."

Rowan lifted a brow.

"I'm worried."

Rowan sighed. "I'll think about it." He leaned in and stole a kiss—likely to shut him up, but Shaw wasn't complaining.

"Just let me know what you're doing," he conceded. "I can come back out here tonight if you need me to."

Shaking his head, Rowan prodded him out of the room. When all he grabbed was his wallet and keys, Shaw knew Rowan would be returning to the Sacred Timber that night. He certainly wasn't making it easy to keep an eye on him. It wasn't as if Rowan was incapable of taking care of himself, but that didn't stop Shaw from worrying.

"You're going to be the death of me," Shaw said as they went out the door.

Rowan laughed at him, which did absolutely nothing to help the situation.

Chapter Ten

"I'M NOT SURE about this," Rowan commented, looking around the meeting room. The board had called together every Guild member currently holding at least one masters to explain the situation they faced with the dark mage, although it had taken until the late afternoon to get them all assembled.

"Neither am I," Tate replied, standing off to the side with Rowan, "but Jorah hasn't been able to track him any other way."

Rowan still had a hard time believing that Jorah of all people had lost the dark mage using a spirit track from the last murder site.

"What, they didn't tell you?" Tate continued, leaning closer and dropping his voice. "There was another kill the other night."

Rowan's head whipped around, almost smacking it with Tate's. "Where?"

"Outside Azmar. Must have been stalking the festival."

Rowan's stomach dropped out. If he hadn't been worried about the mysterious presence at his home before, he was downright terrified now. Had the dark mage been stalking him?

"What did the inspectors say?" Rowan managed to ask.

Tate's jaw clenched as he looked away. "An animal attack. They think she wandered out into the woods and got lost."

"And Jorah?"

"It was the same spiritual imprint he got off the other kill sites. He lost the trail when it doubled back to Azmar. Too many magicae to mix in with."

"Damn it."

Tate nodded in agreement. Things were becoming more complicated. Their time was running out before authorities throughout Osterian would put together the same pattern that they had. After that, it was simply a matter of time before the finger was pointed at the Mages Guild.

"So, what do we do?" Olivia asked once the board was done filling them in.

"Quail has suggested we do a group channeling," Ieus said.

It was Quail himself who explained, "As my students here might recall, spirit walking is a rather difficult area of Incarnum magic. Even a master may not have full control over where they go in such a trance. Therefore, I'm only asking those with a Masters in Incarnum, if you are willing, to journey with me so we can perhaps locate this errant mage."

Frey took over from there. "Ieus and I will be leading the rest of you in the ritual. We will be pooling our energies into helping them succeed, and be here to help draw them back when the spell is over."

Ieus set about getting them into position. "Everyone gather round."

Rowan was cut off by Jorah. Tate looked between them questioningly, but Jorah jerked his head for Tate to keep going. "You're coming on this trip," he told Rowan, his gaze unreadable as always and his words just as guarded.

"I'm no Master in Spirit," Rowan pointed out.

"No, but your testing was slated for later this week, wasn't it? Consider this your exam."

"What?" Rowan's eyes widened. "No, I have no idea how to spirit walk."

"Sacha and I have never done it either."

"But *you* have a masters," Rowan argued. "It should be easy enough for you." It was on the tip of his tongue that he could barely hold his hexes and counters, but he refrained.

"Rowan, this isn't exactly up for debate. We have a handful of mages here that can do this, two of whom aren't going in because they fear what can happen if someone skilled enough isn't left behind to pull us back." Jorah stepped closer to him, eyes like coals piercing into him. "This is too important to sit back and make excuses. If you call yourself a master mage, then prove it."

Rowan was left stunned, attempting to grasp at words but finding nothing would come.

Jorah grabbed his wrist, pulling Rowan toward the circle where Quail and the others were already getting settled. "Make a bigger hole," he gruffed, nudging Quail with his boot. He pressed on Rowan's shoulder to get him to sit.

"Jorah." Frey was looking ruffled as she walked over to them. "What is this?"

"Rowan volunteered to help out."

"Like hell he did. What do you think you're doing?"

"Coddling the boy doesn't get him to high master."

Frey scoffed. "We also don't force people into performing dangerous magic." She looked down at Rowan. "My dear, you—"

"It's fine," Rowan interrupted her. "I may not be able to do it, but at least I can try."

Jorah's lips twitched slightly, but he steeled his features just as quickly. He settled down between Rowan and Sacha, saying, "It's decided."

Frey gave Rowan a long, hard look before throwing her hands up and letting it be.

Quail, who had been casually listening to the whole exchange, reached over and clapped a hand onto Rowan's knee. "You'll do fine," Quail said, a reassuring smile on his face as he leaned closer. "Follow where the energy takes you. Don't try to fight it. Frey and Ieus will pull you back, so there's nothing to worry about."

Rowan nodded slowly, hoping that Quail was right. His stomach was already in knots. He'd been acting out of spite more than anything, Jorah's comment about being a master burning him up inside. While he may have known how spirit walking worked in theory, Rowan had certainly never tried it, and the whole idea was, in truth, terrifying.

"All of you..." Frey said, drawing their attention. "Take a deep breath... Hold... And breathe out." Rowan's eyes fell shut as Frey had them repeat the relaxation practice a few times. "Now, those of you walking, simply follow where we lead."

Low chanting started, rhythmic in nature. Rowan tried not to focus on the words of the spell itself but rather the beat. He found himself syncing his breathing to it. In. Out. In. Out. He let the magic wash over him, allowing it to draw him in.

Rowan felt as though he were being pulled from his own body. His first instinct was to resist, but he remembered Quail's words. Relaxing into the sensation, he gasped as he was tugged forward. He opened his eyes, finding himself in a very different room.

Everything around him appeared to emanate a kind of smoke. The haze extended to the people around the room. However, the other spirit-walking mages stood there in the fog with him, smoke licking around them, almost wisping in and out of existence. It was like being in another realm, ethereal and unnerving all at once.

Rowan went to speak, only to feel pulled by an invisible tether. The world moved around him in a blur before he was dropped into a familiar place. Well, as familiar as the world could look when covered in this strange, muted fog.

He was in the back alley behind his shop. *Why did the spell bring me here?* he wondered. A shape emerged from the shop's window. Trailing smoke, Badger manifested in a partially solid state, just as his fellow mages had been. Something compelled Rowan to follow.

Everything around him moved like it was underwater. His limbs felt sluggish and heavy. The sounds were all a distant murmur. The farther he went, the darker it seemed to become, as if light itself had trouble piercing through the ever-shifting haze.

Suddenly, the form before him changed. Badger was no longer a cat, but a man.

Rowan gasped and the man reacted in kind, turning to look in his direction. There were no features to be made out, as the man seemed comprised of the same muted tones as their surroundings. One thing that Rowan could see was a pair of pale yellow eyes, slitted like a feline.

Suddenly, the world around him warped. He felt the rush of wind as he was yanked backward.

Gasping for air, Rowan reached out, snagging someone's shirt. His fingers curled in the soft fabric. "Breathe, Rowan." It seemed an eternity before Rowan started to do so, shaking as he looked up to find Ieus there. "Take it easy. You're back."

Rowan looked from side to side, finding that the others were recovering as well. Quail reached out to him with a little smile on his face, nodding when Rowan grasped his wrist. "Told you it would be fine."

"I saw him," Rowan blurted, looking back to Ieus. "I saw the dark mage."

Ieus appeared surprised. "You saw him?"

Rowan nodded, stumbling to his feet. Thankfully, Ieus was there to keep him from face-planting.

Jorah's brows were furrowed together as he rubbed his forehead. "I'm not sure what I saw. I think it was the murders but..." He shook his head. "It doesn't make sense."

"He's a shapechanger," Rowan spoke overtop of Jorah.

"A shapechanger?" Frey was helping steady Sacha as she stood.

Rowan understood their skepticism. It was an ancient form of magic, rarely practiced as it was hard to control. However, those who did master it could take on multiple animal forms as easily as any were-creature.

"I saw him transform right in front of me. It was..." Rowan shook his head. "He's been posing as the cat that comes into my shop."

"Goddess preserve us," Sacha breathed.

"He's been under our nose the whole time?" Tate said

Jorah's frown deepened, if even possible. "My own walk makes more sense now. I saw a large predator."

"You connected to those who were attacked," Quail observed. "You saw the terror that they did."

"It's why the attacks looked animal," Tate realized. "How does someone even learn those powers outside of a guild?"

"We should call the other guilds," Frey suggested. "Ask about any members who studied the old arts."

"Or expressed interest in doing so," Ieus agreed.

"It doesn't matter who he is," Jorah said, getting to his feet. "He needs to be taken care of."

"I believe I have a location for us," Quail supplied, accepting a hand up from Rowan. "A cave, in the southern part of the Sacred Timber. It appeared to be on the other side of the Mirrored Waters."

"I know that lake," Tate commented. "It's isolated."

"We find this cave," Jorah said, "and we flush him out. Hit him fast before he has time to react."

"Between all of us," Ieus replied, "I believe we could manage such a thing."

"Not you," Jorah disagreed. "You and Frey should stay behind."

"And why would we do that?" Frey challenged.

"Allowing the whole Masters Board to go after a rogue dark mage isn't the smartest course of action."

"What do you propose?" Sacha inquired.

"Naturally, I will go. Tate, Sacha... Quail, your healing skills might be needed." Jorah looked at Rowan. "You might not have battle experience, but another deft hand in Primal magic will be appreciated."

"So, Tate and Rowan for myself and Frey," Ieus said. He looked over at Frey, who didn't seem very happy about it, but nodded all the same. "Very well. You'll inform us where you find this cave? Just in case?"

Jorah nodded in agreement. "We'll go in tonight. We can't afford to put this off any longer."

Rowan licked his lips, shifting in unease. "Shouldn't we prepare?"

"All the preparation amounts to nothing if the Inquisition is brought down upon the Guild." Jorah met his gaze. "Sometimes you need to jump in headfirst and worry about swimming later."

"An odd attitude for a battlemage."

"I believe," Ieus interjected, "what Jorah is attempting to say is that some things you can't prepare for. You must trust in the people around you and in yourself." Ieus settled a hand on Rowan's shoulder. "Trust your abilities, Rowan. They will not fail you."

Rowan took a moment to process the words before nodding. It appeared he had little choice in the matter, in any case. He simply hoped Jorah knew what he was doing. It was likely he was leading them all to their deaths, otherwise.

ROWAN WAS WEDGED into the backseat of Quail's truck, between Sacha and Tate. They hadn't left until well after dark, partly because Jorah had claimed tactics, but mainly because Frey had insisted they all have time to recover from their spirit walking. Except, that meant Rowan had far too long to think—mostly about the fact they were about to go kill his cat.

He had borrowed a permanent marker from Frey on their way out the door and now sat—almost frantically—putting runes onto his skin. Of course the second he thought to do this, Jorah would be ready to leave. He had no idea how to fight, yet there he was. He would need all the help he could get.

"You need to calm down," Tate soothed, placing his hand on Rowan's wrist to grab his attention.

"Easy for you to say." Tate was trained for various forms of combat by Jorah himself. Even Sacha had a bit of experience to that end with her old guild. "I'm flying blind here."

"You'll be fine," Sacha assured him, hand falling to the nape of his neck. There was a calming force she passed to him, similar to what Shaw could do. It was nothing like his energy though, and all it managed to do was grate against Rowan's own magic.

Grunting, Rowan went back to the protection rune he was drawing on his arm. How many did that make now? He knew at least two for shielding, and there was a mana stabilizing one he could add as well.

Jorah spoke up from the passenger seat in his usual bored manner. "Those won't do you any good if you lose that arm."

Rowan froze.

"Jorah!" Tate scolded, reaching between the seats and shoving him. "Knock it off!"

Rather than curse Tate where he sat, Jorah did nothing more than raise a meaningful brow at him before going back to watching the road. "Wasting mana on protection runes doesn't do anyone any good."

"Rowan's mana reserves will be fine," Quail said. "Now, leave the boy alone."

Rowan was grateful for the vote of confidence—and the backup. At least he wasn't the lone non-combatant they had. Quail was only chosen for his mastery of healing. His job would be to keep them alive. Granted, they were all hoping it wouldn't come to that.

"Here," Tate murmured. He took Rowan's right arm gently, plucking the marker away with his other hand. Tate started to draw out familiar runes and Rowan managed to smile a little. Magic prickled his skin as Tate fortified Rowan's Primal abilities.

"Thanks." Rowan had been hanging around Caleb too long—he had the strange urge to rub his cheek to Tate's head in appreciation.

Tate shrugged it off, passing the marker back. "Is there a plan, Jorah?" he prompted. "Or are you dragging us out here as bait?" There wasn't any question that as the former battlemage they were all deferring to Jorah to lead them.

"Our advantage will be stealth. You and I will draw the mage out, allow the others to stay back and strike if they can. The goal is to get him restrained as quickly as possible. Then we can get him talking."

"After that?" Sacha asked.

Jorah paused. "His answers decide his fate."

Rowan didn't like the sound of that, but he kept drawing his runes. He had something of a gauntlet forming around his left arm. No doubt Caleb would find it cool. Rowan frowned at the thought. Neither Caleb nor Shaw knew where he was. If anything were to happen...

"We do have one advantage," Quail mentioned. "He used his shapechanging abilities the other night. He won't have the energy to use them again so soon."

"Perhaps not his full beast form," Jorah agreed, "but we know he's been able to still change into a domestic cat, so he may be able to use some aspects of those abilities." He glanced back at Rowan. "When was the last you saw him?"

"Umm..." Rowan was thrown for a moment, brows drawn together. "Monday, when I had the shop open." It had been a couple days before the festival and he'd been attempting to organize everything for it. Badger had kept out of the way, for the most part, lying in a spot of sunshine on the counter.

"That cat form must not take a lot out of him then."

Jorah and Quail were going back and forth about more theories on the subject of shapechanging, but Rowan tuned them out. He was still in shock over the fact Badger was no mere cat. How had he managed to hide like that for so long? Why had he kept returning to the shop? There were so many questions Rowan had, yet he couldn't wrap his head around the concept long enough to even start piecing any of it together.

"This turnoff here," Tate directed Quail into the forest off the main road. "There's another road that will take us to a parking area for a trailhead. We can follow that up toward the lake."

"As we get closer," Jorah said, "I should be able to pick up on a soul track to take us to the cave."

Rowan was half paying attention. He shifted to pull his phone out, opening up the texting app. *I love you,* he typed. He entered both Shaw and Caleb as recipients, thumb hovering over the send button. There would be questions, suspicions, on both their parts should he send a text like that out of the blue. Before he could change his mind, he powered his phone off instead, returning it to his pocket.

Sacha must have noticed. She was the one who stole the marker from him that time, jotting lines of runes on the back of his right arm. Rowan allowed for the distraction.

Chapter Eleven

THE CAVE WAS tucked away behind thick brush and trees. It blended in seamlessly with the landscape, even without the powerful magic hiding it. As it was, Quail had to drop the wards they encountered, while Sacha did away with the illusion spell cast upon it.

"Quail, Rowan," Jorah instructed from their place crouched in the darkness, "cast for any traps." They merely needed the surrounding woods and small clearing in front of the cave to be safe. Anything that awaited them inside would never be put to use as they all agreed that being drawn in would mean their deaths.

"At the entrance," Rowan informed them, "there's a tripwire."

"The treetops," Quail added.

"I see them," Sacha said. Her eyes glowed a stunning shade of indigo as she reached out with her own magic, disabling the firebombs dangling in the branches over the clearing. Undoubtedly, they were meant to drop on whoever was following the unsuspecting triggerman into the cave. Just the same, there was no reason to risk them being set off in another manner.

"I'm not picking up anything else," Rowan said. "I guess he figured that would be enough."

"He never expected to be found," Jorah agreed. "He was brazen enough to be near you this whole time."

Rowan scowled.

"Tate," Jorah continued, motioning him forward, "I need you to draw him out." He met Tate's gaze, assuring him, "I'll be right there."

Hanging back in the tree line, Rowan watched while Tate stepped into the open. Jorah moved quickly without making a sound, practically melting into the shadows beside the cave entrance.

"Come out, mage!" Tate barked, summoning an ax from thin air. "It's time for you to answer for your crimes!"

Menacing laughter echoed through the clearing and woods around them. A chill went down Rowan's spine, and he knew immediately that they had been expected.

"Tate!" Rowan yelled, lunging out of hiding and hooking Tate around the waist, taking them both to the ground.

An array of daggers sailed over them, embedding into the bark of the trees. They were glowing black with the taint of dark magic.

Rowan turned as he sat up, Tate already popping into a crouch. The laughter died down to center on the source. Stepping from the darkness was none other than the mage Rowan saw in his vision.

The man in front of them didn't look like someone they would peg as being off at first glance. He was tall and broad across the shoulders. There was scruff from a few days of not shaving and his dark hair was a bit unkempt where it curled at his neck. His jeans and loose-fitting tee were dirty from being in the forest, but really, the mage was rather handsome.

It was the manic smile that gave his true nature away, his sickly yellow eyes glowing like beacons.

Rowan wasn't sure where his self-assuredness came from. Perhaps it was the fact he knew that not only were their lives in danger, but the lives of all the mages in Everstrand should they fail. Rowan didn't want to know what the Inquisition would do to them should they find out, or how many more people this shapechanger would kill before he was finally put down.

Standing defiant, Rowan greeted, "Badger."

The man grinned back. "Nothing personal, Rowan."

Jorah had been slinking into position, as silent as the shadows themselves. However, *Badger* somehow knew he was there, turning and throwing a snare spell Jorah's way. Dodging, Jorah rolled to the side, popping up and thrusting with his staff. At the same time, Tate pushed past Rowan, aiming his ax at Badger's back.

Neither man connected, Badger wisping away as shadow and reappearing a couple of feet to the right. It wasn't a skill learned lightly, but then Badger had already proven to be a man of many talents. He flickered in and out a few more times, dodging every blow the pair could throw.

With a taunting laugh, Badger ensnared Tate's neck with a vine of pure darkness. It caused Tate to fall to his knees. Every time he gasped for air, the spell squeezed tighter. Rowan wrapped his fingers around it to attempt a counterspell and was scalded for his trouble, Tate wincing.

While Jorah went toe to toe with Badger—landing a few hits in the process—Sacha was able to act. "Well, that is enough of that," she stated, literally putting her foot down. Incantation said under her breath, she threw her arms out wide into the air, casting a net of light.

Badger screeched, vanishing completely. As they all blinked away spots from their vision and looked around the area, now lit by bright floating orbs, they all realized the same thing. "Decoy," Rowan growled, immediately on alert.

Tate was coughing, which was a good sign, Quail coming to his aid. "Relax," Quail urged, hand glowing a healing blue.

Rowan couldn't afford to be distracted. Only three of them were currently in the fight and Badger could have been anywhere. Beside him, Sacha gripped her own staff tightly.

"Where is he, Sacha?" Jorah demanded, resting the bladed end of his staff behind his shoulder.

Eyes glowing as she stretched her powers outward, her detection ability came through for them. "There." She pointed toward the lake, visible between the trees, down an overgrown path. "I see a presence."

"There's no point in using stealth," Jorah said. "He knows we're here. Sacha, keep light on us at all times. We're not giving him the opportunity to use any of those same tricks again. Tate, are you alright?"

"I'll be fine." His voice was a bit hoarse, and Rowan saw what appeared to be a burn looping around his neck, but already it was healing, thanks to Quail.

"Good. You and Rowan stay with me. Quail...just try to keep out of the way."

"'Keep out of the way,' he says," Quail grumbled. "What does he think I've been doing?"

Rowan's smirk dropped away when he caught Jorah staring at him. He was always so difficult to read; his face seemed to be permanently set in stone. "Follow my lead," Jorah told them all, despite the fact he was still watching Rowan with that piercing gaze.

They made their way down the path, Sacha casting another net of light when they broke through the trees to view the water. There was nothing there—as far as Rowan could tell—just the lake, with a low layer of fog, surrounded by the woods. Even the wildlife had gone silent.

"Get out here, Badger!" Rowan hollered, hoping to instigate him into showing his hand before he was ready.

Jorah looked at Rowan in disapproval. Still, he added, "You've got nowhere to run. We will hunt you down in whatever hole you crawl into."

"Is that so?" They whirled around, the voice having come from behind, turning once more when the voice spoke from yet another direction. "Seems like you're at a disadvantage."

Tate huffed, having traded out his summoned ax for a swifter sword instead. He twisted it in his grasp, allowing it to absorb light energy, causing it to glow brightly. "I'd like to see you try that again."

Rowan wasn't as skilled with light as Sacha, or even Tate, but he knew how to make a mean fireball. He would have to be careful about where he flung them so he wouldn't burn the woods down around them. He allowed electricity to dance across his fingers, hoping to stun Badger when he showed himself before landing a direct hit with flame.

As with most plans, it didn't exactly work that way.

Jorah reacted before Rowan even knew what was happening, strafing in front of Rowan and holding up his staff diagonally. Badger impacted the force field, snarling as he slashed out with hands that had grown deadly looking claws.

Seeing his chance, Rowan let loose an electrical arc. Badger cast a counter that sent it into a nearby tree. As the wood exploded and splintered, Quail threw up a shield to protect him and Sacha, who was busy holding the array of lights.

Once more, Tate and Jorah worked to encircle Badger, giving him all they had. The light may have prevented him from using the shadows to teleport, but that didn't seem to help them. Both physical and magical attacks didn't penetrate his powerful shield. If they were going to do any damage, they would have to take it down.

Rowan narrowed his eyes. "Dodge this," he spat, pushing out with both hands. The shield shattering spell that had been in his grandmother's old books shot straight through Badger's defenses. In fact, it went so far as to launch him back a good six feet, sending him skidding along the ground.

Badger looked up, yellow eyes piercing into Rowan. "Should have stayed out of it, Rowan," he growled. His shield fizzled as he attempted to bring it back, but Badger appeared unconcerned by the new development.

Tate and Jorah's next attacks were countered, Badger knocking them off their feet with a gust of wind. He threw Sacha and Quail back against the trees near their cover. Thick roots were pulled straight up from the ground, wrapping around all four of them. Thorns prevented them from moving. Jorah cursed, but every time he attempted to cast a new incantation to break the trap, the vines squeezed tighter.

Rowan tried again to hit Badger with a shock spell. Except, Badger did something Rowan had never seen before. He trapped the electricity in a ball of dark energy.

Badger's grin was anything but friendly, too many teeth flashing in menace. "One by one they fall. One by one I'll rip them apart. It's tempting to save you for last...make you watch while there's nothing you can do to stop me."

Hand behind his back, Rowan switched tactics, pulling moisture from the air and cooling it rapidly.

If Badger noticed, it didn't worry him in the least as he stepped closer. "You shouldn't have come looking for me." He brought the electrified dark energy ball up in one hand. "There is *so much* I wanted to show you, Rowan. So much we could have been."

"That's why you kept coming back to the shop?" Rowan spat.

"You *ooze* power," Badger all but purred. "You were like a beacon. It's a shame these fools could never see your potential."

"You're right." Their eyes met. "But looks like you underestimated me too."

Rowan slung the spell, ice shards whipping around to slash at Badger. The ball of energy flew into the air, landing short of Rowan. The impact shattered it—the shock spell dissipating into the air in all directions.

One of the sparks hit Rowan, passing through him before discharging into the ground. Though enough to sting and make his heart skip a beat, he didn't go down. He hated to imagine what would have happened had it been a direct hit.

Badger glared at him, a snarl that was more animal than man leaving his throat. "I'm warning you, Rowan."

Rowan smirked, feeling more confident than he had a minute ago. Badger was bleeding from multiple lacerations, some of them deep. While he could mimic the shapeshifting abilities of others, he couldn't copy their healing.

The blood gave Rowan an idea. His eyes flicked over to Jorah's staff, lying discarded on the ground. Apparently, Badger noticed because he lunged straight for him. Rowan brought up a wall of earth, cutting him off and allowing Rowan to make a play for the staff.

"Ro!" Tate managed to choke out before the vines tightened.

Badger snagged Rowan's leg, tripping him. Rowan rolled to his back, kicking out as he tried to wiggle away. Badger dug his claws into Rowan's leg, yanked him closer, and sneered. "Where you goin', Rowan?"

Rowan heated his hand with fire and lashed out at Badger. Both his wrists were grabbed and slammed to the ground. Badger levered himself farther over Rowan.

When Rowan opened his mouth to shout an incantation, Badger whispered, "Hush." He blew black smoke from his mouth, the spell wrapping around Rowan's vocal cords and stopping him in midsentence. "None of that now, pet."

Rowan felt panic bubble up. Now, he was well and truly trapped at the hands of a psychotic dark mage. Worse yet, his guildmates were unable to do anything to aid him. His eyes must have given him away because Badger chuckled.

"Now, now, no need to get out of sorts. This just gives us a chance to talk properly."

Rowan's eyes narrowed.

"Aww, don't look at me like that." Badger shifted his weight to settle on top of Rowan, bringing their faces closer. "You know, you're adorable when you're angry."

The spell didn't stop Rowan from breathing, so he was able to huff a reply.

"And look what we have here," Badger all but cooed, catching all the runes on Rowan's left arm. He gathered both of Rowan's wrists into one hand in order to run his finger across them. Rowan shivered, feeling the prickle of dark magic as it interacted with the runes. "You can be so naive sometimes." Badger patted his cheek.

Rowan glared. He was very tempted to bite those fingers right off, but he doubted that would end very well.

"One last chance, Rowan." Badger pressed down on him. "We could be great together."

Rowan opened his mouth, no words coming out.

"Did you want to say something, pet?"

Rowan gave him his best annoyed look. *What gave you that idea?*

He had wanted his voice back but wasn't exactly thrilled with the way Badger went about reversing the spell. The lips on his were chapped, though it wasn't so much a kiss. Rowan's mouth fell open in surprise, Badger inhaling to draw the black smoke out. Rowan coughed at the sensation, ignoring Badger smirking above him.

"Well? Don't keep me in suspense."

Rowan glared. "*Vigoréton*," he said, Badger instantly flying away with the force of the incantation. Rowan scrambled up to his hands and knees, reaching for Jorah's staff. "Shouldn't have been so cocky."

His hands, thankfully, wrapped around the staff that time.

Badger groaned from yet another face full of dirt. "I gave you a chance," he growled, watching Rowan rise to his feet. "I would have given you anything. Taught you everything. And you throw it back in my face!"

The bladed end of the staff hovered above Rowan's hand. "No!" Badger shouted. The cut was deep, and Rowan felt delicate ligaments go, but he would simply have to hope Quail could fix it later. This was survival.

Eyes glowing as he tapped into the blood sacrifice for further power, Rowan could imagine the sight he made— blood dripping from his hand, wind whipping around him— as he drew on his Primal abilities. "Could have surrendered," Rowan reminded him, barely recognizing his own voice as it twisted into something not entirely human.

Badger stubbornly refused to just lie down and die, coming at Rowan again. That time Rowan was ready, calling the fog from the lake. Wisping out of sight, the mist enveloped and hid him as he moved to flank Badger.

"Using my own tricks against me?"

"Not quite the same," Rowan answered, his voice echoing in the fog.

At last, he was able to land a shock spell on Badger. The crack in the air was deafening and smelled of ozone. The power behind it was fueled by blood, and even Badger couldn't escape its effects—he was left immobile and barely breathing with nasty-looking burns over most of his body.

Stepping from the mist, Rowan gazed down at him. "Sorry," he offered. There was fear in Badger's eyes—the first flicker of real emotion—when Rowan raised the staff.

The blade slammed through Badger's chest. He opened his mouth in a soundless scream. The yellow glow of his eyes faded, replaced with the blankness of death. Rowan trembled at the sight, releasing the staff and backing away slowly.

The grateful sounds of his fellow mages drew his attention, the vines releasing their hold. They were all covered in cuts and bruises, but they were alive.

"You did it," Tate breathed in relief, rubbing his throat. He was the first to reach Rowan, grabbing his shoulders. "You okay?"

Rowan stared at him, unsure what to say. He didn't feel like he was in his own skin at the moment, which made absolutely no sense. Tate frowned when he didn't answer, looking frantically in Jorah's direction.

"Rowan." Quail gestured for his injured hand. "That was foolish. But, I won't complain about the result."

"Nor will I." Jorah reached out and yanked his staff free, twirling it before tucking it under his arm. He actually appeared concerned as he gazed at Rowan's hand. "Will he be alright?" he inquired of Quail.

"I'll be able to repair the damage." To Rowan, he said, "I'll need to get you some of my potions first. And it might take a couple treatments, but..."

Rowan nodded, thankful to hear it. The magic prickling his skin was gentle as his blood vessels were stitched back together. At least he wouldn't bleed out before Quail could fix the rest of his hand.

"Try not to use it," Quail urged. He wrapped it with one of the bandages he brought with him, immobilizing it. Once that was in place, he tugged Rowan's arm. "Come over here and sit so I can look at that leg." Glancing at Jorah, Quail suggested, "Why don't you and Tate dig a grave while you wait."

Jorah scoffed. "Why bother?"

Rowan looked at Jorah. He didn't know what exactly was on his face, but it caused Jorah to sigh and give in. "Come on, Tate," he muttered.

Rowan allowed himself to be positioned on a downed tree nearby. Quail knelt, rolling up Rowan's jeans to get at the injury on the side of his right calf, Sacha coming over to have a look as well. It burned now that Rowan was paying attention to it.

Quail clucked his tongue. "There's dark magic in the wounds."

"They go awfully deep," Sacha said, not able to hide the concern on her features.

"Hurts," Rowan confirmed, wincing at the gentle prodding.

"Very well," Quail said. "Let's see what I can do here." Rowan barely paid attention as Quail started to work, Sacha offering her aid where she could.

He glanced over at Tate and Jorah, noting the latter had quickly made a hole in the ground, and they were lowering Badger's body down into it. Rowan couldn't watch, instead looking at the mist-covered water.

He felt numb.

Chapter Twelve

HE HAD HALF a mind to call Caleb to ask after Rowan's whereabouts when he found the cottage empty, but Shaw didn't want to worry him unnecessarily. Still, with everything that was going on—the Inquisition stealing magicae, this dark mage running around, the weird activity of Rowan's wards—well, Shaw was a little past worried.

He had hidden his truck off the dirt road and come in on foot, his gut telling him something was wrong when Rowan hadn't been picking up his phone. Rowan's bike was still sitting in the same spot from that morning, the ground undisturbed, and the motor cold when Shaw set his hand on it. Inside, there was no indication of a struggle. Shaw didn't suspect that Rowan would go down without *some* kind of fight. There was no sign of flung spells or lingering magic in the air.

Just to be certain, Shaw pulled out one of the dwindling supply of magic scrolls from Keenan. He slapped the reveal scroll onto the wall, watching the spell ripple through the air and bounce back like a sonar blip. There was nothing hidden there, no cover up of activity. Nothing there suggested Rowan had been taken.

Taking a deep breath, Shaw let it out slowly. He attempted to reason with himself. Rowan had grown up in the Sacred Timber. He knew it like the back of his hand. Hadn't he said that he liked to go and collect ingredients around the woods? Rowan could be out enjoying a walk for all Shaw knew.

At midnight?

Shaw paced in front of the large picture window. The longer Rowan didn't magically appear, the more Shaw worried.

A chime startled him. It took a moment to realize that it was Rowan's wards sounding an alert. Without being a mage himself, he had no idea how to read the message it was sending back to the house. Another chime, a little louder, indicated the inner perimeter wards were being crossed.

He heard the crunch of tires on the drive and pressed himself into the shadows beside the window, peeking out. The lights on the porch and hanging in the trees around the front yard lit up, bathing the area in a low glow. It allowed Shaw to better see the dark-colored pickup truck that came to a halt midturn.

A man got out of the back seat of the cab, helping Rowan out next. They exchanged a few words, the woman in the passenger seat leaning out the window to add her own two cents. Shaw could see there was yet another man in the back seat, in addition to the one who was driving.

He recognized them as members of the Everstrand Mages Guild Masters Board—save the one standing beside Rowan. Identifying them was part of his job as an inquisitor. *What's Rowan doing out with them at this hour?* Shaw had his suspicions, and none of them were good. He stayed hidden from view, not wanting to cause problems for Rowan with the Guild. What he wouldn't have given for Orion's wolven hearing at that point, wanting to know what they were speaking about. Whatever it was remained brief as Rowan nodded, patting the side of the truck and backing away.

Rowan waited while the truck went down the winding drive, before turning toward the cottage and calling, "You can come out, Shaw."

Grumbling, Shaw stepped out onto the porch. "How'd you know I was here?"

"My wards told me."

"Figures." Shaw didn't give him a chance to speak. "Where have you been?"

"Out."

Shaw narrowed his eyes.

Sighing heavily, Rowan said, "I really don't want to do this right now."

Shaw's initial reaction was to argue. Then he noticed that Rowan didn't look so good. "Are you okay?" He hopped off the porch.

Rowan started to shrug, but he ended up shaking his head. "Not so much, no."

Seeing the bandage wrapped around Rowan's left hand, Shaw cradled it as he pulled it up. "What happened?"

Shoulders sagging, Rowan pulled his hand away. "Look, I know you have questions, but—"

"But nothing. I've been waiting for you to come home for hours now."

"I'm sorry." Rowan frowned. "I didn't mean to make you worry."

"Talk to me," Shaw pressed, snagging Rowan's uninjured hand.

Rowan threaded their fingers together as his face scrunched up in pain. He pitched forward, laying his forehead on Shaw's shoulder. Shaw wrapped his other hand around Rowan's back in silent support.

A small shudder passed through Rowan's body. "I can't believe— How did any of this happen?"

"What?" Shaw prompted when Rowan went quiet.

"Badger."

Shaw's brows furrowed.

"He was the dark mage this whole time."

"Hold up." Shaw grabbed Rowan's shoulders and pulled him back. "What are you—?"

"He could shapeshift. He was watching me that whole time!"

Shaw could understand why Rowan was borderline hysterical after that revelation. "How do you even know that?"

Rowan sighed again, walking off toward the pond beside the cottage. There was no missing the limp in his gait as he favored his right leg. Shaw trailed after him. He reached out for Rowan but pulled his hand away, wondering what Rowan needed most—comfort or space.

As Rowan started to explain the spirit walk he and the other masters took, Shaw rubbed his temples. "I'm sorry I asked," he interrupted, noting the brief wry smile it brought to Rowan's face. "So, now what? Please tell me that you guys left an anonymous tip that there's a crazy person in the woods?"

"Not exactly?"

Shaw groaned. "I'm not going to like this, am I?"

"We took care of it." Rowan tried to leave it at that, walking to the water's edge and gazing outward.

Shaw wasn't about to let that go. He went to Rowan's side, demanding, "And how did 'we' do this?"

Rowan crossed his arms, looking down at his feet. "We went out to where he was hiding and I..." Rowan's face scrunched in pain, voice breaking. "I killed him."

Shaw's eyes widened. Rowan may have certainly been capable of taking a life, holding an amazing amount of power as he did, but that didn't mean he had the temperament for it. "*You* did?" he found himself asking.

Rowan nodded, choking back a sob. "We were supposed to just capture him, but... The others were trapped, and I..." Rowan shook his head violently, his body starting to tremble.

"*Sh*, Ro." Shaw wrapped his arms around Rowan's shoulders from the side. "It's okay. It's alright. It's over." He pressed a kiss to Rowan's jaw. "You did what you had to do."

"I took a life!" Rowan argued, yanking free.

"And he would have taken yours." Shaw gave him a hard look, one that was uncompromising. "You may not like it, but you didn't have a choice. And between the two of you, who do you think I'm happy to see come home?"

Rowan tugged at his hair, vibrating with energy.

"Ro, breathe."

Shaw could feel the power radiating off him. Shaking his head, Rowan's magic continued to build, crackling in the air like static electricity. Shaw was torn between stepping back and wanting to help but not knowing how.

When Shaw finally reached out for him, Rowan's head tipped back and he screamed. The resulting force of power pushed Shaw away, and although he stumbled, he managed to keep his balance. Ice rippled across the pond, freezing the entire thing in seconds. The trees were blasted as well, icicles now hanging from branches of frozen leaves.

Rowan hovered on the edge for a long minute before falling to his knees, all energy going out of him. Shaw let out the breath he hadn't realized he was holding, blinking in confusion. It took him a moment to pinpoint the reason he was still standing after such a display; it was the mer scale, warm against his skin. It had created a shield around Shaw, strong enough to block out Rowan's magic from doing him harm.

Kneeling beside Rowan, Shaw ran a hand down his spine. Rowan shivered at the contact but didn't protest. "I've got you," Shaw murmured. "I'm here, okay? You're safe."

Sniffing, Rowan nodded slightly. Settling back on his heels, Rowan looked up and saw the pond. He blinked a few times, surprised by what he found. "Did I do that?" he asked softly, sounding almost afraid to ask.

"You did a little more than that," Shaw answered. Rowan's gaze snapped over to him, looking Shaw over frantically. Shaw snagged his wrists, causing violet eyes to meet his. "Relax, I'm fine." Shaw pulled the scale charm from under his shirt. "See?"

Rowan's fingers passed over the sparkling black scale, nodding in understanding.

Releasing Rowan's wrists, Shaw's hands traveled up his arms, squeezing his shoulders. "Are you alright?"

Rowan's face scrunched in pain; however, Shaw gathered it wasn't of the physical variety. "No," he choked out. "No, I'm not. I could have killed you!"

"But you didn't." Shaw frowned in confusion.

Rowan shook his head. "I can't do this." He tried to stand, but a tug from Shaw landed him on his butt. "You should leave," Rowan snapped.

"Why?" Shaw demanded.

Rowan deflated, looking away, his reply barely heard. "Because it's too dangerous for you to stay."

Shaw huffed, shifting to sit cross-legged on the ground in front of him. "I'll be the judge of that." He held Rowan's unwrapped hand. "I'm not leaving you alone like this. You're upset."

"Which is exactly why you shouldn't be here."

"After that?" Shaw jabbed his thumb over his shoulder at the pond. All the plants and trees were still frozen around them as well, a chill being given off in the air. "Pretty sure even you'll need a recharge."

Rowan shook his head, murmuring, "You don't understand."

"So, explain it to me."

Rowan looked up at him, setting his jaw. Tears welled in his eyes.

"Hey," Shaw soothed, pulling him into his arms. "*Sh*, it's alright." Rowan's fingers curled into the back of Shaw's shirt. "Talk to me."

Rowan's tears spilled over and he sobbed out, "I killed them! I killed my parents!"

Shaw froze, wondering if he had heard that right.

Rowan, however, plugged on. "I don't know how it happened. I was in the back seat of the car. We were going to dinner. And then... Then the car was smashed into a tree." Rowan sucked in a shaky breath. "I don't remember anything. Just sitting there talking to my mom one minute. The next thing I know, I've got a healer bringing me around."

"I don't understand." Shaw lowered his brows, pulling Rowan back a little. He wiped tears from under Rowan's eyes. "How is that your fault?"

"Because the investigators said there was a heavy presence of magic. They suspect it was a factor in the crash, but they've never been able to piece everything together."

"Magic? Surely your parents—"

"If you're about to suggest they used magic to try to prevent the crash or to protect me, don't bother." Rowan's eyes sparked. "I was the only mage in that car." He shook his head, no longer able to meet Shaw's gaze. "My father was mundane. And while my mom was born to two mages, her powers never unlocked."

"Maybe they did in that moment?" Shaw proposed. He had heard of cases where latent mages presented under extreme circumstances.

"It was me. I was the one who came into my powers." Rowan sniffed, shaking with emotion. Shaw just held him again. Rowan rested his head on Shaw's shoulder, turning his face in toward Shaw's neck. "I never showed any signs of being a mage myself, so everyone figured that I wasn't one."

"I still don't understand how the crash is somehow your fault."

"When my magic unlocked, it must have been powerful from what the reports say. I caused that wreck. I just... I know it."

"Or your powers reacted to you being in mortal danger and saved your life."

Rowan shook his head. "There was no other reason for my dad to lose control. They found nothing. That leaves me."

"You don't know that!" Shaw forced Rowan to look at him. "You can't blame yourself for something you don't even know happened. And even if it did, you still can't blame yourself. You were an untrained kid, Ro! How were you going to control a magical purge?"

Rowan's lip quivered. "They're dead because of me. That's all I know." He pulled away, standing with a bit of difficulty and hobbling over to the edge of the pond, gazing at the ice with such a pained expression that it broke Shaw's heart.

"Why do you think I live out here?" Rowan asked after a while.

"I assume because you like nature."

"I do, but it's more than that." Rowan turned around. "If I'm out here, I can't hurt anybody else. I trained hard at the Guild so that I could control this." He flung his arms out to indicate their icy surroundings. "Gram taught me everything she could. She told me being what we are is a blessing and a curse. That the world out there is a dangerous place for us. But the truth is that we're the danger."

"You can't honestly believe that."

"I could have killed you, Shaw!" Rowan's eyes started to glow. "Why do you think part of the enchantment I put on that necklace was to repel my own magic?"

Shaw's teeth clicked together as he snapped his mouth shut.

"I don't avoid the city because it's too far away. I'm terrified I'll lose everything I've trained for and kill someone else. I want to be a grandmaster to prove that I'm better than...than this."

Rowan was barely holding himself together. His voice broke as he continued, "I never wanted to hurt anyone again. And then tonight... Tonight I killed someone with my magic." Rowan choked on a sob. "I swore to Gram I'd only do good with my magic."

"And you did." Shaw stood, snagging Rowan's wrist before he could retreat. "Without you, the other mages would probably be dead." With his other hand, Shaw took hold of Rowan's chin, making their eyes meet. "You did what you had to do to stay alive. And you saved lives doing it. To me, that's the definition of good. Even if you had to do something as ugly as take a life to do it."

Rowan took a moment to digest his words before murmuring, "The needs of the many..."

"Exactly." Shaw stepped in closer. "Do you think I enjoy killing people? I do it because I have to. Doing what I do? It protects the ones who matter most."

Nodding slowly, Rowan replied, "I get what you're trying to say." He took a deep breath, starting to settle.

"As far as this here?" Shaw twirled his finger to indicate all the ice. "You just did something that I wouldn't wish on anyone. You're upset and rightly so. This? This is a productive way of expending that energy buildup. So, don't stress over letting all of the emotions go, okay?'"

Rowan gave a barely perceptible nod.

"We all need to lose it every once in a while," Shaw said. "My method typically involves bullets or a good fight, so this? This is nothing."

Rowan let out a startled laugh. Once he started, his emotional dam burst. "Oh my Goddess... I can't even..." He bent over, forehead on Shaw's shoulder, and continued to laugh.

Shaw smiled, one arm wrapping around Rowan's waist, the other hand lying on the back of his neck. "Better?"

Rowan calmed enough to manage a reply. "Better." Laughter dying down, he let out a sigh that was somewhere between relief and frustration.

Shaw pulled him closer, allowing his own powers to help soothe the poor man in his arms. "Don't beat yourself up over this. Please, Ro." His fingers combed through Rowan's hair.

Rowan squeezed him in return but didn't say a word.

"Don't you think it's time to move on?" The back of Shaw's fingers traced down along Rowan's temple and jaw. "Your parents wouldn't want this."

"I know," Rowan whispered.

"Please, don't blame yourself anymore," Shaw murmured, lips brushing across Rowan's cheek. "Please."

"That's easier said than done."

"I know. But, try?"

Rowan barely nodded.

After holding him a bit longer, Shaw decided to ask, "What's Caleb said about it?"

"He doesn't know. Only Gram ever knew what I suspected."

Shaw was rather shocked that Caleb, of all people, hadn't been told. Then again, Shaw supposed Rowan had his reasons. It also made more sense why Caleb was one of the few people Rowan ever let get close.

"So, what did she say?" Shaw asked, rocking Rowan a little bit.

"Said it wasn't my fault. She went there to check the site herself. All she said was that it couldn't be helped; that I wasn't to blame."

"And you didn't think to believe her?"

"Always thought she said it to make me feel better."

"Hmm, makes sense I suppose. But, still…" The way Rowan talked about her, she seemed extremely powerful in her own right. "She must have been able to, I dunno, piece things together, surely?"

"Maybe she did. I'll probably never know."

"Sure you do. It's exactly like she said it was." Shaw pressed a kiss to Rowan's cheek. "Come on. Let's go inside. I'll make you some tea."

Rowan laughed. "Maybe I should do it."

"Oi! I know how to make tea!" Shaw grinned, snagging Rowan's good hand. He would play along if it kept that smile on Rowan's face.

"I don't know about that," Rowan teased.

Shaw pulled him carefully along, mindful of the limp— they were so having a discussion about the particulars of his injuries later.

"We could always start talking about how pissed I am you ran off to fight a dark mage all on your own," Shaw offered.

There was a beat before Rowan said, "You make excellent tea."

Shaw smirked, ushering him up onto the porch. "Oh, are you gonna...?" He gestured out to the trees.

"Oh." A shadow crossed Rowan's face, but merely for a moment. Shaking his head as if to clear it, Rowan focused on the task. With a simple wave of his hand, the ice melted like a wave, water crashing down to the grass.

Shaw's eyes widened. He didn't think he'd ever get over being impressed by Rowan's casual use of magic. "Wow."

Leaning over the railing, small flames danced across Rowan's fingertips. He blew outward, sending embers to the pond. When they hit the ice, it started to melt away, the water appearing like nothing at all had happened.

Shaw was shaking his head when Rowan turned around. "You're something else." The words were out of his mouth without thought. Rowan smiled, allowing Shaw to pull him in and give him a gentle kiss.

"Now," Shaw continued, prodding Rowan inside. "Tea."

Once the kettle was on, Shaw leaned over and kissed him again, more thoroughly. He held Rowan's chin as he pulled away. "I'm very glad you're okay."

Rowan let out a little huff of a laugh, lips ticking up into the hint of a smile. "You and me both."

Shaw was distracted by the lips that found his, holding Rowan and simply being thankful for his continued existence—only the whistle of the kettle broke them apart.

Chapter Thirteen

ROWAN SLEPT IN fits and starts, giving up by late morning and having a shower. When he got out, there was a cup of tea and buttered toast waiting for him. Shaw coaxed him into having some fresh fruit, as well, before driving them into the city.

"I'm going to check the rumblings at the temple," Shaw informed him. "Call me if you need anything."

Rowan hummed.

"Rowan, I mean it."

"I know." Rowan reached over and laid his hand limply on Shaw's, which covered the stick shift, the bandage scraping. "Just...tone down the protective mode a bit, huh? My head is killing me and I just really want to sleep."

Warmth crept up Rowan's hand, and there was a smile tugging at Shaw's lips.

When the truck stopped beside the bridge to the Mages Guild, Rowan leaned over, pressing a kiss to Shaw's cheek. "Thanks for the lift. I'll keep you updated."

Shaw turned his head quickly, catching Rowan's lips before he moved away. "Don't go getting into any more trouble, yeah?"

"I'll try."

Shaw swatted at him, grumbling while Rowan just laughed. "Careful," Shaw said all the same, leaning across the seat to hold Rowan's upper arm as he lowered himself gingerly from the truck.

Rowan held up his hand in farewell, watching the truck pull out of the parking lot. Looking up at the floating walls of the Everstrand Guild, he sighed, feeling a knot in his gut that shouldn't have been there. He shot off a text to Quail to tell him that he was there, before making the trek across the bridge—it may have been magically stabilized, but the thing still gave him vertigo if he tried to text and walk at the same time.

Temperance Hall was quiet, the apprentices off at their regular high school classes already. While the first floor was set up in a dorm style for them, the next two were private apartments for non-apprentices. Any Guild member could request housing. Some stayed there because it was cheaper, while others—such as Sacha—kept a room there in case of late nights. Only the apprentices were required to stay on Guild grounds, unless their legal residence was within Everstrand.

Rowan knocked on the door of Quail's third-floor apartment. "Come in!" Quail called, the door glowing faintly to allow entrance.

"Why are you so awake?" Rowan complained, finding Quail bright-eyed and bushy-tailed. He was moving around the table, which was already covered in potion bottles, a rack of vials, and a bubbling cauldron.

Sacha sat on a creaky stool, legs crossed. "I don't think he's been to bed yet."

Rowan sighed heavily, dropping his satchel by the table. "Quail."

His chastising fell on deaf ears—hell, it hadn't even begun. Quail shoved a vial into his good hand. "Drink that. Now, where did I put the—ah, and then drink this one." A bottle was set on the table in front of him.

Nose crinkling, Rowan asked, "Why does this smell like feet?"

"I said drink them, not smell them."

Rowan made a vomiting noise, ducking his head when Quail shot him a look, and did as he was told. They didn't taste much better than they smelled. Thankfully, Quail followed it up with a shot of what could have been called cotton candy. Not a flavor Rowan would have chosen, but at least it washed out whatever rotten egg, garbage tastes Quail had him drinking beforehand.

"I should point out how much trust I have in you," Rowan said.

"And I appreciate it immensely." Quail apparently couldn't let an opportunity go to waste, however, as he added, "Do let me know if you feel like you're about to die."

"No, but my leg itches." Rowan lowered his brows.

"Ah, good, the dark magic is working its way out."

Sacha gave a put-upon sigh. "If you don't mind?" she prompted.

"Ah, yes," Quail agreed, "by all means." He gave her a wave, going back to the cauldron.

She motioned Rowan to sit on the stool beside her. "While those potions are taking effect, I'll take care of your hand."

"Fine by me." She and Frey were probably their next best healers, and it was likely Sacha wanted Quail to concentrate on dealing with the dark magic. He did tend to get scattered if he was given too many things to focus on at once.

As she carefully unwound the bandages, she asked Quail, "Do you have any rosehips balm? That won't interfere with whatever you're giving him, will it?"

"Hmm? No, no, that'll be fine." Quail levitated a small bottle over to her.

Shaking her head, she gave the painkilling tonic to Rowan. "I'll use a numbing spell, as well, but it doesn't hurt to have something else already on board for when it wears off. This won't be the most pleasant experience."

"No shit." Rowan managed to find a spot on the overflowing stand beside them for the empty bottle. "Would be nice to be sedated, but I don't think any of us want to explain to the hospital staff how I screwed up my hand."

"Or your leg."

Rowan grumbled.

Sacha cradled Rowan's hand, hovering her other one over it and casting a diagnostic spell. Instantly, a three-dimensional, interactive image of the inside of Rowan's hand appeared. It was far better than any other mundane imaging processes—like X-rays—although hospitals still used them to avoid unnecessary strain on their healer teams. That was why diagnostic spells tended to be reserved for emergency patients and prepping for surgeries.

"You're lucky," Sacha concluded. "I can repair the damage."

"That's a relief." Rowan had started to worry, once the adrenaline had worn off and he was thinking straight again, that he had done more damage than what magic could fix.

That was the thing with magic, even that had its limits. Bone breaks, muscle tears—it would be unwise to simply *force* those things back together again. Rather, any major injuries had to be taken care of the mundane way. Granted, that didn't stop mages from being able to speed the process along in various ways.

"You didn't go as deep as I feared," Sacha assured him, rotating the image. "But, it will scar."

"Not worried about that."

"Let's begin, shall we?" She pressed her fingers to several points around the long laceration and Rowan felt everything start to go numb. "Thank you," Sacha mentioned while she worked, her magic carefully stitching ligaments and tissue together again. "For what you did." Her dark eyes met his.

Rowan tried to brush it off. "Don't mention it."

"What you did was very brave."

Rowan scoffed. "More like reckless." He nodded toward his hand pointedly.

"You used your skills and faced down your fears in order to save us. That is brave." Sacha smiled gently at him, thumb brushing over his cheek. "So, thank you."

Deciding not to argue, Rowan bowed his head and mumbled, "You're welcome."

"How's that leg?" Quail asked.

"Still itches, but otherwise, no change."

Another vial was shoved under his nose. "Have this one. Almost done there, Sacha?"

"Just about."

"Good, I might need a hand with this."

"I don't like the sound of that," Rowan said, brows drawn together. He drank the potion anyway, making a *blah* sound when it tasted like overly sour lemon.

Quail ignored him, going back to his potions. The one he'd been working on when Rowan arrived was transferred into a bottle. It glowed a pale green, and Quail put a stopper in it before moving on to other things.

"Why don't I like the sound of that?" Rowan checked with Sacha instead, more insistent.

"Getting the dark magic out is likely to be painful. Hopefully, Quail managed to isolate it last night. If it spread, that will draw out the process."

"Oh, that sounds wonderful," Rowan groused.

"Just about done."

Sacha wasn't kidding. Rowan had been distracted, yet Sacha clearly wasn't. She was stitching the last few layers of tissue together again. What was left behind was a blazing red line of flesh.

"Salve, please," she said.

Quail levitated it to her, along with a fresh bandage.

"Thank you." Sacha rubbed the gel in, laced with a bit of magic, no doubt; Rowan couldn't feel it, thanks to the numbing spell that was still active. As she wrapped his hand, Sacha instructed, "I want you putting this salve on twice a day, and change the wrapping as needed. Come to me if it looks like anything is wrong with it. Or go to Quail, if you wish."

Rowan side-eyed the large green potion Quail was carrying toward them and said flatly, "I'll take you."

Sacha smiled, eyes twinkling a bit with amusement. "There. Go easy with it for a few days. I did just stitch your ligaments back together, after all."

"I'll try to remember that."

She raised a skeptical brow. "It's just as well I wrapped it snuggly."

Quail interjected, "Yes, yes, now over to the couch with you. And drop your pants."

"What?" Rowan' felt his face heat up.

Sacha laughed, stifling it and hiding her mouth behind her hand. Quail made a shooing motion.

Rowan stood and backed up a couple steps, still bright red. "Seriously, Quail?"

"Boy, unless you want me to rip your jeans, I suggest you lose them. For the sake of the Goddess, no one is about to ogle you. Now, off."

Grumbling, Rowan obeyed. He removed his sneakers and his pants, kicking them into a bunched-up pile beside the couch.

Quail sat at one end and directed Rowan to sit sideways so his right leg was laid in Quail's lap. "Drink," he ordered, working at the bindings.

Rowan popped the cork, a little smoke rising from the potion. "Not inspiring," he muttered, tossing it back before he could think better of it. He immediately started to cough. *What the hell did you put in that?* he thought of demanding but couldn't as he felt his insides roil. He doubled over, the hacking cough shaking his body. Sacha was crouched beside him, making sure he didn't tip over onto the floor.

"Hang on there, Rowan." Quail began to chant quietly, the warmth in Rowan's leg quickly giving way to sharp pain.

"Fuck." Rowan's hands clenched into fists. It only grew worse, Rowan biting his lip until he tasted blood. He thrashed out of instinct more than anything, forcing Quail to hold his leg down, continuing to draw the darkness out of the wounds.

"Hold onto me," Sacha encouraged, taking his fists.

Rowan was enveloped by warm, healing light. Air was forced into his lungs and for a long minute, his mouth was open in a silent scream. Then it all came rushing out and he could breathe once again.

"There you are." Sacha's eyes glowed indigo. "Steady breaths, okay?"

Nodding, Rowan tried to ignore the throbbing in his leg.

"I believe you're safe now," Quail said. Rowan looked over, watching Quail's grip loosen as he sat back, taking a deep breath of his own. "Just need to do a quick diagnostic."

"Allow me," Sacha offered, obviously seeing how much that had taken out of Quail. He inclined his head in thanks. A diagnostic spell confirmed all trace of Badger's magic was removed from the wounds—and Rowan's system as a whole—but it also revealed a new issue. "These punctures are too deep to seal with magic. There's been too much muscle damage."

"Frey offered to stitch them," Quail said. His cell phone was already in hand, presumably sending her a text.

Rowan groaned, putting his face in his hands. He had forgotten about Frey and Ieus. "What did you tell them?" he asked, voice muffled.

"Everything, of course," Quail answered casually.

Sacha, at least, patted Rowan on the knee sympathetically. "Remember what I said about your hand. I'm going back to bed."

He caught her hand with his good one, looking up at her. "Thank you." They shared a smile and Sacha nodded before she took her leave.

Rowan hissed when Quail jostled his leg. "Damn it! That hurts, y'know!"

"Sorry, sorry," he replied, his mind already elsewhere, going straight for his potions. There was a knock and Quail waved his hand. "Come in."

Frey walked in, shaking her phone and huffing. "What in the hell is this even supposed to mean?" she asked Quail. "You sent me nothing but those silly pictures."

Rowan raised a brow.

"Emojis," Quail explained. "They're called emojis. You've got to be hip to these things."

"Okay, now I have to know," Rowan said.

"Maybe you can make sense of it," Frey grumbled, handing him the phone.

It was an arrow, a tree, a face with a medical mask, a needle and thread, and finally, a pair of scissors. Rowan barked a laugh. "That was his way of saying to come over and stitch me up."

Frey threw her hands up. "So why didn't he just say that?" Before anyone could answer, she snapped, "And, you..." She shook her finger at Rowan. "You are in for such a talking to, young man."

Rowan ducked his head.

"Quail, where are my supplies?"

They levitated over and Frey set them out as she would need them on a tray table. She made Rowan twist awkwardly, putting his foot on an ottoman rather than her lap, before she started to numb the area.

"What are we going to do with you?" Frey tsked.

"Sorry?" he mumbled, feeling every bit the child being caught setting off dung bomb spells in the dorms.

After a moment of silence, he looked over to find that rather than appearing angry, Frey was smiling softly. "I'm very proud of you."

"Really?"

"Of course I am, dear. We all are. When Quail and Jorah told us what happened, I wanted to rush right out to your cottage, but Ieus..." She heaved a sigh. "Well, Quail assured us you were in one piece and would be coming here today, so I refrained." She glared at Quail's back and raised her voice as she said, "Although, this doesn't exactly look fine to me."

Without turning around, Quail waved his hand. "It's fine. It's fine."

Frey scoffed and Rowan had to wipe the smile off his face when she looked over at him. "Sorry?" he offered.

Frey's shoulders sagged. "You should have been more careful."

"I didn't know what to do," Rowan admitted, voice barely above a whisper.

Frey reached over, brushing a strand of hair from his eyes. "I told you I was proud, didn't I? Ieus is as well." She started to suture up the wounds, allowing the silence to linger a while, save for the *clinking* of whatever Quail was concocting now. Unexpectedly, she said, "Your grandmother would have been proud too."

Rowan froze. He hadn't spoken to Frey about his grandmother since the funeral, save for a brief mention after he earned his second masters and she wasn't there. They had been best friends, which was why Frey hadn't hesitated to accept Rowan as an apprentice, despite the fact she had a full teaching schedule and hadn't sponsored an apprentice for years.

"You think so?" Rowan's voice was hoarse.

"Dierdre would be crowing about now." Frey huffed. "You two were much more alike than you ever gave her credit for. Your passion for knowledge comes from her; that's for sure. So does that stubborn streak of yours."

It was Rowan's turn to huff and Frey glanced at him with a small upturn of her lips.

She sobered, looking back to her work. "She would be proud of everything you've done, Rowan. This would be no different."

He paused, before repeating the same thing he'd said to Shaw: "I killed someone."

"What choice did you have? Tell me." She had him there. "That's what I thought."

After a few minutes, Rowan said, "I miss her."

"As do I." Frey paused, looking at him. "Do you know there are still days I think of something, and I pick up the phone to call her, expecting that she'll be there on the other end of the line?"

Rowan nodded. He had been guilty of doing the same thing himself. There were things to remind him of his grandmother everywhere. Some days, it was like nothing was wrong, and then others, there was a gaping void that seemed nothing would ever be able to fill again.

"I should go check on the cottage," Rowan mentioned. "It's been a while."

"I'll go with you, if you like. Or take that wolf of yours with you. You shouldn't go alone." It was said casually, but the pinch of her features told a different story. He knew Frey was worried. It may have been roughly six years since her passing, but the memories of her home could still be painful for him.

Rowan had tried calling in the afternoon—their normal time to chat—but when Gram didn't pick up, he figured she was simply out and about. He tried again later and then in the evening. That was when Rowan started to worry. They talked every day, or just about, and he started to ring her phone over and over again.

When still no answer came, he drove his bike the roughly five miles through the woods to her cottage. "Gram!" he called, opening the door. Her car was out front. "Gram! Where are you?"

Rowan wasn't prepared to find her in the bathroom, bundled in her robe as though she were getting ready for the day, laid out on the floor. "Gram!" Her body was stiff as he rolled her, blood on her face, the wall, and pooling on the floor. "No, no, no..."

The healing spells fizzled as he tried to cast them, partly due to his own incompetence, while the rest was because of his shaking hands and hot tears blinding his vision. He wiped his eyes with the back of his hand, fumbling for his phone and dialing blindly.

Caleb had been on the other end of the line. He honestly couldn't even remember anything he said, but it was enough to get Caleb on his way to the cottage. Rowan had called Frey next, who had the sense to contact the police and medics to meet them out in the Sacred Timber.

Rowan's mind must have wandered for a while, because the next thing he knew, Frey was patting his leg. "You're all done."

The puncture wounds were all neatly stitched up. The flesh was still red and slightly swollen with irritation, but it already looked better. Frey was wrapping it loosely with gauze in order to keep the area clean.

"Stay off it as much as possible. Don't lift anything heavy. Keep everything clean and dry," she rattled off. "Quail should have potions for you to take home to help with healing and to keep any infection at bay."

"Yes, yes, just finishing that now," Quail said. He was using a ladle to pour a light blue liquid into a row of small vials. "One week should do it. We'll see how things look after that." He ladled a full spoon's worth into a glass and brought it over to him. "This will start you off. I want you to take a vial every morning."

"Thanks." At least this one was sweet, with a cooling peppermint aftertaste.

"Alright, dear," Frey said, rubbing the side of his head affectionately, "as much as I want to keep you here and go over every little detail of last night, you need to go back home and sleep." She leaned in, pressing a kiss to his temple. "I should scold you for driving yourself out here in this condition at all."

"I was careful," Rowan said, not needing for her to know about Shaw. He pulled his pants back on and wiggled into his shoes.

Quail had already put the vials into his satchel and held it out to him. "Sleep sounds perfect. Just as well all classes were canceled today."

"Well, with three of our teachers worse for wear..." Frey reasoned. She gave Rowan a hug and another kiss. "You go on, dear. I've got to talk with Quail yet."

He nodded, thanking them both again, before leaving.

Halfway down the hall, a door opened and Tate stepped out. "Rowan," he greeted, his hair going in every direction, clothes that he wore the day before rumpled. "Everything good?"

"Still in one piece. You?" Rowan noticed a slight mark left on Tate's neck from Badger's strangling vine spell.

Tate hummed, looking half asleep himself. "Crashed with Jorah last night."

"You headin' home?"

Tate raised a shoulder, but then asked, "You want to grab breakfast?"

"I think it's lunch now," Rowan pointed out, his lips twisting upward a moment. "Sure, why not?" They were both beat, but it would likely do them some good, and Rowan could stand to have the company.

Outside of Temperance Hall, it appeared Ieus was waiting for them—or Rowan, more like. "I'll wait for you," Tate offered.

"Rain check?" Rowan asked instead.

Tate gave him a warm smile, leaning against him a moment and resting their heads together, before heading off.

"Nice to see the two of you getting along so well," Ieus commented.

Rowan shrugged. There weren't all that many mages in the Guild that were in their age group, and Tate was one of the few who had never treated Rowan like a freak of nature.

Granted, they had become closer in the last couple years, since Rowan had been making a conscious effort to allow more people in.

Without waiting for a reply, Ieus looked him over. "Go get some rest."

"No lecture?" Rowan asked.

"Later. Don't worry; I'll be sure to prepare something."

"Wonderful."

They shared a half-hearted smile, and Ieus escorted him toward the bridge. "For now, I am satisfied you are in one piece and healing. The lecturing, as you so put it, on how many years you have taken off my life, can wait until you don't look so ready to fall asleep standing up." He paused in order to pull Rowan into a hug, rubbing his back. "Well done out there, my boy," Ieus murmured.

That choked Rowan up. His fingers curled around Ieus's shoulders. It wasn't that Ieus was ever light on the praise—he gave it when it was due—but all of it was too much at once. If Jorah appeared and started singing his praises next, Rowan was going to spontaneously combust.

"I'll see you later" was all Rowan could manage.

He made it back to the parking lot in a daze—a mixture of the lingering pain and the urge to sleep. Even if he had his bike, it probably wasn't safe for him to drive. He could call Caleb in a heartbeat—he would be home, working on some website design or other for a client—and crash on his couch, but there would be too many questions and Rowan wasn't willing to get into any of them at present.

The only other option Rowan could figure was going to his shop. He wasn't meant to open today, but he could always lay out a few blankets and take a nap between the shelves. He already had his phone out, ready to call for a cab, when the thought hit him.

"Badger." His shop was the last place he wanted to be. It didn't matter that Badger was dead. It may have been safe, but he didn't want to face those memories right now.

Rowan groaned. *What am I gonna do now?* He sat on the curb, leaning back against one of the brick columns of the archway.

He took a deep breath. If he was being honest, he wanted to go home. So he dialed the one person he had left to count on—despite the fact he felt extremely selfish doing it.

"Ro? Everything okay?"

"Can you take me home?" Rowan asked. "I just... I really want to go home."

Shaw must have heard the weariness in his voice. "Yeah, I'll head out right now."

"As long as you're not gonna get in trouble."

"No, no, actually there's been a weird bug going around, and I did walk in looking less than stellar."

Rowan managed the semblance of a laugh. "See you soon then."

"Be right there."

"Just don't get me sick," Rowan mused.

Turned out, more than anything, what Rowan truly needed was someone else to be there. Shaw never complained. He stayed with Rowan the remainder of the day while he drifted in and out of sleep, missing entire chunks of movies.

Shaw's energy was a calming balm, allowing him to rest while they curled up together on the couch. Late in the evening, when Rowan was once again drifting off, he was fairly certain he sent back all the affection he could muster, what he could only describe as love.

Chapter Fourteen

ROWAN SMOOTHED OUT his light-blue robes, the traditional mage apparel appropriate for all formal ceremonies within the Everstrand Guild. The last time Rowan had worn them was when he obtained his second masters. He knew other mages that practically lived in the things, but it wasn't for him. He was well past being an apprentice or a "college mage" as the journeymen tended to be called.

"Relax, would you?"

Rowan attempted a smile as he looked over at Caleb.

Caleb grabbed his arm, giving it a little shake. "You'll be fine."

Rowan let out a nervous laugh. "Not so sure about that." Caleb raised a brow and Rowan knocked their shoulders together.

"Want me to stay?" Caleb offered.

"Go ahead and grab a seat."

Caleb nodded, slapping his shoulder. "Good luck."

"Thanks," Rowan murmured, watching Caleb enter the Hall of Enlightenment.

Rowan had received a phone call from Ieus the previous day, ordering him to be there. Apparently, he was to be presented with a special commendation from the Mages Guild for his actions against Badger. No doubt the whole of the Guild would be filling up the rotunda, along with any of the general public who had read the announcement.

"Rowan." Tate walked up, dressed in his guard uniform. "Looks like you finally got some sleep."

Rowan chuckled. "You too." It may have merely been about forty-eight hours since they killed Badger, but it sure seemed like a lot longer than that. "How's your neck?"

Tate pulled his collar aside to show the barely there bruising. "I'll survive. Think it's you we should be worried about." He nodded to Rowan's bandaged hand pointedly.

Rowan sent him a look. "I've got enough people fussing over me, thank you very much."

The door to the Hall opened. "Ah, there you are," Gabriella, one of their other guards, said. "They're ready for you."

Rowan took a deep breath and let it out slowly. "Alright."

Sure enough, it was a rather full house. He caught sight of Caleb down in one of the first few rows, giving him an encouraging grin and a double thumbs-up. Rowan nodded at him, proceeding to the middle of the ring. His gait was slow and stiff, trying not to show his limp. His gaze was fixed to the raised panel where the Masters Board sat.

"This session will come to order," Ieus announced and the chatter of the crowd died down. "We've gathered here today for a special purpose. Most here know Rowan. Our youngest mage to ever obtain a masters, let alone two. Well, Rowan has once again accomplished an amazing feat that we are here to honor."

Looking down at the arena floor, Rowan felt a blush creep up his face.

"Rowan has shown bravery in the face of incredible danger and insurmountable odds. He put his own life at risk to save several fellow mages in peril."

Because of the public form of these meetings, Ieus could not speak in detail for fear of rebuke from the Inquisition, but many of the mages knew the truth—or at least part of it. Even Caleb didn't know what was going on. Rowan had written it off as no big deal, just a group of mages who had gotten themselves caught off guard in the Sacred Timber.

Ieus looked down at him. "Rowan, for your acts of valor, we of the Everstrand Mages Guild thank you. But we wish to do more than that. Because of your display of skill and power in the School of Spirit, particularly with the use of spirit walking and blood magic, we of the Masters Board are proud to declare you a Master of Spirit."

Rowan's jaw fell. *This can't be happening...*

"Which means, Rowan, you are now officially a high master mage."

Rowan felt himself start to shake. "I... I can't..." Tears flowed over and he didn't bother to stop them. He had never expected anything like this.

Ieus gestured for the crowd to settle, apparently not done. "It has also been decided that from this day hence, Rowan is to be the newest member of the Masters Board."

The crowd erupted once again, but to Rowan, it all seemed far away. His legs felt weak and he could do nothing more than stand there in complete shock.

For a mage to pass a masters exam, they simply had to have a majority favor of the board members present at the time of testing. To add a new member, however, required a unanimous decision by all the board. In that, they had chosen Rowan!

In his daze, he missed the rest of the Masters Board coming down into the ring. Ieus pulled him into a hug, and Rowan buried his face against his shoulder. "Congratulations, son. You've made us all proud."

"Rowan." Frey smiled up at him, stealing a hug of her own.

Sacha was next, smiling just as brightly. "I look forward to working with you."

"Welcome aboard, kiddo!" Quail congratulated him cheerfully, thumping his back with enthusiasm.

Jorah genuinely softened a bit, the hint of a smile on his face as he held out his hand. "Congratulations, Rowan. It will be good to have you."

"Ro!" He turned around in time to see Caleb barreling at him. As he ran into him, Rowan grunted, looking over Caleb's shoulder to where Tate shrugged. The little smirk on Tate's face said he hadn't even bothered to attempt stopping Caleb from coming out into the ring.

Of course, that meant Rowan was able to spot another familiar face. Shaw stood in the tunnel entrance to the rotunda, leaning against the wall and smirking. Rowan felt his face heat again, returning Caleb's embrace. When he had called Shaw to tell him about getting an award, Rowan honestly hadn't expected him to show since Shaw needed to be at work for once. He was rather glad to be wrong.

"This was all quite last minute," Frey spoke up apologetically, "so I'm afraid there's no grand celebration planned. However, we most certainly want to organize a proper feast."

"We'll let you know the details," Ieus said. "For now—" He cut himself off, looking past Rowan to where Shaw was standing. "An inquisitor," he observed quietly. "Perhaps we were not quite so lucky with staying off the radar."

Rowan wasn't about to admit to knowing him. It would involve too many questions. Therefore, he remained silent when Ieus motioned Tate to bring Shaw forward.

"Inquisitor," Ieus greeted diplomatically. "Was there something you required?"

Shaw glanced at Rowan before replying, "Nothing at all Master Ieus." If he was surprised Shaw knew his identity, he didn't show it. "We naturally received the announcement at the temple, and I decided to come observe the proceedings. Though, I must say, I had not expected to see anyone be made a high master, let alone join the board." He turned to Rowan, attempting to hide his slight smile. "Congratulations, Master Rowan."

Rowan smiled in return. Master had a nice ring to it.

"Well, that's kind of you to come," Frey said, with forced politeness. "We wouldn't want to take you from your other duties."

Shaw waved it off. "Really, it's no trouble. Frankly, I've hoped to build better relations with the Mages Guild, but being a newcomer in these parts, it seems my voice falls rather flat with the other ranking members of the Order."

Ieus and Frey didn't bother to hide their surprise. In truth, it was an unusual stance for any in the Inquisition to take, let alone an inquisitor.

"Well, I won't take up any more of your time," Shaw continued. "Congratulations, again."

As Shaw made his way out, Quail was the one to comment, "Well that was strange."

"Do you suppose they know anything?" Jorah questioned.

Ieus meaningfully tilted his head in Caleb's direction. "We'll talk about it later." To Rowan he said, "Why don't you get out of here? Go celebrate with your friends. Frey or I will call you about all the details of your new appointment later."

Rowan was still a bit overwhelmed by everything, so all he did was thank them, and allow Caleb to drag him off. Tate at least managed to get a quick "Congrats" in before they escaped the throngs of people, who no doubt wanted to congratulate Rowan as well.

"This is so awesome, dude!" Caleb barked as they made their way across the courtyard. "I can't believe it!" He shoved Rowan playfully. "Not a big deal, he says. Yeah, right. You sure as hell impressed someone."

"Yeah," Rowan said dejectedly. He had to tell Caleb the truth. Knowing how he would react, Rowan wasn't exactly looking forward to it.

"What's wrong?" Caleb lowered his brows. "You should be happy."

"I am. Just—" His phone chimed with a text message. "Shaw wants us to meet at the shop."

"Great." Caleb brightened a little. "We can all go out to celebrate!"

Rowan couldn't return the same enthusiasm, but Caleb didn't seem to notice.

They took Caleb's Jeep the short drive across town to the street mall. There wasn't any sign of Shaw, so Rowan let them inside to wait for him. Not that it took long.

When the door opened, Shaw was standing there beaming at him. "You're amazing," he declared, meeting Rowan halfway across the room and wrapping him in his arms. Shaw kissed him deeply, pouring in enough passion that the emotions trickled off Shaw and onto Rowan. Shivering at the sensation, Rowan laid his hand on Shaw's neck as he deepened the kiss.

Caleb wolf whistled, breaking them apart. Rowan shook his head, smiling all the same, and Shaw chuckled.

"I'm serious, you know," Shaw continued, holding Rowan's face in both hands. "Congratulations. You did it!"

"I'm glad you were there." Rowan couldn't rightfully explain how good it felt to know that both Shaw and Caleb had been there to see him reach his goal of high master.

"Quite the nice surprise." Shaw gave him another quick, soft kiss. "You deserved it."

"This is insane, Ro," Caleb practically squealed. He was perched up on the counter, kicking his feet. "I can't believe it."

Rowan attempted to smile, but it fell short.

Caleb frowned. "What's wrong?"

"There's something I have to tell you." Rowan sighed, stepping up next to the counter and looking up at him. "I wasn't exactly honest with you over the phone."

Caleb's brows furrowed. "What are you talking about?"

"I didn't just happen to save a group of mages at random. I was there with them on purpose."

"Doing what?"

Rowan heaved a sigh. "There was a dark mage. The Guild had to get rid of him before he killed anyone else, before the Inquisition got wind of it."

Caleb opened his mouth, nothing more coming out than confused noises.

"So, me, Jorah, Tate, Quail, and Sacha went out to the southern side of the Timber where he was hiding out, and we killed him."

"Why didn't you just tell me?" Caleb demanded.

"'Cause when I called you, I was afraid someone could have been listening in." At least that was true enough. "And there wasn't time to get into it between your apartment and the Guild, so I planned to tell you afterward. Now."

"But this didn't just happen. You knew before you ever went out there. You could have gotten yourself killed!" And there was the reaction Rowan had expected. "Why in the hell didn't you tell me before!" Caleb didn't wait for an answer, slipping off the counter and throwing his arms out. "I mean there's a—what?—a dark mage running around killing people and you didn't think to say anything?"

"Guild orders. Most of the mages didn't even know. It needed to be kept a secret."

"Mage secrets. Great." Caleb huffed. "Don't tell your best friend when you plan to go off and get yourself killed." Looking over at Shaw, who was standing off to the side quietly, Caleb gestured to him. "What about you? Why don't you seem surprised by this?" He whirled on Rowan and accused, "You could tell him but not me?"

Rowan felt Shaw's familiar energy filling the shop, sending out calming waves in hopes of helping aid the situation. "He didn't tell me either," Shaw outright lied. It drew Caleb's attention, which also meant that Shaw's empathic abilities worked better. "I had to find out by showing up at the cottage when he didn't answer my phone calls, only to find it empty and then have him come home covered in blood."

Caleb whirled on him, and Rowan huffed out, "Thanks a lot. And it wasn't even my blood." Shaw raised a brow. "Okay, most of it wasn't. That's not the point."

Caleb crossed his arms over his chest, landing Rowan with a hard stare. "You better start talking." At least Shaw's powers had stopped the yelling.

Rowan spilled everything: the Guild's discovery of a dark mage terrorizing Osterian, the attempt to find him before the Inquisition found out, and the spell they cast that showed them the way. "It was Badger."

Caleb gave him a blank look. "What do you mean it was Badger? Badger's a cat."

"Shapechanger."

"Shape—?"

"Ancient form of magic that's hard to master. He could change his form into multiple beasts, which explained why those kills looked animal."

Caleb gaped at him like a fish. "How is that—? He was here that whole time!"

"Believe me, I'm not thrilled knowing he was spying on me either."

"But, why?"

Rowan shrugged and looked away.

"Ro," Caleb warned.

"I think he was looking for a partner maybe," Rowan admitted. "The things he said... I dunno. Maybe he was just looking to try to gain more power, steal mine somehow. It wasn't like he was very sane when we found him."

Shaw was the one looking unhappy now. "You neglected to mention the partner bit."

"Sorry?"

Shaw snorted.

"I was a little scatterbrained if you didn't notice! Hell, I'm still trying to wrap my head around all this."

Sighing, Shaw held up his hand. "You're right. I'm sorry." A bit of calm washed over Rowan like an apology and his lips twitched in response, a silent acceptance.

"So you..." Caleb held his temples. "You killed Badger? Who was really a dark mage in disguise? Who tried to kill you, before you slayed him with blood magic?"

"That about covers it, yeah."

"I need a drink."

"I hear that."

Caleb raised a brow. "Rowan asking for a drink? Shit, you really are fucked up."

"Bite me."

Caleb snapped his teeth in Rowan's direction, drawing laughter from all of them. When it died down, Caleb pulled Rowan into his arms. "Just glad you're okay. I dunno what I'd do without you." Caleb nuzzled their cheeks together.

Rowan squeezed him harder in turn. "I know. I'm sorry I couldn't tell you." He pulled back enough to look at Caleb. "Can you forgive me?"

Caleb tilted his head with an easy grin. "Could never stay mad at you."

Rowan smiled in turn, throwing his arms around Caleb's neck. "Love you," he murmured.

Caleb pressed a noisy kiss to his cheek, making Rowan chuckle. "Love you, too."

"What am I?" Shaw inquired. "Chopped liver?"

For his trouble, Shaw got his arms full of both of them. "I guess we can keep you around," Caleb mused. "You've made Ro happier than I've seen him in a long time."

Shaw's smile was bashful as he looked from Caleb to Rowan. "He makes me happy too."

Rowan felt his heart flutter and his face heat at those words, but he couldn't deny how insanely happy he was in this moment. He was a newly minted high master, with the best friend anyone could ask for, and an amazing boyfriend. In truth, Rowan wasn't sure how it could get much better than this.

THEY HAD DUMPED Caleb onto the couch. After spending the evening bouncing from one bar to the next, they decided to take things back to Rowan's cottage. Not that Caleb had lasted the trip, falling fast asleep in the back seat of the Jeep while Rowan—the sole sober one remaining—drove.

"He's fine," Shaw said, nudging Rowan away. "Wanna sit on the porch? It's a nice night."

"Sure." Rowan flipped on the porch light, the faint glow not extending far. Rather than sit on the porch swing, he leaned against the railing, looking up at the sky.

Shaw joined him. "See? Beautiful." Stars filled the sky, a waxing moon shining brightly.

Rowan lay his head on Shaw's shoulder. They stood there like that for some time before Rowan smiled and stepped off the porch.

"What are you up to?" Shaw asked in amusement, leaning his forearms on the railing. Rowan gave him a wink. Shaw shook his head, watching as Rowan walked into the middle of the yard.

Light danced across Rowan's fingertips. He was chanting a spell under his breath, the light sparkling as it looped around him. Rowan stretched his arms up, throwing the lights above him to hang like a brilliant array of fairy bulbs.

Whirling around, Rowan looked a little surprised, but most certainly pleased. "That's the first time I've tried that."

Shaw beamed, walking down the stairs to meet him. "I told you that you were wonderful." He gathered Rowan into his arms, kissing him softly. Shaw started to hum, spinning them in a small circle.

It made Rowan laugh. "Hold on, I think I've got this part down." Closing his eyes, Rowan said a few more words, the lights starting to shimmer as a soft folk melody seemed to emanate from them. Rowan was smiling down at him when he opened his eyes again. "How about this?"

"Perfect."

Shaw couldn't stop smiling, allowing Rowan to lead him as they twirled around the yard. There wasn't much grace to their dance, but neither of them cared as they held each other close and laughed at their occasional fumbling.

Shaw snagged Rowan around the waist, picking him up and spinning him. After setting him down, he looked up at Rowan and pulled him close. He took hold of Rowan's chin, utterly entranced. "I love you," Shaw said.

Rowan was taken off guard, but his surprise quickly vanished, replaced by a completely fond expression. "I've known that for a while." His lips twitched. "You wear your emotions on your sleeve." Rowan leaned down and kissed him, long and slow, before speaking against his lips, "I love you too."

Shaw rose up on his toes, tugging Rowan as close as humanly possible. When he came to Osterian, not once did he think he would find someone who would so completely steal his heart. Yet that was exactly what had happened.

He laughed a little as he pulled away, face turned into Rowan's neck. "What spell did you put on me?"

"I can ask you the same thing," Rowan answered softly, giving him a squeeze.

Shaw simply replied by kissing him once again.

Chapter Fifteen

SHAW WASN'T ENTIRELY sure he was in the right place, no matter what his GPS was telling him. This neighborhood didn't seem like Caleb's type, despite him being an artist. Nevertheless, when he turned into the parking lot of the row of one-story apartments, he saw Rowan's bike parked next to Caleb's Jeep—both splattered in mud. Not that Shaw's truck was any better with the number of trips he'd taken to the Sacred Timber himself now.

Shaking his head in amusement, he pulled into a vacant space. He was barely out of the vehicle when Caleb came barreling out of an apartment door. "Hurry up!" he called. He grinned at Shaw, bouncing down the steps. "Hey, dude, right on time. Hop in the back."

Rowan was the one left to lock up. "Relax, would you? I can take as long as I need for lunch, and I'm sure Shaw can too."

"Pretty much." Shaw could do as he pleased, for the most part. He didn't even need an excuse usually. It paid to be on Meredeen's good side with an impressive case closure record—never mind the fact he was secretly getting many of them overturned.

Rowan took it easy coming down the stairs, albeit, for the most part, he was walking normally again. It had been almost a week and the stitches were starting to dissolve. Even so, Shaw was well aware his leg was still sore after a long day of activity if Rowan didn't keep off it like he was instructed.

"You look nice," Shaw complemented, giving him a quick kiss.

Rowan attempted to hide his blush by being cheeky. "So do you. Appreciate you losing the inquisitor uniform."

Shaw laughed, allowing himself to be shoved into the back of the Jeep so Rowan could get into the passenger seat.

"What," Caleb complained, "don't I look good?"

Shaw leaned between the seats, looking Caleb dead in the eye. "I hate your hair."

Caleb's pout was epic. "Rowan," he whined, looking for help.

"I like it." Rowan combed his finger through the new emerald locks.

"At least somebody loves me," he muttered, starting the Jeep.

Shaw stifled his chuckle, Rowan sending him a sympathetic glance. Honestly, it wasn't Shaw's fault that he thought it looked ridiculous.

He arrived at the cottage to hang out that night, stopping midsentence as he was greeting Rowan in the kitchen. "Why does it smell like wet dog in here?" Just then, Caleb walked out of the bathroom, a towel slung around his waist and another being used to scrub his hair. "Oh."

It turned out Caleb was making one of his infamous color changes in preparation for the celebration at the Mages Guild. Shaw was still surprised he had managed an invite, but the way Rowan told it, he had discreetly made the suggestion to Frey since Shaw had appeared to extend an olive branch to them. Shaw would prefer to spend the entire party with Rowan and Caleb, instead of pretending to rub elbows with each of the Masters Board members, but at least that included Rowan.

"Tate's been teasing me," Rowan whispered once they were alone. "Apparently, I've been making eyes at you all night."

"Did you tell him it's because I'm irresistible?" Shaw ribbed.

"I told him you weren't bad to look at." Rowan shot him a playful glance, getting back to his other party guests before people got too suspicious of them.

"Y'know," Shaw mentioned, thinking of the celebration for Rowan's advancement the day before, "there's got to be a limit on parties in one week."

"It's not a party," Rowan said. "Some clients couldn't come yesterday, so they want us to stop by, that's all."

"Want you to stop by, you mean."

"Well, I'm not going to have lunch alone."

"Besides," Caleb said brightly, turning on the CD player, "we're the best."

Shaw swore it was Caleb's revenge for the earlier comment about his hair when the volume was cranked on an old rock song. It had a punk vibe to it, and it sounded oddly familiar. It wasn't a true betrayal until Rowan started to sing—well, more like yell—along to it as well.

"Oh, come on!" Shaw shouted above the noise.

Caleb winked at him in the rearview mirror, tossing that damned green hair. Rowan turned, grinning. Shaw gave him a pitiful look, and Rowan must have been swayed enough because he at least turned down the volume to a level that wasn't about to make his ears bleed. Though they were still ringing when they arrived at the cafe.

Nyx's Coffee was a standout among the other shops on the block with its bright, sky-blue canopy over the entrance. There was an enchantment on it so that a small, cartoonish nixie flitted across the canvas, creating ripples. Shaw could take a guess at who had done the work.

Rowan linked his arm with Shaw's, Caleb holding the door for them. It was a charming little place that transported Shaw outside rather than in. The ceiling appeared to be branches of tree canopy, the lighting mimicking sunlight, while the floor looked like fallen leaves and other forest debris—he half expected to hear the crunch under his boots. When he caught a good look at the staff, he realized the reason for the decor—they were nymphs.

"Rowan! Caleb!" one greeted from behind the counter, waving happily. What looked like leaves in her hair and vines along her dark skin, where veins would be, pegged her as a dryad.

"Hey, Lilium," Rowan replied.

The other woman had light skin, and silver hair that moved like water—in fact, her whole body did—and there was no doubt to Shaw that she must have been a naiad. "Nyx, Rowan's here!" she called.

Someone came barreling from the back. She wasn't a nymph, rather an elf from Lefalas. Snow elves, people called them, because of their rather obvious features, including white hair and light-colored eyes. Shaw couldn't recall seeing one since he was a boy—they didn't often venture from their far northern city.

"Congrats!" Nyx wrapped herself around Rowan, rocking him back and forth. "I'm so proud of you!"

"Thanks. Sorry, you guys couldn't come."

"I could have watched the store for a couple hours." The voice was male, dry. Shaw followed it to the source, an elf sitting off by himself in the corner. His hair was also white, but nothing else about him made him look like a Lefalas elf.

Nyx rolled her eyes, waving him off with the ease one did an old argument. "You must be Shaw. I'm Nyx. That's Lilium, Pyrus"—she pointed out the naiad, now wiping down tables—"and ignore Taron."

"Whatever," Taron muttered, going back to reading his book.

Caleb stepped closer to Shaw and dropped his voice. "No, seriously, ignore him."

"You slept with him, didn't you?" Shaw guessed.

Caleb dug his elbow into Shaw's ribs.

"You guys have a seat," Nyx said, "and I'll bring you out some drinks."

As they were settling at one of the round tables, Shaw looked around to the empty cafe. "I know we did late lunch, but everyone sure cleared out fast."

"Yup," Caleb replied, "it's always slow about now. That's why we waited. So much nicer when it's quiet." He paused before raising his voice to add, "Except for Mister Grumpy Pants."

"Eat me," Taron said, almost absentmindedly.

Turning in his chair and leaning it back on two legs, Caleb cooed, "Only if you ask nicely."

Taron glanced up from his book and gave Caleb an unimpressed look. He eventually asked, "Free tonight?"

"Tomorrow?"

Taron sucked his teeth. "Text me."

"Will do." Just like that, the conversation was over. Caleb turned around, chair legs clunking back to the floor, arms flopping onto the table, with a smirk on his face.

Shaw looked over at Rowan, who was shaking his head, and back again. "Okay then." He had been under the impression that things between Caleb and Taron hadn't gone well, but apparently that wasn't the case at all.

"We're not about to hang out, but we're good for a hookup when we need one," Caleb explained with a shrug, flipping his bangs a bit.

"Maybe you should trim those," Shaw suggested, reaching over to try to push them out of Caleb's face for him.

"Would ruin my look."

"You did that yourself when you made your hair green."

Suddenly, the lights went out, and Shaw stilled. He was on alert, his hand inching toward the knife attached to his boot. The singing stopped him—"Happy Birthday." The cafe lighting came back up to a twilight mode, and a small cake was slid in front of him.

"Happy Birthday, Shaw," Rowan said, smiling at him. Caleb followed suit, along with Nyx and her nymphs, maybe even Taron too. Shaw wasn't certain since he was too busy watching Rowan.

"How did you know?" Shaw asked once Nyx had taken the cake over to the counter to cut up.

"I stole your ID, remember?" Rowan's smile was coy. It morphed into slight embarrassment, likely recalling the whole mess that it caused. "Anyway," he barreled on, "I remembered the date, so Caleb and I decided to surprise you."

"Green tea lattes," Lilium announced happily, setting the drinks down on the table—complete with heart-shaped foam. Shaw chuckled and thanked her, watching her light up at the simple praise.

"Here you are," Nyx said, giving Shaw and Rowan a piece of cake each. When Pyrus served Caleb a piece, Nyx leaned over to brush a kiss across her cheek, and they shared a warm smile before Pyrus left to help Lilium. "Anything else you need, just let me know, hon."

"So, we had to get Nyx to make you one of her cakes," Caleb supplied, before taking a giant bite.

Shaw had to admit it was pretty damn good. He wasn't a dessert person, but this was nice. The peanut butter cake was nice and fluffy, while the chocolate buttercream was rich and creamy. "Consider me surprised." Shaw licked frosting from his lips. "And very grateful."

He took Rowan's hand, which happened to be his left. There was no bandage on it today. That meant when Shaw turned it over, he was able to see the raised line going across Rowan's palm—a scarred reminder of his fight against Badger. Shaw ran his thumb gently across it.

Rowan wrapped his fingers around Shaw's hand, causing him to look up and meet his gaze. Shaw smiled softly, remembering himself. "You didn't have to do anything," Shaw insisted. "I stopped givin' a damn 'bout birthdays a long time ago."

"Well, being old does that," Caleb fired back, giving him a cheeky grin around his fork.

Rowan smacked Caleb's arm, ignoring his faux complaint, and said, "We got you something else too."

"Oh?"

Rowan licked his lips. "We weren't really sure what you might want. Normally, we'd just ask you, but we didn't want to ruin the surprise, so if you don't like it..."

Caleb nudged him when he trailed off.

"When we talked about fishing, you mentioned that you liked doing that and wanted to try it out on the ocean one day, so..."

Shaw's brows rose, and he looked between the pair. Thankfully, Caleb supplied, "We found a charter boat that does fishing tours in the Galst Deep. We've got a long weekend booked."

"When?" Shaw asked, feeling excited at the idea of finally getting to go deep sea fishing.

"Not this one, but the next. Will you have work off? Summer rush isn't for a while yet, so we can rebook if we need to."

Shaw's initial excitement waned. "Yeah... Work."

Rowan cursed under his breath, apparently knowing exactly what path his mind had strayed to. After a long pause, Rowan said, "We'll go another time."

"I'm sorry." Shaw felt bad now for ruining their thoughtful gift.

"What?" Caleb's brows were lost behind his hair. "Why?"

Shaw and Rowan shared a look. "There are some... things," Shaw answered, "going on."

"Why do I have the feeling I won't like this?"

"'Cause you won't," Rowan muttered, then took a sip of his latte. To Shaw, he checked, "Are you sure?"

Rowan didn't have to finish that statement—*was it smart?* Likely, Rhys would kill Shaw for even allowing Rowan to know about his mission, let alone Caleb. Shaw couldn't argue necessity in either case. But, in no way was he worried that either of them posed a threat to his safety or the integrity of the mission therein.

"Maybe we should take this out to your place," Shaw suggested to Rowan. He quirked his lips at Caleb next. "Good thing you didn't make plans, I guess."

Caleb snorted. "Why do I suddenly feel like I need alcohol?"

"I actually have been thinking about..." Rowan drifted off, waving his hand in a circle to encompass the Inquisition dilemma. "I have an idea."

"Definitely will need to stop for alcohol," Caleb concluded.

Shaw clapped Caleb on the shoulder, giving him a little shake. "Oh, you have no idea."

Caleb gazed back carefully. "Is it seriously that bad?" he asked after a long moment.

"I'll tell you in the car."

"I DON'T LIKE this." Caleb crossed his arms over his chest.

"Which part?" Shaw snarked from his perch on the counter.

"Any of it." Caleb narrowed his eyes at Shaw. The image was somehow ruined with the emerald locks falling into his face.

"You're acting like I like it any better."

Caleb's piercing gaze went to Rowan, not that he even seemed phased by the look. "You lied to me," Caleb accused.

"I didn't lie."

"Bullshit!" Caleb barked, hands slamming down onto the kitchen table between them. "The day after you went home with Shaw, what did you tell me?"

Rowan looked like a kid who got caught with his hand in the cookie jar. He refused to look at Caleb as he murmured, "I said everything went fine."

"Conveniently leaving out the part where you found out he was a witch. And then, when you learned the truth about this undercover shit, you left me in the dark! Just like you did with the goddamn shapechanger!"

"You already yelled at me for that," Rowan shot back, brow lowering.

"Who the hell am I gonna tell?" Caleb growled. "You seem to forget that you're my pack!"

Rowan reeled back as though he'd been slapped.

Shaw slid off the counter, moving to intervene. "Everybody chill out, okay?" He pushed his powers out, trying to bring the situation under control.

He watched Rowan's eyes fall shut, taking a deep breath as he absorbed the familiar energy.

Caleb twitched, shaking his head. "Well, that's annoying," he grumbled. Shaw could see him visibly relaxing all the same.

"Now," Shaw continued, when the atmosphere in the cottage calmed down, "what happened, happened. Can't change that. Right now, we move forward."

Caleb was looking elsewhere when he spoke to Rowan quietly, "I get why you didn't say anything about the mage. But, why not tell me about all this? You're supposed to trust me."

"I do." Rowan reached out, grabbing Caleb's arm as he came around the table. "That's why I'm telling you now." He rubbed Caleb's arms up and down, tension leaving Caleb's body. "I get that you're upset with me. But, what kind of person would I be to tell you something that Shaw told me in confidence?"

Caving, Caleb dropped his head onto Rowan's shoulder, arms coming around to hold onto the back of Rowan's shirt. Rowan drew him closer, wrapping him into a hug. "I'm sorry," Caleb said, voice muffled.

"You were worried," Rowan replied, rubbing his back. "I get it." He nuzzled his nose against Caleb's cheek.

"So," Shaw ventured, "can we get back to the part about how this plan isn't the smartest?"

"I hate to agree with him," Caleb said, "but I think it's stupid."

Rowan shoved him. It was more out of good-natured scolding than anything antagonistic. "I'd like to see either of you come up with better." Shaw and Caleb traded a look. "That's what I thought."

Shaw sighed, pinching the bridge of his nose. "Let's go over this again."

"What's there to go over?" Rowan retorted. "You take me in, book me for a made-up offense. If they're taking powerful magicae, they won't be able to resist, and they'll move me to wherever it is they're holding the others. You follow. You expose them. Job done."

"Except for the part where how we're supposed to follow you," Caleb replied, looking pointedly at Shaw. It was a clear message; Caleb's involvement wasn't up for debate.

"I'll make a charm, obviously."

"Doesn't a tracking spell require you to have a charm on your end?" Shaw checked. "They're not going to let you keep anything."

"They have to let me keep my blood." Rowan smirked.

"Well," Caleb snarked, "or at least most of it."

Shaw wet his lips, brows pinched together. "Blood magic."

Rowan looked at him carefully. "You can't tell me you're still nervous about that."

"No, I just don't know enough about it. I'm not sure how it would work."

"Easy enough." Rowan pulled his necklace off, the aqua aura gem glinting as the light hit it. "You know how scrying works? It'll work like that." He gently moved the crystal in a circular motion. "The charm will be keyed to my blood, so it will locate me wherever I am, at any given time."

"And we're testing this out first, right?"

Rowan gave him a look that fell somewhere between exasperation and fondness. "Yes, Shaw, we can do some trial runs."

"That gets us to the kidnapped magicae," Caleb pointed out the obvious, "but what about getting you out?"

Rowan shrugged. "That part is more Shaw's department than mine."

Shaw rubbed his jaw. "The problem is that we don't know where they're being held. They could be taking them back out of Osterian once they get here. Unless they are in Calagon, my squad can't help us. But, Rhys can get us intel, pull strings. I can probably arrange it so that the appropriate military gets tipped off."

"Allow them to lead the raid," Rowan figured.

"It's the only way to go about it that would be legal. I risk political blowback should anyone know I was involved in an assignment like this."

"That's why they call it black ops," Rowan said with a little smirk, repeating Shaw's explanation of what he did for a living.

Caleb didn't seem as amused. "So, basically we're gambling that we won't be able to get Rowan out."

"We'll get him out," Shaw replied, tone brokering no argument. "I'll go in and get him myself if I have to. This shit ends here. These assholes won't take anyone else from me."

Rowan laid a hand on top of Shaw's clenched fist. Shaw hadn't realized he'd allowed his anger to show that much. He forced his hand open, pressing his palm flat to the table, absorbing the feelings Rowan was sending him.

Shaw turned his hand over, wrapping his fingers around Rowan's. "Thank you," he murmured, returning Rowan's soft smile.

"We can do this." Rowan's voice was gentle but also filled with confidence.

In that moment, Shaw believed him with all his heart.

Chapter Sixteen

IT TOOK A few days to get the supplies he needed. Rowan didn't typically use vials for charms, so it wasn't something he kept on hand. He brought everything to the cottage, knowing full well that what he was about to do would be draining. It was safer to be home, shielded from the rest of the world behind his wards—all shored up with added barriers after the whole Badger ordeal.

Shaw had insisted on being there. Rowan wanted to tell him no, but seeing the worry on his face, Rowan had caved. At least Shaw was staying out of the way, watching from the couch. The coffee table had been moved, creating a work space in the middle of the room, where Rowan sat.

He took a small glass vial from the box. He also grabbed one of the titanium casings. If he had to order a whole dozen, he figured he may as well have picked nice-looking ones he could potentially use in the shop too.

"Can you come hold this for me so I don't spill it?" Rowan asked.

Shaw hesitantly sat cross-legged in front of him, holding the vial. "What's that for?" he inquired of the small bottle Rowan produced.

"Lotus oil." Rowan used the dropper to put three drops in the vial. "It will help enhance the spell."

"If you say so." Shaw shifted uncomfortably.

Rowan picked up the small knife he had prepared beforehand, making sure it was sharp and disinfecting it. He pricked the pad of his thumb on the tip. The sting was brief and blood welled immediately. He held his thumb over the vial, squeezing it with his other hand to let the blood drip a little faster.

Under his breath, Rowan spoke the incantation, linking the vial to his energy signature. When it was nearly filled, Rowan pulled his hand away. Rubbing his thumb and forefinger together, he felt the tiny wound heal.

Rowan took the vial, putting the stopper in, before slotting it inside the metal casing. It was sleek and modern looking, rather attractive to counter the slightly morbid contents. He gave the vial a good shake to mix the blood and oil together. Looking up at Shaw, he announced, "Here. All finished."

Shaw took the offered charm, turning it over in his hand.

"I'll put it on a chain," Rowan continued, "but it's all ready to go if you want to test it out."

Shaw gazed intently at the vial, frowning.

"What's wrong?"

"I'm worried."

Rowan smiled a little. "I know you are, but I honestly think this is our best shot." He took the charm back, rooting in one of his boxes for an appropriate chain. "The maps you wanted should be sitting on the printer in the other room. I forgot to grab them."

Shaw got up without a word, going into the turret room where the wireless printer was kept. Normally, Rowan would never think of letting anyone in his magic space unsupervised, but he knew he could trust Shaw. Like with all things since meeting him, Rowan simply went with the flow of his feelings, rather than trying to fight them.

"There." Rowan held the necklace up like a pendulum, smiling at Shaw when he returned. Rowan passed it over and said, "Try it for yourself."

Shaw held the necklace over the map of the Sacred Timber, startled when the pendant yanked and hit the page right where they were currently located. He looked at Rowan wide-eyed.

"Told you it would work," Rowan said with a smirk.

Shaw's lips curled up into a smile. "I never doubted you. It's the rest of this plan I'm concerned with."

Rowan leaned forward, brushing their lips together. "I'll be fine."

When Rowan sat back, Shaw gazed thoughtfully at the charm once more. "Since I have a way to find you, maybe I should let you have one of these for me." He looked up, biting his lip.

"Really?" Rowan wasn't sure what else to say. Shaw had already proven leery about blood magic, yet there he was, not only suggesting he partake but that Rowan would always know where he was. It was flattering in a way, and it clearly involved a lot of trust on Shaw's part.

"Yeah. I'm yours, Ro. I want you to know that."

Rowan's lips tugged up at the corner. All the same, he shook his head. "You don't have to prove anything to me."

"I'm not. It's just..." Shaw sighed, chewing at his lower lip a moment. "I don't know how to explain it. What's between you and me? I've never felt anything like it."

"Can't argue there," Rowan agreed softly.

"All I know is that if witches and mages had mates, then you would be it for me."

Rowan's heart skipped a beat. "I...I hadn't thought of it like that before."

"Well, I've been thinkin' about it a lot," Shaw admitted, a hopeful smile on his face. "There's nobody else for me out there."

"You are—" Rowan shook his head, launching himself at Shaw and holding on tightly as he chuckled. "I love you." It was all he could think to say.

Shaw held him in return, nose falling into Rowan's hair. "I love you, too."

As they stayed like that, an idea came to Rowan. "You know," he mentioned, "I think there's a way I can bind the charms together."

"Wha' do you mean?"

Rowan pulled away, resting back onto his heels. "There might be a way to use the blood charms to create a mating bond. Of sorts." He twisted his hands together, looking away as he started to babble. "I'd have to look at some of Gram's books. Maybe call Sacha for advice. But, I think I could figure it out if I have the time to—"

Shaw silenced him with a kiss. Rowan sank against him, lost to emotion and forgetting about the details for the time being.

"Well," Shaw said, cupping his cheek, "if you do figure it out? We'll do it."

"You mean that?" Rowan breathed.

Shaw smiled. "You make my soul sing."

Rowan felt the heat on his face and tried to cover it with his hand, but Shaw took his wrist, chuckling a little.

"Who's to say that we don't have soul mates?" Shaw continued. "Even science can't explain how it all works. Hell, they can't even explain what a soul is, let alone the specifics of a mate bond."

"You make a point," Rowan said. "Never put much thought into it." There was no reason for him to—not when he would never have a mate—or so he believed.

"See?" Shaw's fingers were rubbing the inside of Rowan's wrist. "No reason we can't have soul mates ourselves."

"Can't deny the way I feel about you. It's not anything I can explain, but maybe we don't have to."

"Really, isn't that what mates are anyway? Something unexplainable by any test, any measure, any—?" Shaw cut himself off with a sigh, shaking his head ruefully. "Now I'm the one rambling."

Rowan leaned forward to press their heads together. "You're right. It's something they know at their cores, a pull that brings them together." He let out a little laugh, almost in disbelief. "And that's exactly how I feel about you."

Shaw kissed him, hard and fast, taking him off guard. There was a familiar prickle of magic on his skin, warmth spreading through him. "That mean I can keep you?" Shaw asked, brushing their lips together.

"Long as I can keep you."

"It's a deal." He grabbed Rowan, yanking him forward and causing them to topple over. Rowan was laid out on top of him, and he shook his head at Shaw's cheeky grin.

"We're supposed to be doing something," Rowan pointed out.

"We can finish that up later." Shaw's fingertips ran along Rowan's ribs, his other hand hooking around Rowan's neck to bring him down for another long kiss.

Rowan wasn't going to complain about where things were heading. He still remembered their first night together, how high he had flown. In hindsight, he realized why it had felt so magical—because it was.

Shaw groaned, apparently picking up on Rowan's lustful feelings. Their positions were flipped, the vials clinking as the box was hit.

"Is it always like this?" Rowan panted.

"No." Shaw was taking deep breaths of his own. "I've had intense before," he clarified, "but never like this."

Rowan was strangely satisfied by that. Perhaps because it reflected his own experiences, as well as their talk of soul mates.

"So, when do I move in?"

That took Rowan off guard. "Excuse me?"

"Well, I figure being bonded means we get to sleep in the same bed," Shaw teased. "Among other things."

Rowan scoffed but was smiling all the same. It faded as he fully considered Shaw's original statement. "You'd really move here? What about your home? Your squad?"

Shaw looked rather confident as he answered, "They'll understand. I love them—don't get me wrong—but I love you more. And you? I know you'd never leave this place."

Rowan worried his lower lip. "I don't know. I've never thought about it... Maybe?" Even he could hear the doubt.

Shaw laughed. "You're not very convincing."

"Well, it's not like there's ever been anything to consider."

"Don't." Shaw shifted off him to sit. "This is your home, Ro. That means it's mine too."

Rowan was touched, but at the same time, he couldn't justify Shaw throwing his whole life away. "What about your job?"

Shaw shrugged. "Might be able to work something out."

"But, your friends—" Rowan tried again, only to be cut off by a fierce kiss.

"I'm going to have to keep using that trick," Shaw mused.

Rowan swatted him. "You're not getting out of this," he warned. "We need to have a serious talk about this."

"Later." Shaw stood, reaching down to help Rowan up. "Right now, I have other things in mind."

"Damn you," Rowan muttered, letting himself be led toward the bedroom. "That is just *not* fair."

"Never claimed to play by the rules, darling."

"I DON'T LIKE this plan," Caleb said—for the third time since arriving.

"Caleb?" Rowan looked over his shoulder. "We've got it, alright?"

Caleb huffed but stayed quiet. Which was fine by Rowan, who went back to looking through his grandmother's books.

They were in the turret room, which meant Caleb started to wander, touching everything. Rowan didn't mind, knowing Caleb wouldn't break anything—at least not on purpose. Really, it was about Caleb leaving his scent behind, whether he realized it or not.

"Why are there two?" Caleb asked. He was holding the blood vial necklaces where they were hanging from a hook on the side of the bookcase.

"One's Shaw's."

Caleb quirked a brow, letting go of the vials. "Yeah, that was the plan. The other mine, then?"

"No, one is Shaw's *blood*."

"What? Why?"

Rowan's lips twitched up into a brief smile. "He wanted me to be able to find him too."

Caleb's face softened. "That's...that's actually really sweet."

"Romantic at heart," Rowan teased.

Caleb gave him a little shove. "I'm just happy you're happy." He leaned back against the table, glancing at the book. "Whatcha doin' anyway? Been glued to that thing since I got here." Caleb was getting nervous, not wanting Rowan to be alone, as though somehow the Inquisition were going to figure out their plan. Thus, he'd shown up shortly after Shaw had left for the temple.

"Looking to see what Gram had about bondings." There was no reason to lie about it.

"Bondings?" It was said carefully. "Ro..."

"I love him." Rowan looked over, meeting Caleb's honey eyes. "He's the one."

"I don't doubt that." He twined their fingers together. "But we're not talking marriage here. You're talkin' about bonding." Caleb licked his lips. "What's wrong with waiting a while? If you're certain, then he's not going anywhere."

That made Rowan grin. "Since when are you the reasonable one?"

"Fuck off," Caleb said, shoving Rowan, but he was chuckling all the same. "I mean it. Have you thought this through? You're not just jumping into this?"

"I have," Rowan assured him.

Caleb was pensive. As the silence stretched, while Caleb was clearly debating on something, Rowan raised a brow. Sighing, Caleb asked, "Have you ever considered the fact it could be false? Planted emotions?"

Rowan was horrified by the mere suggestion. His argument was cut off before it even began.

"No, listen. It's a fair question. The guy's an *empath*. I don't want to think that he's taking advantage. I mean, I think he's being genuine. But, how well do we really know him? He could be projecting anything he wants onto you."

Rowan shook his head. "He wasn't allowed to use his abilities on me. Not until recently."

"Really?" Caleb appeared relieved. "That's... That's good."

There was more, though; Rowan could tell. "What?"

"We still don't truly know him, Ro. It's been—what?—a couple months?"

"You think he's using me?" Rowan crossed his arms over his chest.

"What if he is?"

Rowan threw his hands up, walking away as he muttered, "Unbelievable."

"Ro! Don't be like that! It's a valid concern." He snagged Rowan's arm, spinning him around. The beseeching look made Rowan hear him out. "This guy showed up out of nowhere, working for the Inquisition and keeping secrets. What else isn't he telling us? What if it's a ruse to, I dunno, get ahold of someone like you for their fucking experiments? We could be playing right into their hands!"

Rowan understood the concern, but he still had to reason. "Seducing me helps how? If they wanted me so bad, they'd simply arrest me."

Caleb opened his mouth, then closed it. He tried once more, holding up his finger, but that time Caleb cut himself off with a grumble. "You make a point."

Rowan chuckled, holding Caleb's shoulders. "I love you. And I'm glad you're looking out for me. But...put aside the conspiracy for a moment? Please? Just..." Rowan sighed. "Lose all the shit going on with the Inquisition. Look at *us*." He paused, meeting Caleb's eyes. "What do you think?"

Caleb licked his lips, gaze drifting away. Rowan let him think a bit. When Caleb looked at him again, it was with a smile curling at his lips. "It's kind of ridiculous how you two work."

Rowan let out a breath he hadn't realized he was holding. "You mean that?"

"Ro, I'd have to be blind not to notice."

"So," he ventured, "you're okay with this?"

"I don't really think it's the right time, given what's goin' on, but..." Caleb heaved a sigh, smile growing. "I love you, and I'm happy for you."

Rowan pulled him into a bone-crushing hug, both of them laughing. "Thank you."

"Hey, I can't say I blame you." Caleb looked a little sheepish as he admitted, "I'm kind of a little jealous, honestly. I can't imagine how it feels, to find that person and just know."

Being a were-creature meant Caleb would be able to identify his destined mate by coming into physical contact, although wolves were known to pick them out by scent alone. Caleb was more than a little heartsick, waiting to feel that pull, distracting himself with pleasure and companionship where he could find it. While some might choose not to trade bites and seal their mate bonds, for Caleb, it would be a dream come true.

Rowan smiled gently, nuzzling at Caleb's cheek. "You will."

Caleb held him in return, rubbing their heads together.

HE WOULD BE expected at the temple soon, not that Shaw cared. He had to change clothes, but his real purpose of going back to the apartment was for the privacy it offered. It didn't hurt that there were silencing spells put on the walls, floor, and ceiling.

Even knowing they had left for their mission already, that didn't stop Shaw from dialing Thalanil's phone. It would be in his footlocker—all their cell phones would be—but the message would be waiting when they returned.

"Hey, Thal, can you put this on speaker?" He waited a moment to allow for Thalanil to do so before saying, "Hope you guys are all okay. I'm going a little crazy even thinking about it. I'll want a full debrief, you know. But that's not why I called. I, uh... Shite, I didn't really think this through. That mage I mentioned, Thal? Well, we're getting bonded. I don't know when or anything. Hell, we could be already by the time you get this. I just—I needed to share. I know you guys will love him as much as I do." Shaw took a deep breath. "Well, call me when you can. Hopefully, I'll have Marcus back soon."

Hanging up, Shaw felt his happiness wane into unfulfillment. Being an empath, he was always more in tune with his emotions than other people. Not having that sense of excitement returned was threatening to make him slip to the other end of the spectrum.

Yeah, and who do you have to call? Shaw thought bitterly. His only friends were his squad. He supposed he could now count Caleb among them, but Rowan would want to speak with him first, no doubt. Rhys was a commander, not a friend, and he didn't speak to his parents.

"Hale." A slow smile spread across Shaw's face. Hale may have been Marcus's sire, but he had rather adopted the whole squad—he was naturally paternal that way. Shaw dialed before he could talk himself out of it.

"Shaw? Is everything alright? Have you found him?"

He was hit with a pang of guilt. Of course Hale would assume that was the reason he would call. "Nothing's wrong," Shaw assured him. "I've got a new lead. It should take me straight to wherever Mar is."

Hale sighed. "You have no idea how glad I am to hear it."

"You and me both. Believe me." Shaw grew more frustrated with every passing day that Marcus wasn't back at his side.

"I assume you weren't calling about that. Nothing Rhys couldn't have told me."

Shaw smirked, teasing, "You're good."

"I raised eight kids. I know the tricks."

"Touché." Shaw had no reason to feel nervous about his announcement, but his gut twisted all the same. "I met someone."

"Oh?"

"Rowan. He's a mage. Actually, he just made high master and was put on the Masters Board for the guild here." There was no keeping the pride out of his voice. "He's brilliant, selfless, funny, warm..."

Hale chuckled. "You sound absolutely smitten."

"Who the hell uses that word anymore?"

"I'm almost a thousand. I'm fairly certain I can use whatever words I like." Hale sounded amused. "Now, no changing the subject. Tell me more about this Rowan."

And Shaw did. He talked at length about Rowan's achievements, his personality, and may have gone on a little too long about those gorgeous purple eyes of his. "He's just... He's perfect. And I don't mean that he doesn't have flaws."

"Only that he's perfect for you," Hale finished.

"Exactly."

"So, when's the wedding?" he asked knowingly.

Shaw cleared his throat. "Well, it's funny you should mention that."

"Don't tell me..."

"We got to talking last night and...we discussed being blood bonded."

"That's a dangerous endeavor, Shaw. That's even ignoring the fact this is all very soon."

"I know it is, but he's the one. I feel it!"

"So, go down to the courthouse. Better yet? Wait until you find that pain-in-the-ass son of mine, and your squad is back, and have a nice little wedding somewhere. Why a blood bond?"

"It's not like we can have a true mating bond. This is the closest thing we'll ever have."

Hale hummed, and then after a moment, sighed. "I understand. I can't exactly say you shouldn't. However, blood magic...? Well, we know our share. I worry about how well he could perform such a binding. It's not exactly a process that's taught anymore."

"I hear ya." Shaw couldn't blame Hale for his concern. It was more than valid. "Ro knows what he's doin' with blood magic, though, like I said. He wouldn't do anything he wasn't sure about." Shaw smiled, thinking of Rowan bent over his books. "You should see him when he's working."

"Smitten," Hale reiterated, trying not to laugh. "If you're certain, then I wish you all the best in the world, Shaw. For you and your Rowan."

"Thanks, Hale."

"And if he wants to discuss blood magic, you give him my number. We have no shortage of resources here for him."

Shaw chuckled. "Knowing him, he's probably gotten it all figured out already."

Chapter Seventeen

THE POND BESIDE the cottage was bathed in moonlight. Fireflies danced around them, crickets chirping, with the frogs occasionally chiming in. An owl hooted, taking flight and crossing over the water. The night was undoubtedly, in a word, perfect.

"You're sure about this?" Rowan checked.

Shaw smiled up at him. "Are you seriously asking me again? Look," he continued, cutting off Rowan's reply, "I'm not about to try and explain whatever this is between us. We're soul mates. It's just something I know."

Rowan smiled in return, ducking his head to kiss him gently. "I feel the same. Just good to hear you say it."

Shaw held out his hand, showing the blood-filled vial necklace that matched Rowan's own. "Let's do this."

It had only taken Rowan five days to figure out the proper bonding spell. Well, four days, actually, but he had spent a final afternoon going over it again, just to be sure. It had already gotten a seal of approval from both Sacha and Hale—it turned out that Marcus's sire really knew his stuff—but it hadn't stopped Rowan from making doubly sure.

Cradling Shaw's hand, Rowan took his necklace off. He placed both of them on Shaw's palm, putting his hand on top so the vials were sandwiched in-between. "Ready?"

Taking a deep breath, Shaw nodded. "Just repeat what you say, right?"

"That's right." The corner of Rowan's mouth ticked up. "Relax. You'll do fine."

It was Rowan's turn to take a deep breath, his eyes glowing as he tapped into his magic. He started the spell, pausing after each word to hear Shaw's echo. *"Cuore."* Heart. *"Anima."* Soul. *"Sangue."* Blood. *"Vincolato."* Bonded. *"Coniugo."* Mate.

Shaw gasped and Rowan's mouth fell open, but nothing came out. They were frozen in place, with a sensation that all the air had left them and they were suspended in time and space. Rowan swore he felt his heart stop.

After what seemed to be an eternity, an energy slammed into them with such force that it knocked them backward. Rowan stumbled, coughing as air rushed into his lungs.

Shaw grabbed him, gulping in air as well. "What... What was that?"

Rowan took a deep breath, looking over at Shaw. A smile slowly appeared on his face. "That," Rowan answered, "was our energies binding together."

Slowly, Shaw smiled back. Then he started to laugh. Straightening, he pulled Rowan into his arms and proceeded to kiss him breathless once again.

Rowan could feel the magic ebbing and flowing between them. The overwhelming emotions were running on a loop from Shaw—nothing that he was able to control. Rowan fed into that, pushing out with all the love he was experiencing in that moment.

"Take me to bed," Rowan panted against Shaw's lips.

Shaw's grin held intent. "Read my mind, darlin'."

Rowan's quip about "That's not part of the bond" was cut off with a fierce kiss.

THERE WAS A pleasant ache of muscles to accompany the thrumming of energy in his chest. Shaw knew he was smiling like an idiot as he stared up at the ceiling. One arm was behind his head, the other was snaked around Rowan's back, supporting him as he snuggled against Shaw's side.

Rowan's touch was featherlight against Shaw's skin. "I could stay like this indefinitely," he whispered, pressing a kiss to Shaw's shoulder.

"Me too." Shaw turned his head to brush his lips across Rowan's temple. "I think, eventually, the rest of the world's gonna have something to say 'bout that."

Ignoring his comment, Rowan played with the blood vial lying on Shaw's chest. "When I have time, I'll attach this to your mer scale. It can sit behind it."

On one hand, Shaw felt like arguing against hiding it, but he realized what Rowan meant. "The scale will protect it; that's for certain."

"Mine will be a bit more tricky."

Shaw scrounged between them to get hold of both Rowan's vial and that brilliant blue stone of his. "They don't really go together," he agreed, the two charms clinking.

"Maybe I can carve out a piece of the gem," Rowan suggested. "I can inset the vial, without the casing."

"Now that will look pretty wicked." Shaw leaned over to kiss him. Modifying the charms like that was greatly symbolic of Rowan bringing Shaw so deeply into his life, into himself—whether Rowan had meant it that way or not.

"Mmm, be right back," Rowan said as he reluctantly extracted himself.

Shaw heard him go into the bathroom. He rubbed at his chest at an odd sensation there, dismissing it as nothing important. It was that lack of feeling once he heard Rowan move from the bathroom into the kitchen that made him pay attention. There was no pain, just a distinct lack of... something.

Before Shaw had time to truly question it, Rowan returned with two glasses, as did the unknown feeling. A flood of warmth swept over his body as he stared at Rowan open-mouthed. "What in the world...?"

Momentarily taken off guard himself, Rowan eventually smiled and sat on the bed, one leg pulled up under him. He passed over a glass of water after Shaw sat up. "That's the bond. We can sense each other's presence now. I suspect it will grow stronger over time. And your empathy's likely to make it more sensitive, I imagine."

"That's incredible." Shaw laughed, shaking his head.

He hadn't genuinely known what he was getting into with this bond. Admittedly, he'd simply jumped in headfirst. It wasn't as if Rowan hadn't explained the process thoroughly, but even he hadn't been sure of all that might happen. Ancient magic no longer performed didn't exactly come with a manual.

"Wonder what other tricks we've picked up," Shaw mused.

Rowan lifted a shoulder. "From what I could find in Gram's books, and after talking it out with Sacha, that seems to be it. I certainly didn't add anything on top of the bonding itself either. Too risky. And also wasn't the point," he added as an afterthought.

"You're likely right," Shaw said. He reached out and touched the vial around Rowan's neck, the one with Shaw's blood sitting in it. "Will we have to be wearing these for it to work?"

"No, we'll always be bonded." Rowan smirked. "Like I told Caleb, we've always got our blood with us."

Shaw's face fell, and Rowan's expression faltered.

"Don't start," Rowan warned.

"I know we've been over it, and we're as prepared as we can get, but I'm still allowed to worry about it."

There was nothing he could say, so instead, Rowan set his glass on the nightstand, motioning for Shaw to do the same. "I want to show you something. Lie down." Shaw did so, and Rowan moved to lay beside him.

Rowan clapped his hands together twice and the lights went out. Then the room was flooded with a completely different glow. Above them, stars twinkled and galaxies swirled in the distance, splashing color here and there.

"Wow," Shaw breathed. "This is..."

"I can bring it down too," Rowan said, before making a gesture with his hand. The stars zoomed in, washing across the whole room, making it feel as though the two of them were floating in the middle of space.

"How did you even do this?" Shaw reached out for a nearby star. Touching it released a pulse of light.

"A project I worked on over the years, since I was young. Had to recreate the effect here once I moved."

Shaw turned his head to gaze at Rowan, seeing the look of wonder as he viewed his work.

"I've always loved the stars," Rowan said. "Were really comforting as a kid. Better than any nightlight."

"Like sleeping outdoors," Shaw agreed, looking back at them.

Rowan pushed his hands out, letting the stars return to the ceiling. "Save the bugs."

Shaw chuckled. "There is that." He took Rowan's hand, continuing to stargaze, as it were. "I think I'm going to like it here." He felt a tug on his hand.

"We never finished having that discussion," Rowan reminded him.

"And I recall telling you your home was my home."

"Not letting you get away with it that easy." Rowan rolled over, straddling Shaw's hips. He sat down heavily, causing Shaw to grunt. "You can't just avoid talking about it."

"Sure I can." Shaw grinned mischievously. His hands were resting on Rowan's thighs, sending lustful thoughts his way.

Rowan's eyes fluttered before closing. He huffed. "That's cheating."

"Never claimed to play fair, darling."

Apparently deciding to drop it, Rowan leaned down and captured Shaw's lips. "We're still talking about it." Or not.

Chapter Eighteen

"HE'S BOOKED," SHAW announced when he came through the door of Caleb's small apartment. "Any movement?"

"Not yet," Caleb replied, the blood vial necklace in his hand still hovering in a tight circle over the area of the temple.

"Alright." Shaw woke his laptop on the end stand. They already had a detailed map of Everstrand on the coffee table—the same Caleb was currently using—as well as a regional and country map. Depending on the area where the charmed necklace led them, Shaw would be able to print off new detailed maps to help pinpoint a location.

"What if they don't move him?" Caleb asked from where he sat cross-legged on the floor. He put the necklace down, flexing his fingers and rotating his wrist.

"They're not stashing the kidnapped magicae on site," Shaw insisted, plopping onto the couch. "I've been through there a thousand times."

If Rowan disappeared without the charm indicating him being off the property, they had a whole new level of problems. No, thanks to the hidden camera footage, Shaw had witnessed the Inquisition taking a shipment of magicae out of the prison, in the dead of night, using some kind of truck. The problem was not knowing their destination. He had been debating on how to get a tracking device into the next batch, but he hadn't considered making that "device" a *person*.

"How long?" Caleb asked, staring at the map.

"They have to arraign him within forty-eight hours. That's how long they have to make him disappear."

Caleb gave a curt nod, gaze darting to the necklace. It was a long moment before he grabbed the chain, picking it up to check on Rowan once more. Shaw leaned forward, grabbing Caleb's shoulder. He knew what Caleb was feeling, and there was no point in trying to reassure him. Instead, Shaw offered companionship in the silence they settled into.

Out of the blue, Caleb asked, "So, how long before you make it legal, you think?"

It took Shaw a moment to realize Caleb was talking about marriage. "Dunno. Once this is over with, the squad's likely due some R&R. Might have to take advantage of it."

Caleb nodded. He had jokingly given Rowan a hard time for not being at their bonding when the trio went out to dinner to celebrate. In reality, Caleb understood the couple wanting to share that night just between them. There would be some type of legal ceremony in the future to attend—after all, it wasn't as if any government was about to recognize their blood bond as is.

"Honestly," Shaw continued, "I don't think Ro cares much about doing the legal bit. When I brought it up, seemed he agreed more 'cause I wanted it."

"Sounds about right," Caleb chuckled. He nudged his shoulder against Shaw's leg. "You're what matters to Ro. Not some piece of paper."

The corner of Shaw's mouth turned up. "Well, I'd still feel better knowing he's protected if somethin' happens to me, y'know?"

Caleb gave him a look of approval before laying his head on Shaw's knee.

The charm didn't indicate any change until after midnight. It made sense they would move Rowan in the early hours of the morning under cover of darkness. Prisoners would be asleep, along with most people in the city. It was the perfect time to make someone vanish. Too bad for the Inquisition that Shaw was watching.

He was holding the charm above the map lazily, not expecting anything to change, when suddenly it darted to the side. The vial dropped onto the map in the area of the southern gate. "We've got movement," Shaw announced, half in awe, half in excitement.

"They didn't waste any time," Caleb said, practically knocking Shaw over as he scrambled off the couch to join him on the floor. "Ro was right."

"Remember what he said, now. We need to wait five minutes before trying again." It was more to remind himself, since Shaw wanted nothing more than to keep at it. However, unless they waited, they wouldn't learn anything new.

After a long five minutes, when Shaw checked, the location had moved again, heading out of the city. Another five minutes told them they were heading north along the main highway. Yet another five, and a switch to the regional map, had them on the same route, so Shaw felt comfortable making the phone call.

"Rhys, I need you." Now those were words Shaw hadn't thought to utter, and he could practically hear Marcus's voice grumbling in his ear about not needing anything from the likes of Rhys. "What do you got for satellites over Everstrand right now?"

"Hold on." Rhys yawned loudly into the phone. "Do you know what time it is here?"

"Almost time for you to get the fuck up anyway," Shaw replied blandly, knowing it was nearing six in the morning over in Tolhollow.

"Fuck you too." Shaw could hear movement, so he decided to bite his tongue. "What's this about anyway?"

"I'm getting us the location of where the kidnapped magicae are."

That perked Rhys right up. "What do you need?"

"Heading north on Highway 10, right now, is a truck. I have no idea what kind. But in there is their latest victim."

"Do I even want to know what you've done?" Rhys inquired skeptically.

"Maybe later."

Rhys sighed. "Lemme get down to command. Back to you soon," he said before promptly disconnecting.

"Umm," Caleb ventured, "so is he gonna help us, or what?"

"Give him a minute." Shaw didn't exactly want to wait either. Thankfully, Rhys wasn't messing around. "What have we got?" Shaw asked after answering the phone.

"Thermal imaging is up. Multiple vehicles. Can you give me more?"

"Hold on. Caleb, try the charm."

"Who's Caleb?" Rhys didn't sound angry, mostly curious.

"Another long story."

"Here," Caleb said when the vial smacked the table.

"Alright. We are about...sixteen klicks out from Everstrand."

"Copy. Zeroing... We've got a sedan, a big rig, and a box truck."

Shaw nodded. "Could be either of those last two. We're not sure the exact type of truck they're using to transport."

"Well, we may get an answer. It looks like the rig is heading down a westbound exit. The truck's still traveling north."

"Give us a couple minutes."

"We don't have long," Rhys reminded him. Satellites didn't give indefinite coverage, after all.

"Acknowledged," Shaw said. "Can we get a check on all the airstrips? It's unlikely they would travel with an official flight plan, but I want it ruled out anyway. I don't want them leaving the country without us knowing about it."

Apparently, Caleb didn't want to wait the allotted time. Shaw heard a soft *thunk* and looked to find out where the vial had landed.

"Hey, I've got updated coordinates," Shaw said, rattling them off.

After a moment, Rhys confirmed, "That's the box truck. We'll keep an eye on it from here and get back with you."

Shaw breathed out. "Thanks." He hung up, looking over at Caleb. "Well, we've got our truck."

"Good." Caleb nodded, placing the vial on the coffee table and sitting back. After a moment, he rested his head against Shaw's shoulder. Shaw set a hand on Caleb's thigh, letting a little warm calm seep into him.

Waiting seemed to take forever, while it was in reality about ten minutes before they got the call back. Shaw put the phone on speaker, setting it on the coffee table.

"The truck stopped at a dock on the Neul Channel and loaded cargo onto a boat. We're going to be losing coverage, Shaw."

"Damn it." Shaw ran fingers through his hair. "We'll keep tracking on our end."

"I don't want to adjust positioning until we have final coordinates," Rhys said. "We can't risk alerting anyone. Especially Osterian brass."

"Understood. We'll keep you updated."

"Now what?" Caleb asked, crestfallen.

"We keep at it." Shaw tapped his finger to the maps.

They continued to track Rowan across the channel and into the barren zone. No country had claim to the region since it was considered uninhabitable. The land there had been constantly covered in ash because of volcanic activity to the east. Despite the fact those same volcanos now sat dormant, the damage had been done; the land was dead, and no one lived on it.

"I don't understand," Shaw said, printing off more maps to lay out on the table. "Where could they be going?" The lone possibility he could see was that perhaps they were going to cross the barren landscape and the next channel to the east into the lands of the Eskaria Empire. If they went into the territory of Calagon's greatest enemy, things would become complicated.

"No idea." The charm landed back on the map again, Caleb furrowing his brows. "I think they might have stopped."

Shaw perked up, taking in the location that Caleb indicated. It was at the base of the Ash Mountains, so named because they were still washed in volcanic fallout. "That makes no sense." Shaw printed another map that showed that area of the mountains with greater detail. "Here, try to get it on here." The charm quickly fell on the spot and Shaw took note of the coordinates.

There shouldn't have been anything built out there, yet the charm kept indicating that Rowan had stopped. When thirty minutes had passed and there still was no movement, Shaw rang up Rhys again. "I have a location for you."

"Are you sure this is right?" Rhys asked after repeating the coordinates back. "The Ash Mountains?"

"What's there, Rhys? We need eyes on it."

"Agreed." There was a pause before Rhys relayed, "I'll have that satellite within range in about five mikes."

"Mikes?" Caleb hissed under his breath.

"Minutes," Shaw explained.

"Let me know if anything changes," Rhys ordered.

It didn't though. No matter how many times they verified with the necklace, it kept assuring them that Rowan was right there. "You don't think..." Caleb said, obviously not wanting to think of the possibility, yet still fearing the worst.

"If he were dead..." Shaw shook his head. "No, Ro's alive. I know it." He nodded his head toward the charm. "And that thing agrees." The blood in the vial was still a dark red, not black as it would be with the death of the subject. "He's too valuable alive."

Caleb replied softly, "I hope you're right."

The phone's ring made them both jump, and Shaw couldn't answer it fast enough, once again putting it on speaker.

"You are not going to believe this," Rhys began their conversation. "I'm sending you an encrypted file."

Shaw pulled his laptop over, bringing up a data packet of satellite images. "You've got to be kidding me."

Caleb was peering over Shaw's shoulder. "What am I looking at?"

It was Rhys who answered. "*That* is what is sitting at the coordinates you gave me. There's a facility sitting at the base of the Ash Mountains."

"Holy fuck." Caleb's eyes widened, looking over at Shaw.

"If this is where your informant is," Rhys continued, "we're to assume it's an Inquisition-run experimental prison facility. We've given it the designation Ashgate Prison, and we're running this operation under the codename Winter Storm."

The facility looked to be a decent size with three wings coming off the main building. "Probably at least one of those wings is housing," Shaw said. "They wouldn't want a lot of activity coming and going from the site."

Caleb laid his chin on Shaw's shoulder, looking through the array of images with him.

"You're likely right," Rhys agreed. "That would logically leave one for holding cells and another for whatever experimental equipment they have." Rhys paused to listen to another report from his end. "We estimate a small force of knights on site. They wouldn't waste the housing space they could use for their scientists, and their location lends itself to not being found."

"No reason to keep much security on hand," Shaw concurred.

"I want you to get up there and do a visual scout. Once I get on-the-ground intel, I can tell you how to proceed."

"Oh, it's rather simple. I'm scouting for an in, and then me and Caleb here are going and breaking up the party."

"I'd rather send you backup."

"The squad's already out on mission," Shaw reminded him.

"I could send in another one. The point is that we don't have to worry about stepping on political toes here. They're in unclaimed territory, which means we're well within our rights to hit it."

It was a fair point, but Shaw worried about the time it would take to mobilize any kind of joint effort. Or how they were supposed to write off by what means they came about their information. Osterian most likely wouldn't be happy to hear a Calagon agent had been sent in undercover in their capital city without authorization. At the end of the day, that was Rhys's problem.

"Okay," Shaw said. "We'll get out there by first light." It would be tough to make the trip in that time, but Shaw had already packed all his gear and had it piled in the corner of Caleb's living room.

"Check in at 0700," Rhys ordered.

"Yes, sir." Shaw hung up the phone with a sigh. "Looks like it's time to move out."

IT WAS HARD to tell if what was blowing around them was snow or ash. Either way, it helped to conceal their position up on the crest of a hill overlooking Ashgate Prison. Shaw would have left Caleb behind, but in truth, it was too risky to go alone. Besides, his nose would probably come in handy.

They were looking through binoculars, observing the entrance to the facility, and spotted two men standing guard in a small shack. Traffic in or out was likely kept to a minimum, so the lack of security presence wasn't surprising. It also made their job a whole lot easier.

"This place is huge," Caleb said. He put his binoculars down, looking over at Shaw. "How the hell are we gonna find Ro?"

"Should be rather straightforward once we get inside." Caleb didn't seem convinced. "Just trust me on this."

"You're the pro," Caleb relented, going back to observing.

"There'll be more guards in a central control room. We have to get in there and take it before they can get word out."

"Aren't we supposed to wait for the military backup Rhys promised?"

"Do you really want to leave Rowan in there any longer? It takes time to mobilize troops, no matter how good Rhys is."

Caleb huffed. "Fair enough... So, we take out anyone between us and that control room, yeah?"

"From there we'll be able to see the full layout. We need to clear any areas where more guards or other staff would be. Once everything's secure, we can get those prisoners out."

"Alright." Caleb paused. "How exactly are we doing that?"

"Well, personally, I'm gonna shoot 'em. That seems to work."

Caleb scoffed.

"You, well... I don't suppose you have any experience with a gun?"

"Not in the slightest."

"Well, then, goin' furry seems to be your best bet. But, not till I tell ya. We wanna get the jump on them."

"I can do that."

Shaw went back to watching the prison. Looking at the tire tracks leading from the building, he had an idea. "Did you see those Inquisition trucks at the docks?"

"Yeah?"

"We're gonna go commandeer one."

Caleb's brows shot up. "And how are we gonna do that?"

Shaw patted his shoulder. "Leave it to me."

Caleb snorted.

"Oh, ye of little faith."

"More like ye who likes to live," Caleb grumbled, following all the same as Shaw grabbed his gear and slipped away.

Chapter Nineteen

THERE WERE TWO docks with a small building that served as an outpost. On their way to Ashgate, they had noted a half-dozen crew leaving on the barge. Now, it looked like only a few men had been left there.

"Are they waiting for another shipment?" Caleb asked, watching the knights playing cards inside the building.

"Could be. People, supplies—they'd need both to keep the prison operational." Shaw looked at the pair of light, open-top Humvees. "If we steal one outright, they might notice it missing and call it in."

"So what do you suggest?"

Shaw grinned over at him. "I turn on the charm."

"Oh, right. We're dead then."

Shaw shoved Caleb right onto his ass. "Shut up, and put this on." It was a spare inquisitor tunic from the duffel bag of goodies, along with a hat to cover up that crazy hair of his. Shaw slipped his own tunic on over the winter camo, hoping it and his acting would be enough to get what they needed. "Hang onto this"—Shaw handed Caleb his bag—"and wait next to the Humvee." He paused before leaving. "Just act pissy and like you're more important than anyone else here."

"Right," Caleb dragged out the word, not even bothering to hide his skepticism.

Shaw walked up to the door and took a deep breath. Putting his best scowl in place, he slammed the door open and yelled at the startled knights, "What in the hell is going on around here? Do you people have no concept of time?"

"Wha—? Who are you?" one of them demanded.

"Who the fuck do I look like?" Shaw barked, getting in his face. He dumped some oppressive emotions into the air for good measure. "I'm your goddamned superior officer, and you will address me as Inquisitor or sir. Do I make myself clear?"

The knight's eyes widened. "Sir, yes sir! Sorry, sir, we, uh...we weren't expecting—"

"The hell you were not! I was supposed to be en route already to check on things up the mountain. Instead, I've been standing out there waiting for a knight to come out and give me my bloody Humvee!"

"Our apologies, Inquisitor," another knight stammered. "We weren't told about your arrival."

"My boat dropped me off nearly five minutes ago, Knight," Shaw informed him. "And you're going to sit there and tell me you knew nothing about my being here?"

"No, sir. We swear, sir."

Shaw huffed. "Well, somebody is going to pay for this oversight. And I better not find out that you were lying to me."

"Not at all, sir," the third knight assured him, hopping up to grab a set of keys by the door. "I can drive you up there right now, Inquisitor."

"That won't be necessary," Shaw said, snatching the keys. "My colleague and I can find our way."

The knights followed him out, pausing when they saw Caleb. He was leaning up against the Humvee looking thoroughly unimpressed. Caleb had no doubt heard the entire conversation because he grumbled, "Oh, so we can finally go now?" He took the keys from Shaw. "Don't ask me to be happy about this little trip." Caleb tossed the duffel into the back of the Humvee and asked, "Sure I'm not allowed to kill anyone on general principle?" before climbing into the driver's seat to start it up.

Shaw's grin was anything but kind to the knights. "You boys just consider yourselves lucky I was the one to come in and chat with you."

They all nodded, continuing to grovel as Shaw got into the Humvee. Seeing they were sufficiently scared, Shaw slapped the dashboard a couple of times, letting Caleb drive off without another word.

Once they were out of earshot, Caleb burst out laughing. "Oh my God, that was great!"

Shaw smirked. "Told you to have some faith."

"My apologies, Inquisitor," Caleb replied sarcastically. After a moment he admitted, "I suppose someone who has been playing the game this long would know how to pull something like that off."

"You weren't so bad yourself." Shaw patted his shoulder. "Now, we need an encore performance at the gate. Don't say anything if you don't have to. I'll handle the talking."

"So, we're here as an inspection detail?" Caleb checked the story.

"Right. We report directly to Knight Commander Zane."

Caleb snorted. "Now there's a pompous ass I'd like to meet in a dark alley."

"You and me both," Shaw muttered. "Put your game face on," he said when the prison came into view.

When Caleb's face set into a scowl, Shaw smirked briefly. Caleb was a pretty damn good actor. Granted, Shaw was fairly certain it wasn't all that hard to feign displeasure, given their current mission.

One guard stepped out of the shack into the road, holding his hand up in a motion for them to stop. Shaw wasn't about to say anything when Caleb halted the Humvee mere inches from running the knight over. Shaw's attention turned to the knight still in the guard shack.

"Inquisitor Shaw," he introduced, flashing his credentials. "This is my partner, Inquisitor Bane. We're here for a surprise inspection of the facility."

"I wasn't informed of any—"

"That's why it's called a surprise, Knight," Shaw spoke blandly, playing up the bored angle.

"Yes, sir. My apologies, sir." The knight glanced to his partner, clearly wondering what to do.

"Are you letting us past, Knight?" Shaw inquired. "Or am I making a phone call to the Knight Commander to explain why I don't have the information he wants?"

"No, Inquisitor. Go right on through. I'll inform Commander Trin of your arrival."

The large steel gates swung open, allowing them to pass into the prison. There was a secondary gate just beyond it that opened after the first closed. "A thermal barrier," Shaw explained. "Helps keep most of the cold out when the transports come and go."

"And another gate to get through if you wanted to escape," Caleb noted with a growl. As he drove the Humvee through and into a vacant parking spot to the side, he asked, "Bane?"

Shaw lifted a shoulder. "He was a wolf I worked with in S.O.D."

Caleb cocked a brow in confusion at the term.

"Special Operations Division... Anyway, you kinda remind me of him." Shaw smirked. "Hotheaded."

Caleb scoffed, muttering what were undoubtedly insults under his breath.

They stepped right up into the main room from the small parking area. There was a horseshoe-shaped desk with high counters and a bank of monitors. It appeared that each of the three wings was accessible from here.

"Inquisitors," a woman greeted them. The navy sash around her waist and patches on her shoulder helped identify her as a commander in the knight branch. At least they had the advantage that no one here was likely to recognize Shaw from the Everstrand Temple.

"Commander Trin," Shaw assumed, offering his hand. "Inquisitor Shaw." He once more introduced Caleb as Bane, not missing the scowl he gave the woman as he crossed his arms over his chest. Shaw leaned in toward Trin and stage-whispered, "He's a bit on the grumpy side today. Don't mind him."

"Screw you," Caleb huffed. "Let's get this over with. I want to be back at the temple before the day's out."

"Of course," Trin said. "You'll have to excuse my knights. We were told by Knight Commander Zane that we would function with very little oversight."

"Yes, well," Shaw replied, "Zane wants to cover his ass. He's been hearing...murmurs."

Trin lowered her brows. "What kinds of murmurs?"

Shaw brushed it off. "Shall we?"

"Yes, of course." She gestured off to the right—"Our science wing"—straight ahead—"cell blocks"—and to the left—"and personnel housing. Where would you care to start?"

"Do you have a central control? I would like to look over operations there. As well as where you're conducting these experiments." Shaw sniffed in distaste. "Frankly, I'm not concerned with the holding cells, except to check your containment methods. How your knights live is not my concern." He paused. "Unless you believe there is anyone who poses a security risk?"

Trin froze. She took the bait. "That's what Zane is concerned with. A leak." She pursed her lips, looking over to the pair of guards on duty at the desk. "I personally cleared all the knights who work here. I trust them. The science team, however... I have my doubts about them. They stay in quarters on the second floor. My knights have the ground level."

Shaw nodded. "I'll be sure to have you give me a tour." He walked forward enough to catch what the knights at the desk were doing. They appeared to be processing paperwork. The few security monitors there contained footage from the front gate and the cell blocks. "For now, the control center?"

"Yes, right this way, Inquisitors."

Shaw and Caleb shared a look as they followed behind her. Caleb gave him a brief smirk, Shaw returning it. Sometimes it was just far too easy to manipulate people.

They were led to an elevator beside the entrance to the prison wing, which took them straight to the control center. Windows looked out over the entrance area, as well as into the cell blocks. There were only two guards in here as well.

"Your staffing seems light," Shaw mentioned.

"We don't need a large force," Trin confirmed. "Everything runs like a well-oiled machine. The knights here monitor the entire facility. There's a pair stationed in each cell block. The knights you saw down in processing are there during intakes and for completing paperwork. Redundant, otherwise."

"But, no oversight in the science wing," Shaw noted, having been looking over the array of security monitors.

"Just guard postings." Trin didn't appear happy about it either. Shaw would have to play that to his advantage.

"Who oversees the science team?"

"Borek." Trin scoffed. "He has no concept of security practices. He wants his fodder and we're meant to provide without question. Never mind that it's my knights I have to put in harm's way."

Shaw nodded, walking around the control room. On the outside, he may have appeared apathetic, but in reality, he was taking in all of the equipment.

It was Caleb who asked, "What about these two doors?" They were heavy, with keycard locks, sitting at the other end of the room.

"One is to the second floor of the science wing, and the other goes to the blocks—up on the catwalks." Trin was quick to assure, "They're only accessible from this side. They allow a fast response, if needed, until the knights off duty can be there."

Caleb nodded to the weapons locker. "What are they armed with?"

"Everyone on duty carries a sidearm. The ones on the cell block floor are given their choice of a rifle or shotgun. The rest of the weapons are kept secured in lockers here and in the armory near the housing wing. The quartermaster and I have keys."

Shaw was looking out into the prison area. Two cell blocks, each with two rows of cells, plus a few in the very back. By his quick estimate, there were at least forty of them. "What's the current occupancy? Zane didn't give us many details on operations before sending us."

"That's Zane, alright," Trin remarked. To answer his question, she said, "We're currently at forty-two. There was upward of sixty not that long ago, but the science team… Well, they've lost their share to whatever games they're playing."

Caleb's jaw tightened and he turned away to hide his expression. Shaw hoped his face didn't give anything away.

"They've become reckless lately," Trin continued. "Something about breakthroughs and new theories. The details of which I'm not made privy to. Zane and the other Knight Commanders involved are the ones with that information."

"Always makes our jobs so much easier, doesn't it?" Shaw asked sarcastically. He knocked his knuckles against the glass behind him. "Two-way?"

"Of course."

"Good, I don't want anyone knowing we're here until we get to them." He looked between the two knights working pointedly. "Understood?"

They looked to Trin, who nodded before answering, "Understood, sir."

"Good." Shaw looked to the door going to the science wing. "What's the procedure for prisoner transfer?"

"We have at least four knights to move prisoners. Borek refuses to have them in the rooms. Claims they would cause problems for his people: get in the way." Trin scoffed. "So, they sit at posts on the far end of the wing, two on each floor, once they're done with all the transfers. They're set up for six prisoners maximum at one time. Borek has fought me on it, but I refuse to budge. At least Zane saw fit to back me on that, if nothing else."

"I assume you have to take the prisoners through the main area." Shaw didn't see any other connection between the wings.

"Correct. One prisoner at a time, ankle chains and handcuffs for everyone. Depending on what they are, we might need more security. Nothing different from the temple jails—magic-dampeners on the cuffs and cells themselves, silver-infused cuffs for were-creatures and anti-shift collars at all times. Really, it's all to Inquisition standards."

"Do the science team have access to firearms?"

"Hell, no." Trin scoffed. "Another thing I put my foot down about. They don't have the training, and I wasn't going to allow people I couldn't control running around here with weapons."

"Smart," Caleb grunted. He was hovering next to one of the guards, reading over his shoulder and making the knight highly uncomfortable by the looks of it.

"Impressive." Shaw practically choked on the word. "You run a well-oiled machine, Commander."

Trin offered him a smile. "Thank you. I take pride in my knights." She paused before saying, "I refuse to be held responsible for what Borek does with his people."

"Noted." Shaw tipped his head toward the computer bank. "Do you know where they're working today?"

"Of course. Prin," she ordered the knight not being harassed by Caleb, "bring up the logs for today."

Shaw quirked a brow. "Prin?"

They both smirked at him, a perfect reflection of the other, and it was Prin who supplied, "Siblings."

Shaw felt a pang of guilt for what they were about to do. It was possible some of these knights were decent people caught in the crossfire. If it was true Trin had no knowledge or control over what was taking place in the science wing, it could be argued they were all simply prison guards doing their jobs.

The fact remained, however, that they were all very aware of what illegal actions they were taking. They would know these people were stolen, stricken from all records, and being tortured in any number of ways. Whatever else they might have been, these knights were contributing to that.

"We have six prisoners currently out. We also received three new ones today." Trin huffed. "Borek wanted to take one of them immediately. Some mage. Cursed me up one side and down the other when I told him no. That's not how this works. All new arrivals require processing and assignment. Borek doesn't get to jump the line because he wants a new toy."

Shaw was thankful to hear Rowan was safe at least. "Sounds like Borek is going to be a problem."

"I'll be thrilled if you could somehow take care of that for me."

"I'll see what I can do." Shaw took a deep breath, running everything over in his mind as he looked out at the cell blocks. He wanted to make sure he had all he needed before they acted. "The knights you mentioned are the only ones on duty right now?"

"Yes. Shift changes are staggered but don't start for another five hours. While not on duty, they're restricted to housing. There's a rec room, kitchens, and whatnot to occupy them."

Shaw nodded. "I'll speak with them last. For now, I think it's time to speak to Borek and his team."

"Agreed," Caleb spoke up, meeting Shaw's gaze.

"I'd like to do that alone, if you don't mind, Commander."

"Not at all." Trin huffed. "The less I have to see of that man, the better."

Shaw smirked. "This should be interesting. Can you radio your teams in the science wing so they know we're coming?"

"Absolutely." Trin patted her brother's shoulder to have him go ahead and alert the knights. "Will there be anything else you need?"

"Not right now. We'll go check the science team, and do a cursory inspection of the cell blocks, before checking on your little problem in housing."

Trin nodded. "I appreciate any help you can give me, Inquisitor."

Prin looked up at them. "The teams on duty have been informed to expect you, Inquisitors."

"Good." Shaw looked over at Caleb. "Shall we?" There was a glint in Caleb's eyes and Shaw knew he understood.

In a flash, Shaw drew his sidearm, firing on the siblings. Prin was shot in the temple, Trin catching one in the throat. Her eyes widened, grabbing at her neck to try to stem the blood flow. "Sorry," Shaw said, taking pity on her and putting the next bullet between her eyes. Trin fell to the floor in a heap.

Looking over, he found Caleb had tackled the other knight, banging his head off the floor repeatedly. "Caleb... Caleb!" Caleb looked up at him, eyes glowing red—his Alpha magic had come to the surface. "He's dead. Let's go."

Caleb growled, flashing canines that were far too large for his human form. He let go of the knight, revealing the claws that had grown, covered in blood. Shaw was glad he wasn't on the receiving end of Caleb's wrath.

Because Shaw used a silencer, no one would have heard the shots, so the rest of the knights were none the wiser. He took the earpiece from Prin's corpse before pushing it out of the way. "We can listen in on their comms," Shaw said. "Now, just to get into their system."

Caleb grunted in answer. Shaw didn't have time to worry over him at the moment.

The computer was easy enough to navigate, and Shaw was able to shut down the alarms. He pulled out his phone once that was done, punching in Rhys on speed dial. "Winter

Storm is a go. Infiltration team has seized the first objective."

"Shaw," Rhys growled, "you were supposed to wait!"

"Control center is secure. We're moving to secure the rest of the facility now. No one has been alerted to our real purpose."

Rhys grumbled, "You keep it that way. I'm scrambling everyone now. They can be at your location in about... twenty-five mikes."

Shaw synced his diving watch to that time. "Copy. I'll have the facility secured for their arrival."

"Don't do anything stupid," Rhys warned. "No risks."

"Can't make any promises, sir." Shaw disconnected and looked at Caleb. He had reined in his Alpha side, although he was shaking a little. "You alright?"

"Yeah." Caleb's voice was rough. "What now?"

"Now," Shaw replied, rolling Trin to take the master keycard off her body, "we take out the guards over here and see about these scientists."

"I say kill them," Caleb grunted.

"We should try to keep as many of them alive for interrogation as possible," Shaw said, even if he personally hated the idea. "Kill anyone who poses a threat, but leave the others."

"Fine."

"Play it cool with these guys. We keep the act as long as we can."

"Yeah, yeah, let's go."

Shaw sent Caleb a look, holstering his handgun.

He used Trin's keycard, knowing that once the door closed behind them, they would be stuck in the science wing until they made their way back to the main room. It was a risky move, as they could end up cornered, but it was a risk they would have to take.

"Showtime," Shaw murmured.

The wing wasn't as long as the cell blocks, and as they walked down the hall, they passed three different rooms, all closed up with no windows and no sound emerging. "They must have soundproofing," Caleb mentioned under his breath, apparently unable to make out anything either.

The two knights were sitting at the end of the hall as Trin had said they would be. They looked bored out of their minds behind the desk, one with his feet propped up and watching a game on TV, the other playing on his phone.

"Working hard, I see," Shaw said, slipping back into the role.

"Yeah," Phone Guy replied, "the excitement is too much."

"Where's Borek?"

"Downstairs today. All I know." He didn't even look up from his phone.

"Where are they working up here?"

"Everyone piled into room five a little while ago, chattering about an amazing result." Phone Guy rolled his eyes. "Got me. They don't pay me to follow what it is the eggheads do."

"Thanks for the info," Shaw replied, jerking his chin to Caleb.

Not needing any further signal, Caleb lunged forward, grabbing the man by the throat and slamming him into the wall. TV Guy didn't even have a chance to react as Shaw drew his gun and put one in his head. He turned his gun on Phone Guy next, doing the same. Caleb dropped him, looking at the body in disgust.

"Let's go see what's in room five," Caleb suggested.

"Try to keep behind me," Shaw urged, changing the magazine of his gun despite having rounds left, just to be safe.

Shaw swiped the keycard through the lock on room five, pleased when the light turned green and the magnetic locks gave a low buzz. Apparently, no one heard it over the screams of their prisoner, the sound slamming into him when he opened the door. Shaw froze in the doorway, stunned by the sight of the bloody mess before him.

"What the hell?" one of the scientists demanded. "Who are you? Who let you in here?"

Shaw growled, bringing his gun to bear. "Fuck you."

It was rather like shooting fish in a barrel, five of the staff gone, just like that. Shaw stood there a long moment, teeth bared and arm shaking, until Caleb pressed his hand to Shaw's arm.

"And you were worried about me." He spared Shaw a concerned glance, before going over to the man strapped to the table. "Fuck," Caleb breathed. The prisoner had stopped screaming, but now he was convulsing. Caleb looked to Shaw, wide-eyed. "What do we do?"

Shaw stepped forward, looking down at the man. His entire body was covered in severe burns, blackened and peeling. His eyes were rolled back in his head as foam started to come from his mouth. Shaw bit his lip, shaking his head. "Nothing we can do." He raised his gun again, this time to grant someone a small mercy. A single casing hit the floor. The man's body stopped moving.

A whine caught in Caleb's throat before he let out a rushing breath. "What did they do to him?"

"No idea." Shaw looked down at the chart that hung on the end of the bed like an old-fashioned hospital. "Subject AD-3572. Mage." Suddenly, the prisoner's condition came into grim focus. He had combusted with fire magic, whether by design or a reaction to whatever they did, it didn't much matter.

"We have to keep moving," Shaw said, dropping the chart on the floor. "Let the inspectors work this out."

"We should check the other rooms," Caleb replied. "Trin said they had six prisoners today."

"You're right."

Room six contained an elf who was heavily medicated but breathing. She was wheeled into room four after they cleared it and found a terrified werelion. He was no more than fifteen, with a barbaric anti-shift collar on—spikes sitting against his skin that would kill him if he changed forms. Caleb chucked it across the room after removing it, eyes flashing red.

"You're safe now," Shaw assured him. "The rest of the team is on the way, but right now we need you to stay put, okay?"

"I will."

"Can you watch after her? Keep her safe?"

The teenager looked over at the unconscious elf, nodding. "Yeah, I can do that."

"Good." Shaw offered him a soft smile. "I promise our friends will be here to get you out real soon. Caleb and I have to finish taking out the knights first. Make sure it's safe before we move you."

The boy snagged Caleb's wrist. "Thank you."

Caleb's shoulders sagged and his whole demeanor softened looking down at the battered and bruised teen. "Stay put." Caleb dropped his hand on the werelion's head briefly. To Shaw, he said, "Let's get the rest of these assholes."

Shaw slid a fresh magazine home in his gun. "With you."

Chapter Twenty

THEY DIDN'T BOTHER playing nice with the knights they found at the bottom of the staircase, both too wound up from what they'd just seen. Shaw killed the first knight to enter his sights, weapon quickly training on the other as he ordered, "Hold it right there. Don't touch a damn thing."

The knight held up her hands.

Caleb checked around the corner. "It's clear." He growled at the knight, letting his eyes flash red. "What rooms are they using?"

"A-a-all of them." The knight's gaze shifted between them.

"How many scientists?" Shaw demanded.

"Two in each room."

"Which room's Borek in?"

"Three."

"Thank you." Shaw pulled the trigger.

Caleb crinkled his nose, blood having splattered on his face. "Now what?" he asked. He picked up a piece of the knight's shirt, where she was laid out over the desk, and wiped his face.

"We're going to have to hit each of them fast in case somebody comes out. Let's get this one here"—he nodded to room three—"and then you can guard it while I get each of the others. I'll force them back to you."

Caleb let his claws grow—or perhaps they did on their own—eyes glowing red. "Ready."

Shaw entered the room first, holding the pair at gunpoint and ordering them to the ground. "Watch them," he told Caleb needlessly, both scientists too scared to lift their gazes off the ground—they'd figure out which one was Borek after they secured the wing.

The next room was of no incident, Shaw able to take them by surprise as well. He herded the scientists down the hall and forced them inside room three. They shied away from Caleb's flashing eyes and sharp fangs, cowering in the corner with the others.

In the final room, Shaw caught them while one scientist was holding a syringe that was promptly propelled in Shaw's direction, barely missing him. That one was shot for his brashness. The other scientist tried chucking a tray. Shaw was tempted to shoot her, too, but instead, he snarled, cuffing her by the collar and dragging her back to room three.

"Grab the restraints," Shaw ordered Caleb, confiscating all the keycard lanyards from the scientists. "Which one of you bastards is Borek?" He toed at one of the men who had been in the room.

"I am," the other answered. "Who are you? What do you want?"

"Me? I'll just be happy when you're strapped into a nice electric chair with the power cranked to max."

Caleb sneered, shoving a piece of cloth in Borek's mouth and tying it behind his head. "Hope you choke on it."

They bound and gagged the scientists with a variety of cuffs and hobbles that were in the locker, chaining them to the furniture for good measure.

"We need to check on the prisoners," Shaw said, looking to the one in this room for the first time. It was a woman, a vampire according to the chart. She was thankfully out cold, her breathing relatively steady. "Let's get her out of here."

"Nice knowing you, assholes," Caleb crooned, shutting the door behind them.

Wheeling the cot into the next room, they found this patient awake. Restrained to the table with straps, he thrashed against the binds. Shaw removed the cloth covering his eyes, shushing him. "Relax," he urged. "You're safe now."

Caleb worked quickly to release the straps while Shaw took the gag out of his mouth. "Easy now," Caleb said, squeezing the guy's leg when he tried to move too quickly.

"Who—?" His voice cracked.

"We're the cavalry," Caleb answered. "But, you need to stay put."

"This place isn't secure," Shaw said. "We need you to stay here. Watch after her, alright?"

"Alright." By the way the guy practically collapsed back down on the table, it didn't appear he'd be getting very far, even if he tried. It was just as well that watching after his fellow prisoner was mostly a ploy.

In the third room, they found another unconscious victim, except this one was barely breathing. With all the machines he was hooked up to, and neither of them having a clue what they were doing, they deemed it best to leave him where he was.

"You good to go?" Shaw asked, reloading his gun once again to be safe. Checking Caleb over, he made sure his claws and canines were receded and his eyes were back to their golden hue.

"Yeah," Caleb replied, taking a deep breath and adjusting his hat. "Let's do this."

Shaw holstered his weapon, adopting a cool demeanor. Caleb was like a coiled spring, waiting to go off.

The two knights at the desk were still there, and Shaw greeted them casually enough. "Can you radio those knights out front? We want to speak with them about a few things."

The knights exchanged concerned glances but did as they were asked.

"Thanks." Shaw grinned before drawing his gun and killing them both. "Chuck them under the desk," he said, attention already turning toward the doors—and the next threat. "Stay up here." He jogged over to the inner doors, lying in wait off to the side.

Caleb shook his head, walking to the other side of the desk and leaning a hip against the railing of the steps.

The pair of knights entered shortly thereafter, approaching hesitantly. "You asked to see us?" one inquired.

Shaw moved up behind the guard trailing a few steps behind. He snapped the knight's neck in a practiced movement, bringing his gun up as the man's partner whirled around and received a bullet in his head for the trouble.

Caleb looked down at the corpses apathetically. "Remind me not to piss you off."

Shaw smirked briefly. "Come on." He slapped the back of Caleb's shoulder on the way by. "Let's finish this."

They took the elevator back up to the control room using Trin's key card. The comms had been quiet, confirming the remaining knights were none the wiser to their activities. "I'm gonna lock the personnel housing wing down," Shaw said. "I shut off the alarms, but they still may figure it out. Especially once the shooting starts."

Caleb nodded. "Just be careful."

Shaw looked over at him, Caleb gazing back in concern. "I'll be alright. This is what I do."

"I trust you." Caleb wet his lips, looking out the window to the cell blocks. The four men out there were oblivious to what was about to happen. They were the last people standing between them and Rowan. Looking back to Shaw, Caleb growled, "Go get 'em."

Shaw smirked in response. He pushed the lockdown button, confirming that the remaining off-duty knights wouldn't be able to interfere in what was about to happen. Then he picked an assault rifle from the weapons locker. "I need you to stay in here to open the door back up for me," Shaw said, hitting the charging handle of the gun and loading a round into the chamber.

Caleb grumbled but went to open the door. "Already starting to stink in here."

"You'll live."

The door slid open and Shaw stepped through, the buttstock of the rifle nestled against his shoulder. He put the first knight in his sights. Popping off a couple of rounds, he was able to get the next knight without either having time to fire.

The knights in the next block were alerted, however. As soon as Shaw got them into view from up on the catwalk, he popped one in the shoulder. The second knight opened fire, and Shaw darted sideways into cover. He waited for a lull in the fire before creeping out. Squeezing the trigger, Shaw took the shooter down, finishing off the wounded knight next.

Shaw took a deep breath, letting it out slowly. It was a long moment before he lowered the rifle. The rest of the world trickled back into focus.

The door opened behind him and Shaw slipped inside, met by a frantic Caleb. "Are you okay?" Caleb's hands patted him down and his nose twitched, probably searching for blood.

"Caleb." Shaw grabbed his shoulder, giving him a little shake. "I'm good."

"Right."

Shaw's watch alarm sounded, and he grinned. "Looks like we're right on time." He hadn't heard any chatter on the comms—the place must have had very good soundproofing—but it probably wouldn't be long before they noticed inbound helicopters outside. "How about we find Ro and get these people out of here?"

Caleb grinned, tossing his hat. "Won't hear any arguments from me." He started to pull off the inquisitor tunic next.

Shaw initiated another emergency protocol, this one releasing every single cell in the blocks, along with the wing's entry doors. He opened both gates into the prison, giving the incoming teams easy access. Last, but not least, he figured Caleb had the right idea by losing the inquisitor garb. He shed his tunic, leaving them both in their winter camo.

"I will happily never wear that thing again,'" Shaw said, throwing the uniform aside.

"Amen to that." They bumped fists as they got into the elevator.

Returned to processing, Shaw gestured to the block on the right. "Take that one. Try to get everyone to head out here. I'll take this one."

"You got it." Caleb disappeared into the cell block.

Shaw hesitated, hearing the familiar whir of helicopter blades. Backup had arrived, along with medical help for everyone here.

Need to find Ro.

Shaw jogged into the cell block, discovering prisoners hesitantly emerging or lingering in the doorways of their cells. "It's alright!" he called, putting the strap of the rifle over his head so it could hang freely. Shaw used his empathy to project as much calm as he could. "We're here to help! Soldiers are coming in now to get everybody out!"

More prisoners appeared, each in various states of health. "Come on," Shaw urged. "If you can walk, head on into the processing area."

"Thank you!" a woman cried out. She threw her arms around his shoulders, sobbing in relief. "Thank you so much!"

"It's okay. You're all safe now." He rubbed her back a moment before gesturing to another woman. "Here, take her. Get out to processing."

He continued down the block, seeking out Rowan. He paused to steady a man who appeared worse for wear, but he was walking at least. There were others who were being coaxed to their feet by healthier cellmates. One man was practically being carried between two others who looked barely able to stand themselves. That's when Shaw felt it. Warmth blossomed in his chest. It had been mere days since their bonding, yet it was already so familiar.

Rowan appeared from a cell, helping a man keep his feet. He looked up, eyes latching onto Shaw. A grin split Rowan's face and he asked someone else to help his ill cellmate as Shaw started running.

Shaw slammed into him, enveloping Rowan in a crushing embrace. Every fiber of his being sang with the contact. "Damn it all! You had me so worried!"

Rowan had the nerve to laugh. "I told you I would be fine. I trusted you."

"I oughta smack you right now," Shaw groused.

Rowan laughed again, kissing Shaw to shut him up. "Come on," Rowan said. "Let's get out of here." As they made their way out with the others, he asked, "Caleb?"

"Getting the other block. He's fine," Shaw was quick to assure him.

Rowan was looking around at the prisoners and frowned. "Goddess, this place is a hellhole. The things I saw in a few hours? What Zaeed told me?"

"Zaeed?"

"My cellmate." His thumb jabbed back to where said man was slowly making a go of it. "Apparently, you're missing a master healer and alchemist back in Calagon." Rowan growled under his breath. "They were trying to unlock some kind of mana coding in the mages, trying to steal their powers."

"That would be useful," Shaw said, disgust in every word.

They found a squad of soldiers was already inside, posted around the main room, alert and ready to act if the need arose. They were trying to gather everyone together, encouraging them to have a seat. Shaw gave Rowan's hand a squeeze, moving toward a trio of them. There was no way to tell anyone's rank when they all wore nondescript urban tactical clothing and riot gear, complete with balaclavas.

"Captain Shaw?" one asked, stepping forward.

Shaw nodded. "You in charge?"

The man lowered the cloth over his nose and mouth. "Captain Lawrion, Osterian Special Tactics and Reconnaissance."

"We've got forty-two prisoners." Shaw paused, frowning as he recalled the dead mage. "Forty-one," he corrected. "Five are in the science wing. They'll need help getting out. There's also five members of the science team bound and gagged in room three, including Borek. He was behind all the experiments."

Shaw jabbed his thumb toward the housing wing as he continued, "We're secured everywhere but there—personnel housing. I have it on lockdown. Expect upward of a dozen knights. They shouldn't have anything more than sidearms, but it's likely they've noticed your arrival."

"Understood," Lawrion said. "We've got a second squad outside with one of yours. Medical's inbound." He nodded toward the housing wing. "We can't leave them in there to stew too long. Might get smart and barricade themselves. Can't go in with civilians in the line of fire. We'll need to get them outside."

"Agreed."

"I'll call in my second squad to give them a hand," Lawrion said.

Shaw's attention was drawn to the other cell block where Caleb was emerging with another person in tow. "That everyone?" Shaw called out. At the sound of his voice, the larger man leaning heavily on Caleb snapped his head up to look at Shaw. "Marcus?" Shaw stood there with his mouth hanging open. He managed to snap out of it, rushing over and practically knocking the pair over as he crashed into Marcus. He drew Marcus into his arms, tears stinging his eyes. "I can't belie—Damn it, Marcus!" Shaw fisted his hands into the back of the grimy shirt Marcus wore.

It took a moment before Marcus responded, clearly as shocked by the reunion as Shaw. He let out a broken laugh that twisted into a sob. "Shaw," he breathed. With seemingly great effort, Marcus removed his arm from around Caleb, putting all his weight on Shaw as his arm wrapped around him instead.

The sudden shift of weight set them off-kilter, and they ended up stumbling to their knees in a rather ungraceful move. Even so, Shaw caught them before they tipped over and ate concrete. Both of them knelt on the floor, their holds tightening on each other.

"Shaw," Marcus repeated softly, over and over. His words caught on unshed tears, face turning to nestle into Shaw's neck.

Rowan had joined them and asked, "What's wrong?"

Shaw wasn't sure who he was talking to. It was Caleb who answered, "We need to get him out of here. He needs a healer."

"Shaw." Rowan's hand was on his shoulder, giving it an urgent squeeze.

When Shaw pulled back, however, he didn't acknowledge Rowan outside a quick "Yeah." Instead, he took Marcus's face in his hands, feeling an overwhelming amount of relief. "Let's get you home, yeah?" Shaw's gaze wandered over Marcus, in wonder at first with him being alive, but then with increasing concern. Marcus was thin, and despite being a vampire, he had never been pale. His skin was practically ashen now, his cheeks sunken. Ebony hair that would scarce be out of place was tangled and greasy. His normally bright, aqua eyes were dull, laced with pain. Shadows danced there, the nightmare Marcus had been living reflected in them.

It was then Shaw noticed what the others already knew. The long-sleeve shirt Marcus wore was threadbare and far too large. But that didn't account for why the right sleeve hung limply without anything appearing to be underneath. "Mar...cus..." Shaw's voice drifted off as he grasped for a limb that was no longer there.

"We need to get him out of here," Rowan repeated, squeezing Shaw's shoulder again.

"What? Yeah...yeah." Shaw was already scrambling to his feet, reaching to help Marcus.

Except, Caleb beat him to it. He swooped in, bending to slide his arm around Marcus's waist. "Come on," Caleb encouraged, holding the arm that once more fell across his shoulders. "I've got you. Put your weight on me."

Once Marcus was upright, Caleb's arm locked firmly around him, holding onto his pants in an effort to keep Marcus standing. He pressed their sides together, insisting Marcus lean on him more. "I can handle it," Caleb promised. "I'll protect you."

Marcus's lips twitched upward, for a brief moment a flash of his former self. Marcus let his head drop onto Caleb's shoulder, murmuring what sounded like "Thank you" as he allowed himself to be supported. Caleb was left to practically manhandle him into motion.

When Shaw—who had been taken aback by Marcus's strange behavior—went to help, he was startled by a snarl. Caleb bared his teeth at Shaw and growled, "I've got 'im!"

Shaw took a step back in shock, bumping into Rowan. "It's okay," Rowan said softly. Shaw had no idea what brought that on, but he trusted Rowan to know Caleb better than he did. "Go on ahead and make sure everyone gets out safely."

Already, most of the magicae had been ushered outside to the awaiting teams. "I'll have healers on standby," Shaw assured them. With an objective, Shaw slipped back into the soldier mindset, jogging to catch up with the escaping prisoners who needed him.

"HERE," ROWAN OFFERED Marcus, "this might help a little." He placed a hand on Marcus's right shoulder as they slowly made their way toward the exit. Now that he was far enough away from the cells where the magic-dampeners were located, he was able to at least take the edge of pain away. He watched as Marcus's body released more tension.

"Thanks, Ro," Caleb murmured sincerely, accepting the added weight.

"Anything for your mate."

Caleb huffed air from his nose, shaking his head. "Figures you'd know."

"You *are* rather easy to read."

Caleb didn't answer, instead adjusting the weight at his side. "Almost there, Marcus."

The light was shockingly bright after being kept in darkness. Rowan flinched, walking blindly a few steps. He was hit with a powerful wind, hearing helicopter blades before opening his eyes to see them.

"Sir, this way," a soldier urged, holding onto Rowan's arm to steady him. "Are there any more behind you?"

"I think we're the last out," Rowan yelled above the noise, the other stragglers passing them by.

The soldier turned to his men, signaling them to move into the prison, while others remained behind, creating a perimeter. The medics and healers were spreading out through the groups of prisoners, evaluating them.

Shaw jogged over, a lithe battlemage in tow. "Here," she said, flicking out a tarp, "lay him down here. You said his name's Marcus?"

"Yeah," Shaw answered, helping them get him settled.

"Marcus," she said, trying to get his attention, "my name's Primrose. Can you hear me?" Her hand glowed above him in a gentle, healing light blue.

"Primrose?" he asked, voice still a bit rough. "Your parents must have really hated you."

Shaw huffed, hanging his head. "He's fine," he grumbled, moving aside to let Primrose work.

To her credit, Primrose chuckled. "Better than my sister." In answer to Marcus's challenging brow, she said, "Fauna."

Even Rowan had to cringe a bit and he wasn't exactly one to talk. However, Marcus was almost smiling, and a bit more conscious than he was before, which certainly counted for something. Caleb remained next to him, holding Marcus's hand as he was examined. Rowan moved to stand next to Shaw, who was gazing at his long-missing friend with a mixture of emotions.

"They're mates," Rowan mentioned.

Shaw's attention snapped up to him. "What?"

"Marcus and Caleb."

Shaw let out a little laugh of disbelief. Rowan smiled at him and took his hand.

After a moment, Shaw looked toward the prison. "Once they've secured the facility, they'll bring in the investigators. We should have the survivors airlifted out as soon as everyone's been stabilized."

Rowan nodded. He was distracted by observing Primrose work and watching Caleb as he combed fingers through Marcus's hair.

Something moved into Rowan's vision—a necklace with a small glass vial of blood inset into an aqua aura point. Looking over, he saw Shaw's lips twisting into the start of a smile. "I believe this is yours," Shaw said. A glance at Shaw's chest showed the mer scale necklace shielding a blood vial of his own.

Smiling softly, Rowan took the necklace, sliding the chain over his neck. As it settled into place, he felt the charm warm against his skin. "Thank you," he whispered, taking a deep, steadying breath.

Reaching out, he snagged Shaw's arm and drew him in. He needed his bonded close, needed to feel that hum of energy between them. There was a spark of emotion from Shaw as his hands curled into Rowan's prison-issued shirt. Relief was mixed with anger, tinged with sorrow and regret. Rowan had no doubt in his mind that their bonding had allowed him to recognize them so easily.

Shaw sighed heavily, and with it, a wave of determination followed. "I love you, Rowan." Shaw squeezed him around the middle.

"*Mon l'sangé,*" he murmured into Shaw's ear, managing a smile. "My bonded blood, I adore you."

Shaw kissed him with a flood of emotion as hard as the kiss itself. That time, Rowan only sensed overwhelming love. He smiled against Shaw's lips before nipping at them. Shaw chuckled, the pair of them standing there, lost in the moment as they looked into each other's eyes.

A grunt of pain and a curse brought them hurtling back to reality. "Shaw!" Marcus yelled.

"*Sh*, I'm here. What do you need?" Shaw knelt beside Caleb, grabbing Marcus's hand.

"Don't leave me," Marcus pleaded.

Primrose seemed to have other ideas, flagging down one of the assistants. "He needs to go out with the first group," she ordered. "Get me a stretcher."

"I'm going with him," Caleb said. When she tried to argue for room, Caleb growled, "He's my mate." Primrose nodded in agreement. To Shaw, she said, "We need space for the criticals."

Marcus squeezed Shaw's hand tighter. "Don't you fucking leave me," he repeated.

"Hey now, hush..." Shaw leaned over him, obviously trying not to look at the bandages seeping through with fresh blood, covering the stump of Marcus's arm. "You know the procedure: evacuate the wounded, cover their escape, then pull out."

Marcus shook his head, body starting to tremble.

"Caleb's gonna be with you the whole time, you hear me?" Shaw was brushing the hair from Marcus's face. "Your mate's gonna be with you."

Marcus's eyes slid over to Caleb. "I'm here," Caleb assured him, bending to press their foreheads together.

"I'll be right behind you," Shaw said.

As a pair of soldiers with a stretcher appeared, Shaw gave Marcus's hand a final squeeze before having to visibly force himself to back away. Rowan wrapped him in his arms for support, Shaw's back to his chest. There were no words to make the situation better, so instead, Rowan offered his presence, chin resting on Shaw's shoulder.

"Your friend's strong," Primrose offered. "He'll pull through." She nodded to them before going to lend aid elsewhere.

They stayed put, watching in silence while more patients were loaded onto the medevac as the blades spun up to speed. The first helicopter took off, their best friends on board, and all they could do was watch as it headed toward Everstrand without them.

As the helicopter faded farther away, Rowan took a moment to observe the activity around them for the first time. A sea of soldiers and healers moved among the frightened former prisoners. Some were crying, clinging to the closest person. Others gazed off into space, apparently numbed to it all. Somehow they had all managed to survive.

Victims were carried out from the prison, piled quickly onto another helicopter—more critical patients to be rushed off. At the end of the group, a body bag was placed gently to the side to be taken care of later. Shaw turned his face into Rowan's neck, and he didn't ask.

It wasn't truly hitting him yet—the sheer scope of what had been going on here. Rowan was certain it was a form of shock, though nothing like what the others were going through. Still, he felt lucky to be alive.

"We'll catch a ride on one of the copters here soon," Shaw said, loosening his hold on Rowan. "Let them get out any more criticals first."

"Don't you need to stick around?"

Shaw shook his head. After a minute, he said, "I'm not even supposed to be here, remember?"

It was ridiculous, but Rowan barked out a quick laugh. Shaw's lips managed to curl into a smile. "Still," Rowan reasoned, "won't that captain be expecting your help?"

"He has his own troops, his own operation. My part's done." Shaw looked up at him. "Right now? I take care of my men."

Rowan nodded. "We'll do it together."

That brought a true smile back to Shaw's face. He looked around, noticing there was a large group of prisoners being led to one of the small helicopters. They were walking under their own power, despite how banged up they looked. Another group was gathering as well, a little worse for wear, but far more stable than others they'd seen.

"Oi," Shaw called to one of the soldiers, motioning him over. "You with Captain Lawrion's squad?"

"Yes, sir."

"Let him know Captain Shaw flew out with the prisoners."

"Can do, sir."

Shaw pulled Rowan along toward the closest helicopter, having to raise his voice to speak above the noise. "Any of these heading to Everstrand?"

"No, they're going to other hospitals," the battlemage yelled back. "That one's going to Duneshore Base." He pointed out the helicopter in question. "They had room for more after we sent them some of those criticals."

"Thanks!" To Rowan, Shaw said, "We'll be able to get a ride out to Everstrand from there."

"It's only about an hour by car," Rowan agreed, following after Shaw.

"Car? Try another helicopter."

"You have that much pull?" Rowan asked skeptically.

"I have to call Rhys once we get there to give him the short version anyway."

Shaw managed to get them a couple of spots at the door, the blades whirring to life. Rowan's grip on the frame tightened when the helicopter started to hover, his other hand grabbing at Shaw, who was sitting on the floor next to him, legs dangling over the side. Shaw laughed at him, but the sound was caught by the wind.

Rowan poked his head around the doorframe, watching the ground grow farther away. The snow-covered facility was still crawling with activity, and the soldiers were nothing more than dots of black against the backdrop.

A hand passed into his view and Rowan looked from it over to Shaw. He was smiling softly, waggling his fingers in invitation. It took convincing from Rowan's brain to let go of his death grip. Fingers twined with his, and Rowan sank against the edge of the doorway, gratefully, with the reassurance and love Shaw sent him.

The wind whipped at their hair and clothes, the land and water passing below them in a blur. Despite hanging on the edge of death, Rowan felt content. He gave Shaw's hand a squeeze, leaning sideways to press a kiss to his jaw.

Shaw smiled, stealing a proper kiss of his own.

Rowan could barely believe what they'd just pulled off. They had rescued countless magicae and exposed the Inquisition for what they truly were. Marcus had been alive after all and, unbelievably, was Caleb's mate, as though fate herself had intervened. The fight wasn't over, not by a long shot. In fact, it was only the beginning. This was a new start to his life, as well—a new bonded, with a new circle of friends—and for once, Rowan didn't fear what was to come.

Appendix

Schools of Magic

CONJURATION:
  Summoning
      Creatures
      Weapons
  Shields
  Necromancy

ENCHANTMENT:
  Wards
  Charms (affect people)
  Enchanting (affect objects)

ALTERATION:
  Transmutation/Alchemy
      Shapechanging
  Glamours
  Light/Shadow
  Sound
      Sonar
      Throw voice
  Detect Life/Nightvision
  Quantum (a new, experimental form of magic that works side-by-side with non-mage scientists working on Quantum Theory)

PRIMAL:
    Earth
    Water/Ice
    Fire/Electricity
    Wind

SPIRIT/INCARNUM (former name):
    Blood Magic
    Healing
    Hexes/Curses
        Mana Draining
    Spirit Walking/Dream Walking
    Spirit Tracking

UNOFFICIAL FORMS OF MAGIC (anyone can learn to do these, but they can be enhanced by magic and are often offered as courses by a guild):
    Herbology
    Divination
    Runes

Races

MAGES:

Everything about them is human, save for one biological difference. There's a force of magic every mage is born with, known as mana. This condition is hereditary and it's possible to appear in a child even when a family hasn't had mages for generations. A small percentage of people born with mana will never manifest their powers—usually a mage's powers will awaken before puberty, especially with a mage parent(s).

Mana is a naturally replenishing element within a mage's body, secreted through an organ known as the manara, which feeds their magical abilities. Without mana, a mage will not be able to use magic. They train their bodies and minds, allowing them to use less mana for certain spells, and even to increase the rate their bodies replenish mana. There is artificial mana that a mage can take, but typically guilds frown on its use. However, it can be commonly used by battlemages during combat. Another way to get around the use of mana is blood magic, in which a mage can use their blood, or another's, as an alternative power source—which is one reason it's a controversial area of magic.

A quirk of mages is that their eyes will glow when using a decent amount of mana/power—this seems to vary mage to mage—and the color they glow is as unique as the mage, not necessarily matching their eye color.

They can live longer than humans—up to one hundred and fifty years—and medical experts have surmised it's the way that mana interacts with the body that causes this.

WITCHES:

They are humans, but with special abilities. Unlike mages, witches don't have mana, so they don't rely on that for their powers to work. However, they can still drain themselves mentally and physically from using their abilities too often and they can train to combat this. While mages can learn any number of spells, witches are born with a single ability. Their powers tend to be mental in nature—telepathy, telekinesis, empathy, etc.

WERE-CREATURES:

They can be born or changed—though not all races are capable of becoming were-creatures, likely due to certain genetic markers. Born were-creatures won't shift for the first time until they hit puberty.

Were-creatures are bound to the moon. As such, they can be forced into a shift on these nights. One can learn to control it, and older were-creatures are typically good at resisting a full moon shift. It's believed that born were-creatures are better at controlling this than changed ones because they've lived with the animal their whole lives and thus are more connected to their other halves. Some were-creatures choose to wear anti-shift devices laced with magic to help inhibit the change.

There's also Alpha werewolves to consider, who seem to hold an even greater affinity with the moon. Qualities bred over time have created a werewolf stronger and faster than their regular counterparts, but they also have some unique magical abilities—for example, Alphas can heal pack members. They are easily identified when they let their Alpha nature surface with their glowing red eyes and the smoky shadows that surround them.

Were-creatures can detect their mates through physical contact, and sometimes scent. Cross-species mating results have been passed down through packs/clowders/clans, knowing what works and doesn't. To set a mate bond, they trade bites. Another were-creature couldn't be changed by the process, nor can vampires, while other races can—and often are—changed to become were-creatures themselves for a stronger mating.

In their animal forms, they typically tend to be larger versions of their normal animal counterparts. They have enhanced senses, also relative to what type of animal they are—a werewolf might have better smell than a werepanther, who has better hearing, and so on. Their lifespans reflect those of average humans, not their animal counterparts.

Silver can be deadly, as were-creatures have developed a severe allergy to it. Small amounts can be relatively safe—more akin to an irritant—thus silver is infused in tattoos or piercings for were-creatures to make them stay. Otherwise, their natural accelerated healing would heal them over.

VAMPIRES:

They are daywalkers. This wasn't always the case, but they evolved to it, and in doing so, their abilities have changed. Their night vision diminished as their tolerance to daylight increased. To find a vampire who still has the skill to change into mist or shadow is rare, and such vampires are most likely intolerant to the sun. Most of their unique abilities, such as blood and shadow magic—typically passed through bloodlines—have vanished alongside their nighttime habits. They have natural regeneration allowing them to heal at an accelerated rate. They're extremely fast, though agility is relative to the individual.

They can be immortal. They can be killed through major trauma—brain or heart damage, blood loss—or starvation. They aren't immune to disease, but they have a higher tolerance to viruses and bacteria.

A vampire can be born—though it's considerably rare—or a human can be turned into one—other races haven't been successfully turned for one reason or another. The process involves draining a good deal of the human's blood and then having them drink the blood of their sire. The change itself may take anywhere from three to five days to be complete. While they eat and drink as any other race would do, they require blood as well. New vampires and injured vampires require more blood than their older or otherwise healthier counterparts.

Like were-creatures, vampires also have mates. They have the ability to sense their perfect match, which can be of any other race. Depending on the race, a mating bite can be given and received, bonding them together. Vampires can then detect their mates at greater distances—the strength of the bond will affect how far that can stretch—pick up their feelings, their health, etc. It's similar to a sire-childe bond, but stronger, and a mate bond will typically dull a sire-childe bond, though it couldn't get rid of it. Science isn't sure how exactly such a bond works, especially not between a vampire and another race—what vampires understand of various cross-matings has been passed down through covens—but science does acknowledge it being different from a soul bond.

ELVES:

The immortal elves were one of the first races to reveal themselves to the humans, helping to bridge the gap between mundanes and magicae during the early years of integration. They are brilliant inventors and scientists in their own right, and have helped advance technology and medicine in big ways—helps when you have ages to study findings.

While they may still have their elven cities as seats of culture for their people, they have fully involved themselves in society as a whole. Still, the call of nature is in their bones, and thus most elves found living in cities are likely half-elves—humans, both mundane and magicae, have been found to be compatible with elves to create offspring.

Because of their immortal nature, young elves age rather slowly—about half that of humans. Once their bodies reach a state of full maturity, the aging process halts. They are able to be killed by trauma or illness, though they have better immune systems than other races, and some slightly advanced healing that stems from their own natural brand of magic. It's not as complex as mages, or even were-creatures and vampires, but it's there.

While they can't tell who their mates are like some races, they do believe that the Earth Mother has a soulmate for everyone, somewhere out there—race, gender, none of that matters. Elves are able to perform an ancient ritual of soulbonding, where the two partners—though there have been cases of trios—have their souls physically linked together. It allows the partners to not only sense each other as other mated pairs can, but they can also speak telepathically. A downside is that should one of them die, the other is usually soon to follow, as a literal piece of themselves is now missing.

Most elves still follow their ancient teachings on the Earth Mother. It is, quite obviously, a nature-based religion, believing in the balance of all things. They believe that in death, their bodies return to the earth, while their souls travel to the Beyond to be with the Earth Mother and all those who came before them.

MERPEOPLE:

Mers have been known to live for centuries. Their long, scaled tails and fins can be found in every color imaginable. For protection, they have sharp spines down their vertebrae and forearms, along with claws, and sharpened teeth that are similar to a shark's. Their skin is porpoise-like in texture, though the color is as varied as humans are. Their facial features are also very similar to humans, including their eyes and hair. Despite the gills on the side of their necks, they also possess a pair of redundant lungs that allow them to breathe above water and talk. Below water, they speak in clicks and whistles like other sea mammals.

They reside in clans spread through various oceans. Mers typically do not stray from the clan they're born into. They hold to migration patterns as the seasons and waters change. There are few places where multiple clans gather in peace, which is usually the only time they'll be seen interacting. They use this time for trade, sharing news, and—sometimes—mers will choose to go with another clan when they part ways.

Some clans are sociable to land-dwelling races—whom they call Topworlders—while others stay far from shores, ports, and passing vessels. It isn't a wonder, since there are still nations that hunt merpeople for sport and profit, refusing to recognize them as a sentient race of free beings.

NYMPHS:

A type of fae that come in a variety of subspecies, such as dryads and naiads. Though they have historically been guardians of nature, they are fascinated by the modern world. They have fallen in love with people and can now be found rather commonly in cities. They tend to be natural healers, or anything that involves working with the public. Despite their sociability, it would not be wise to disturb their sacred homes. All nymphs are bound to a natural space—usually the place of their birth—and they will defend it viciously, even giving their life to keep it safe.

Their appearance varies by species, a reflection of their nature. For example, a dryad—which is a forest nymph—has bark-like skin and foliage in their hair, while a naiad—a water nymph—is often pale with features to match, moving more like liquid than a solid being.

Nymphs are unique in that their magic allows them to reproduce without regard to gender.

They are long-lived, up to half a century easily. They can be killed by normal trauma or disease, although they are a bit more resistant to illness than some other races. But the sure-fire way to kill a nymph is by destroying their sacred home, which is the heart of their power. Also, a sick nymph could be a sign that it's actually their sacred home that's "sick."

Acknowledgements

Special thanks to my local writers group and my NaNo writers group for all their help in making this trilogy become a reality.

As always, thanks to my soul mate for being my greatest supporter, for pushing me to go after my dreams, and raising me up to reach the stars.

About the Author

"Everyone deserves a Happily Ever After."

For Casey, writing equals existence. History nerd, film enthusiast, avid gamer, and just an all-around geek. Casey has been known to spend a lot of time dancing around the kitchen to music while cooking. Add in an unapologetic addiction to loose-leaf tea, and you get the general picture. Married, with furry, four-legged children, Casey lives happily in the middle-of-nowhere, Ohio.

Email: authorcaseywolfe@gmail.com

Facebook: www.facebook.com/authorcaseywolfe

Tumblr: www.authorcaseywolfe.tumblr.com

Website: www.authorcaseywolfe.wordpress.com

Other books by this author

One Bullet

About the Author

"Everyone deserves a Happily Ever After."

For Casey, writing equals existence. History nerd, film enthusiast, avid gamer, and just an all-around geek. Casey has been known to spend a lot of time dancing around the kitchen to music while cooking. Add in an unapologetic addiction to loose-leaf tea, and you get the general picture. Married, with furry, four-legged children, Casey lives happily in the middle-of-nowhere, Ohio.

Email: authorcaseywolfe@gmail.com

Facebook: www.facebook.com/authorcaseywolfe

Tumblr: www.authorcaseywolfe.tumblr.com

Website: www.authorcaseywolfe.wordpress.com

Other books by this author

One Bullet

Also Available from NineStar Press

Connect with NineStar Press

Website: NineStarPress.com

Facebook: NineStarPress

Facebook Reader Group: NineStarNiche

Twitter: @ninestarpress

Tumblr: NineStarPress

9 781949 340204